I0682046

THE BOOK WITCH
SEQUEL TO THE BOOK ADDICT

ANNETTE MORI

ALSO BY ANNETTE MORI

Single Stories
The Dream Catcher
Free to Love with Ali Spooner
Captivated
The Termination
The Review
The Ultimate Betrayal
Locked Inside
Out of This World
Asset Management
The Incredibly True Adventure of Two Elves in Love
(Affinity 2014 Christmas Collection)
Love Forever, Live Forever
The True Story of Valentine's Day
Vampire Pussy…Cat
Nicky's Christmas Miracle X3
(*It's in Her Kiss*, Affinity's Charity Anthology)

Series
Unconventional Lovers
The Organization with Erin O'Reilly

The Book Addict
The Book Witch

THE BOOK WITCH
SEQUEL TO THE BOOK ADDICT

ANNETTE MORI

Affinity
Rainbow Publications

2019

The Book Witch
© 2019 by Annette Mori

Affinity E-Book Press NZ LTD
Canterbury, New Zealand

1st Edition

ISBN: 978-1-98-854993-4

All rights reserved.

No part of this book may be reproduced in any form without the express permission of the author and publisher. Please note that piracy of copyrighted materials violate the author's rights and is Illegal.

This is a work of fiction. Names, character, places, and incidents are the product of the author's imagination or are used fictitiously and any resemblance to actual persons living or dead, businesses, companies, events, or locales is entirely coincidental

Editor: CK King
Proof Editor: Alexis Smith
Cover Design: Irish Dragon Design
Production Design: Affinity Publication Services

ACKNOWLEDGMENTS

A huge thank you to all of my beta readers: Gail Dodge, Ali Spooner, Carrie Camp, Ameliah Faith, Dana Holmes, Elle Hyden, and Danna Micoletti, who made great suggestions to improve the initial draft. Of course, once again, I have to acknowledge Erin O'Reilly, who is a constant support and encouragement to me. I am honored to call her a friend and to have her support me in my journey. I would also like to express my gratitude to Affinity Rainbow Publications and the wonderful trio (JM Dragon, Erin O'Reilly, and Nancy Kaufman) who continue to provide feedback to tighten up manuscripts that need assistance and publish my unconventional work. My other family members who are also very supportive, include my nephew, Aaron and his wife, Chelsea, my older sister and my father who struggles to read my books with one eye. I always enjoy working with the beta editor, Nancy Kaufman, who is so skilled at finding plot holes. Thanks to CK King for her magic as the final editor. She is a joy to work with. Inevitably, there are those pesky final errors that slip through, and I am thankful for the final proof editor, Alexis Smith, who catches those before the book goes to print. Thanks to Nancy Kaufman for the final cover. Nancy is also a promoter extraordinaire. A huge thanks to all the other readers and fellow writers who have sent personal e-mails, written reviews, and posted nice things on Facebook (you know who you are). The Affinity authors are an especially supportive group and often share posts or send words of encouragement. Finally, my wife, Jody, continues her support even when it interferes with our time together on the weekends.

DEDICATION

To all the readers who like a little spice with their contemporary romance and can appreciate elements of Urban Fantasy mixed into their Romance for a Romash.

And, as always, to my wife who always supports me.

TABLE OF CONTENTS

CHAPTER ONE

Tanya loved visiting her girlfriend at her bookstore, The Enchanted Page. *Girlfriend. Yeah, that word has a wonderful ring to it.* She'd almost resigned herself to the notion of living the rest of her days alone, or almost alone. She did have Tolstoy, her cat, to keep her company and her feet warm. Meeting Elle had turned her world upside down.

As unbelievable as it seemed, her girlfriend was more than a bookstore owner. She was a book magician with the power (Or was it ability?) to transport those most in need of adventure smack dab into the middle of a book. The chosen were literally participants in the story in a way that created an adventure never forgotten by the recipient of the magic. Tanya should know. She was one of the chosen. Unbelievable? Sure, yet Tanya had accepted magic as fact almost immediately, which had surprised Elle.

While Tanya had appreciated her adventure, there were certain ethical issues they were still working through regarding the absence of choice. How the book magicians and their male counterparts, book wizards, decided upon the chosen was an especially thorny subject. Being one of the chosen made Tanya feel like a pathetic loser. Book magicians decided on the chosen based on a belief that the nonmagicians needed an adventure to liven their dull existence. A book adventure to be specific. Yet, she had to admit the romantic adventure she experienced with Elle was exactly what she had needed in her life.

Saturday was usually busy at the bookstore, and Tanya suspected that made Elle happy. Elle didn't need the money. She craved the excitement and the interaction with various people. She still believed her work as a book magician served a useful purpose. Lately, she'd shown signs of restlessness, and Tanya wondered when a new plan would burst from her mouth.

The Enchanted Page wasn't a normal, run-of-the-mill bookstore. A few carefully selected books contained the magic necessary to send the chosen into a book adventure. As long as the nonmagicians were told their options, Tanya didn't have a problem with what they did for a living. She'd somehow joined the ranks of the book magicians after discovering she possessed the skills. As Director of E-book Magic, she was bringing the book magicians and wizards into the twenty-first century.

Moses Lake was a nice enough place to settle, but Tanya suspected that digging in and enjoying the quiet life was not in Elle's DNA. If Tanya wanted to show her love for her girlfriend, she knew she had to be willing to jump on the merry-go-round for the next adventure around the bend. Elle had mentioned buying a bookstore on Whidbey Island. At least the island was not clear across the country and still offered the soothing effects of water. If she were honest with herself, the notion of living in the gateway to the San Juan Islands, where all the orcas hung out, was extremely appealing. Tolstoy might raise a ruckus, but he'd adapt in time.

Tanya propped her chin on her hand, sure that she had a dopey expression on her face, and watched her beautiful lover weave her magic with a customer. The magic Elle was creating had nothing to do with the chants that could send someone into an adventure. Elle had a gift with people, and she was spinning her magic on a young girl who Tanya knew was an outcast in her school. Joining the Chess Club wasn't exactly the preferred method of fitting in. Tanya had tried to talk with her while coaching the team but hadn't managed to bring the awkward girl out of her shell. That was a first for Tanya. Normally she had the magic touch with socially awkward teens, because she could relate.

"You know, in ten years, all those cheerleaders and football players will fade from any notoriety they now possess. Your intellectual prowess as a chess player will provide you with the needed skills to anticipate future challenges in life. Intelligence eats popularity for lunch and spits that shallow noun out as something unworthy of digestion," Elle said to the young girl.

"Really, Miss Elle?"

"Absolutely."

When a frown began to mar Elle's beautiful face, Tanya followed her gaze to a striking woman with flowing red hair and piercing emerald eyes who glided into The Enchanted Page. She wore a smirk on her face that seemed just shy of arrogance. Something about her impish smile told Tanya that perhaps it was all a ruse. Maybe the beautiful woman hid her real emotions so far inside that even she wouldn't know where to look for them. Tanya was curious about who she could be.

She strode to Tanya with what appeared as manufactured confidence. "You are significantly more attractive than the rumors," the stranger blurted out.

"Pardon me?" Tanya tilted her head.

"You are the famed book addict, the nonmag recently promoted to Director of E-book Magic. Are you not?"

Tanya's mouth hung open. She wasn't comfortable with the moniker, "famed book addict." She *had* bound that scrotumface, the former Grand Wizard, to the book he'd tried to trap her in. Apparently, the prophecy told of a nonmagician who would perform an incantation in a similar fashion to how Niviane trapped Merlin in the stone chamber. The Grand Council of Magicians had convinced themselves Tanya was this person.

Elle slammed down the book she was holding onto the counter. The chess player jumped and scurried from the store. "Imara," Elle said through gritted teeth. "Where's your broom?"

"Oooh, temper, temper, Elle. I was just saying hello to your lovely…uh what is she exactly? Not your wife, so no need to get too possessive." Imara cackled.

"Why don't you take your inferior spells someplace else? Oh, by the way, have you found any new warts in delicate places? I've heard vaginal warts are a bitch and so common to your kind."

Imara narrowed her eyes. "You know that is a complete falsehood. Book witches have never suffered from warts of any kind, you loud-mouthed, inarticulate book apprentice. You never could manage to refine the art of truly bringing a book to life like we do."

"Reckless, that's what you are. Completely devoid of any ethics whatsoever. Characters in books are supposed to stay put." Spittle flew from Elle's mouth.

Tanya had never seen her girlfriend so angry before—not even when their very lives were at risk when Gordon had set them up to perish inside the book's adventure.

"Reckless? Oh, that's rich. I'm not the one who sends their chosen into dangerous adventures and has to have her mother bail her ass out." Imara's beautiful face transformed into a snarl.

Tanya thought she heard an audible pop and turned to her left as Bea materialized inside the store. "Enough," Bea yelled. "You're interrupting my afternoon delight with your negative energy. Your father was about to rock my world, then I felt your infantile anger rear its ugly head. Imara, why do you always have to needle Elle?"

"Ew, Mother, I did not need to hear that," Elle groused.

"Hiya, Mom. Give me a hug."

Bea crossed the small space and accepted the hug from the stunning woman.

Tanya looked from Bea to Elle to Imara. "Who are you?"

Imara bowed. "Imara the good book witch at your service. Elle and I go way back. She used to be a lot more fun than she is now."

Elle crossed her arms over her chest. "That was before I knew what a total bitch you are."

"Aw come on. You're not still sore about Misty, are you? Trust me, she wasn't that good. I did you a favor by stealing her away. Honestly, she was a total bore. Now look how much better you've done. Unless…oh, I get it. You're afraid I'll steal this delectable creature away from you."

"As if." Elle hmphed loudly.

Tanya closed the distance between her and Elle and kissed Elle's cheek. "No one could ever steal me away from you."

Elle smirked. "What's your skanky ass doing here anyway?"

Imara held out her hand. "Truce. I promise I won't make a move on your beautiful book addict if you help me out. We used to be a good team…"

"Ha. Can't handle it on your own, huh?"

"This one is special. Besides, I heard you were buying the bookstore on Whidbey. She lives in Coupeville, so I thought we could team up. She meets both our criteria. Who knows, she could be as special as your book addict here."

"Hey, this book addict has a name." Tanya's irritation was growing.

"Sorry. It's Tanya, right?" Imara asked.

†

Tanya hated when the book magicians acted like she wasn't there and talked about her as if she were a sofa. It seemed as though *this* book witch was perpetuating that subtle discrimination. Elle, Bea, and Clara didn't treat her like a second-class citizen, but sometimes the others did. Tanya respected Oren, a powerful wizard on the Magicians' Council, but even he fell into old habits. Fay, the current Grand Magician, would remind her lover not to be a snob and to recognize Tanya's talents. With a woman leading the council, the men no longer called all the shots, but they were still a long way from the antiquated views that lingered from the old wizards.

Fay was a powerful book magician who that same council had once banished after Gordon set her up. She'd returned at the right moment to help them catch Gordon red-handed in his evil plan to discredit all female magicians and secure control for the wizards. Oren had played a pivotal role in helping Elle and Tanya permanently bind that scrotumface to a very nasty place in the book. Poetic justice. Gordon's plan had backfired, and they'd left the slimy bastard in a dangerous book. She hoped he'd spend the rest of his living days in terror. He'd tried to do the exact same thing to Elle, with Tanya as collateral damage. Well, turnaround was fair play.

Tanya admired Fay, but change was hard and slow. Too slow for Tanya's liking. The old guard continued to give her fits. Only Sidell, Oren, and Brendan were on her side. Sidell's surprising turnabout was enough for a majority, but the old-timer was getting up there in years. Tanya feared Sidell would leave the council before young Brendan earned the esteem and ear of his senior colleagues. Tanya was still a bit surprised the council had voted a woman as their Grand Magician and doubly astounded when they asked a nonmagician to work with them on expanding the magic beyond paperbacks.

Hadn't Tanya brought the book magicians into the twenty-first century as Director of E-book Magic? Tanya hmphed to herself. She had to give this arrogant, little book witch a lesson or two in decorum.

"Yes, my name is Tanya, and if you ever refer to me as a nonmag again, I'll be providing you a lesson in etiquette and respect."

"Ooh, she is a feisty one." Imara winked at Elle. "I'll bet she's a hellcat in bed."

Tanya poked her finger at Imara. "You aren't listening, are you? Typical snobby magician—"

"I am not a lowly book magician. I am a book witch." Imara puffed out her chest. Tanya waited for her to stick her nose to the sky, feigning an air of superiority.

"Why you—" Elle took a step in Imara's direction.

"I said stop it, or I'll send both of you into a book of my choosing, like I used to when you were little," Bea exclaimed.

7

Imara shuddered. "Oh God, not that. You always picked the most mundane books. We'd nearly die from boredom. Sorry Bea, but book magicians and book witches are not the same. Haven't you taught this book addict that?"

Tanya threw her hands in the air. "I give up. Maybe someday you'll learn my name."

Bea sighed. "Our kind hasn't really mixed much with yours lately. That ridiculous feud is still going strong."

"What feud?" Tanya asked.

"Book magicians and book witches often select the same individuals to bless with their magic and have different perspectives regarding which is more beneficial to the chosen. I largely blame the wizards and warlocks. They are the ones who began beating their chests, trying to prove who was better. Imara, frankly, I'm surprised you've jumped onto the bandwagon," Bea answered.

Imara looked genuinely regretful. "I'm sorry. You know, deep down, I don't feel that way. I can't understand what's come over me lately. I've missed you. I've even missed Elle. Although, she is a bigger pain in my ass than when you used to send us to Boringville. Or worse, those disapproving incantations. You know, the ones where you inserted overwhelming feelings of guilt into us after whatever half-baked antic we'd thought up."

"Do all witches exaggerate so much?" Elle asked. "They weren't that bad. You're making her sound like some crazed parent."

"I know. I was just kidding, but I do have permanent scars from her disappointment chants. They were a far greater punishment and stuck with me a lot longer than when she sent us into those books."

"Hmm…good to know something stuck. Do you really want Elle's assistance with a special case? Maybe if the two of you work together this silly war between magicians and witches will end. I miss those spectacular shindigs the book witches threw. I know you all didn't name them that…"

"It's okay, Bea, I called the Witchfests and Paganicons shindigs but never within earshot of another book witch. I would have been on the receiving end of a very nasty spell if I had."

"Right, right. It's been so long. I forgot," Bea answered.

Pop

Tanya turned her head. "Clara!"

"I thought I felt a disturbance in the air." Clara grinned.

"Aunt Clara, you old cougar. How ya been? Miss me?" Imara stepped into Clara's open arms and accepted a hug.

"I did miss you. You and Elle always stir things up and make everything a bit more interesting."

"I'm trying to entice Elle to help me out."

"Sounds fascinating. Can I come along?"

"Sure, the more the merrier. We can even take the little book addict with us." A sly smile appeared on Imara's lips.

Something about the way Imara had mentioned Tanya as an afterthought and the expression on her face seemed disingenuous. It appeared as though Imara was playing a role or acting for their benefit. Tanya didn't get a chance to explore her gut reaction, because Elle cut into the conversation in her defense.

"Hey, don't underestimate Tanya. She may not have been born a book magician, but she has more power and knowledge than most of the stuffy, old wizards. It was her chant that sent Gordon packing."

Imara raised her eyebrow and shot Tanya an appraising look. "Wow, I thought that was simply hyperbole." Imara scooted over and slung her arm over Tanya's shoulder. "How about it, book addict. Are you ready for a real adventure?"

"Stay the fuck away," Elle grounded out.

"Ooh, touchy. Does she have you on a short leash, hon?" Imara grinned.

"I'm warning you, Imara. Tanya is not interested in participating in any of your hairbrained ideas."

That was it. Tanya loved Elle, but this overprotective, jealous streak that caused Elle to make all kinds of assumptions about what Tanya did and did not want to get involved in was pissing her off. "Tanya can speak for herself. Thank you very much." Her voice was dangerously low and had a sharp edge that she rarely used, especially with Elle.

Elle deflated. "I'm sorry."

"Give us a minute, will you?" Tanya directed her question to Imara, then pulled Elle up the stairs to the loft apartment they often stayed at when they weren't spending time at Tanya's condo.

†

Tanya tugged on Elle's sleeve and pulled her down on the love seat. She picked up the remote to turn on the electric fireplace. The fake fire didn't put out a lot of heat, because it was mostly for show, but both of them thought it was the next best thing to having a real fireplace. A relaxing space was the idea. "What's going on? Where did my confident, adventuresome book magician go? I've never seen you act like that."

Elle absently moved her thumb back and forth over Tanya's hand. Tanya recognized Elle's gesture as a way to further calm herself. "I'm sure you can tell. Imara and I have history. We were nearly inseparable when we were younger. After her mother basically abandoned her, Mom sort of adopted Imara. Aunt Clara too. We, uh, had similar proclivities... so would go after the same girls. It became competitive. She always won. I was constantly under her shadow. I didn't mind at the time. Being in her presence was like a drug.

"Then I met Misty... First loves are hard. I told Imara Misty was important to me. I asked her not to turn on the charm and give us a chance. I suppose she couldn't help herself. Everyone loves that rogue cockiness she's had since she turned thirteen. Misty wasn't immune. My first heartbreak."

"Well, I find her brash and irritating. You don't have to worry about me falling for her nonexistent charms. I'm in love with you. Nothing, not even a witch's spell, has a chance at breaking that love." Tanya brought her lips to Elle's, sealing her declaration.

"You want to help her, don't you?" Elle quirked her eyebrow.

Tanya smiled. "It has gotten a little rote around here lately. I'm not exactly involved in the more interesting aspects of book magic."

"I thought you'd had a lifetime of excitement with just one adventure."

"Apparently, I'm another kind of addict. Who knew, huh? I got a small taste of adventure, and now I'm craving more."

"Book witches still haven't resolved the ethics around bringing characters to life. The issues become especially gnarly when a character falls for a nonmag—oops, I mean chant free."

Tanya grimaced. "Okay, I officially hate the replacement word for those of us who don't possess your special skills. Chantfree really is lame, isn't it?"

Elle nodded. "You know, you can't really be classified as a nonmag anymore because of how you took care of that donkeyhole, Gordon. I know you hate the term nonmag, but hon, I have no idea what else to call the others not like us.

Maybe we can borrow from those Harry Potter books, even though they got everything wrong about magicians."

Tanya groaned. "I loved those books, but no, just no."

"How about humbles? That has pleasant connotations," Elle suggested.

Tanya stroked her chin. "How about we don't use labels at all?"

"Both of our worlds immerse themselves in labels. It's the way we organize things."

"It's also lazy and chock full of ways to look at one class of individuals differently—kind of like book magicians and book witches. The divide seems like it's based on your differences, rather than on finding common ground. I suspect both sides think the other is less valuable, less relevant, less important, less ethical... Shall I go on?" Tanya quirked her eyebrow.

"You are far too intelligent for my own good. I'll never win an argument with you. I suppose Imara has her positive attributes. I'll not ever admit that to her, but she was fun to hang out with. Imara did manage to increase the excitement in my life, even when she got us in hot water with Mom. The one area both book magicians and book witches agree on is bringing adventure and self-worth into the lives of the chosen."

"Let's do it then. We can buy the bookstore on Whidbey. It'll be a first, major step toward commitment and eventually marriage. A combination store and cozy loft for us to live in. I've always wanted to live on an island. Of course, Hawaii was my first choice, but as long as I'm with you, any island in the Pacific Northwest will do fine." Tanya laid her head on Elle's shoulder.

"Are you going to sell your condo? What about the store here in Moses Lake? This place has grown on me and not because you're here."

"Maybe we can keep both. We can start a bookstore franchise," Tanya joked.

"I doubt bookstores have the same appeal as fast food restaurants or hoity-toity coffee shops."

"Who can ever predict what the masses will want? For God's sake, those little twirly things are selling like hotcakes." Tanya's head popped up from Elle's shoulder.

Elle laughed. "Do you mean the fidget spinner?"

"Yeah. I mean who thought that up? It's almost as bad as the pet rock."

"Aunt Clara loves hers. She says it calms her."

"There must be a whole group of magicians devoted to making us regular folk fall in love with useless gadgets. I'll bet they're all laughing their asses off about it. They're probably called the fad magicians."

"There isn't, I swear. Besides, I thought we'd already determined you're anything but regular."

Tanya ignored the comment alluding to how she was special. "I've often wondered what constitutes beauty. Are there beauty magicians who decide what is appealing? Same thing. I don't like the idea of always buying into what everyone else thinks is beautiful, relevant, worthy…oh, you know what I mean."

Elle pulled Tanya into her arms and soundly kissed her. "Mmm, I love it when you get all feisty like that. Don't ever change."

The clip-clop of shoes registered on the stairs, and two short raps on the wall announced Imara. "Hey you lovebirds. I think I've aged ten years waiting for you to finish having make up sex. Can we please move on to devising a plan to help a very deserving chosen one?"

"Ten more minutes," Elle answered and grinned at Tanya. "So…considering Imara thinks we're already having sex, maybe we should sneak in a quickie?"

"Nope. If we're going to have make up sex, I want the full-meal deal. Imara, if you're still there, we need another forty-five minutes. Minimum. Try catching up with Bea and Clara. I'm sure y'all have plenty to talk about."

"I love how your mind works." Elle didn't waste any time leading Tanya to the bedroom and beginning her slow exploration.

CHAPTER TWO

Jaiden sat on the end of the dock and reached for her sling pack, where she'd stuffed the cut-up apples and cheese. Thank God summer had finally arrived. She couldn't remember a time when the island had endured such a harsh winter. The students weren't the only ones who had complained about the school year leaking into their summer vacations. By the final day of classes, the teachers were grumbling and whining louder than the entire student body during a pep rally. Of course the entire school had a student body just shy of 300, so pep rallies weren't very loud to begin with.

Every day it snowed, the school administrators had decided to cancel classes, shortening the summer break to compensate. Those decisions meant less time for Jaiden to catch up on her reading during the summer break. Since snow was a rare occurrence on Whidbey Island, for the safety of the students, the school had shut down a record-breaking ten days. None of the teachers were able to take advantage of the few days between the end of school and the beginning of the tourist season. The now bustling island would remain overrun with visitors until the start of the new school year.

Jaiden operated a modest crystal shop in the summer months as a way to augment her small teacher's salary. Not working all summer long wasn't feasible if she wanted to save enough for retirement. There were exciting places she intended to visit once that blessed day came. Coupeville wasn't as hippy-dippy as Langley, but the town attracted their fair share of tourists who gobbled up her crystals and other New Age wares.

"Hey Jaiden. Whatcha doing? Reading again?" Franklin asked.

Jaiden kept her groan from becoming audible. *Captain Obvious strikes again.* "Um, yeah. I was taking a lunch break and thought I'd sneak in a few chapters."

"Anything I might be interested in?"

"Not unless you're dying to read a good lesbian romance." Jaiden reminded the science teacher he didn't stand an ice storm's chance in hell of wooing her away from her interest in women. She wished that interest went further. In her thirty-five years, Jaiden had never found *the one*.

"I'm open minded. Maybe I would like the book." Franklin smiled and showed his crooked yellow teeth.

Jaiden tried to rein in the unkind thoughts that snuck into her brain. *I'll just bet you are if there's lesbian sex in the book.* Franklin tended to surround himself with science journals and all things academic, but he was a man after all. She shuddered, imagining him trying to interject himself in a sex scene. She almost burst out laughing, as she looked at his ridiculous 70s-style glasses and silk, disco shirt. She thought

16

maybe he should try to catapult himself back into that era, because it was definitely a time in history he obsessed over.

"This one doesn't have a lot of sex scenes, mostly fade to black," Jaiden answered.

"Oh. Hey do you think—"

"No," Jaiden cut him off. "Franklin, you're a nice guy, but you are definitely barking up the wrong tree." She held up her tablet.

"I hear bisexuality is all the rage…"

Jaiden sighed and pointed to a mark on the dock. "Let's go through that continuum again, Franklin. This is someone 100 percent straight." She moved her finger a foot. "This is someone who is bisexual. Moving her finger another foot, she added, "And this is someone who is 100 percent gay." Jaiden placed her finger six inches farther from the last place she'd pointed to. "Now pay attention, Franklin. See this spot that my finger is on? That's where I fit on the continuum. Six degrees from 100 percent lesbian, which means I possess less than zero interest in men. Does that help your scientific mind grasp what I'm trying to communicate?"

"No need to be sarcastic. You could have said I'm not interested because I'm not bisexual," Franklin huffed.

"I have, but so far that hasn't gotten through to you. We've had this conversation at least ten times. You're a bright guy. People don't change their sexual orientation on a whim."

"Okay, I just thought it would be nice for you to have someone to go to the movies or dinner with. You're always alone. That isn't healthy."

Jaiden couldn't argue that point. Lately she had felt very alone. Coupeville wasn't exactly the perfect hunting ground for possible mates. *Oh brother, is that what I have evolved to, talking about love like I'm some prehistoric lesbian getting ready to capture an unsuspecting woman?*

"I'm probably going to regret this, but if you want to go see the new Wonder Woman movie, we can go as friends and ogle the Amazons together."

Franklin bounced on the balls of his feet. "Great! I'll pick you up at six."

"No. I'll meet you at the theater, because this isn't a date," Jaiden reminded him.

After Franklin left, Jaiden looked at her watch. She was getting ready to stand and head back to her shop, when she heard a commotion down the dock. Glancing in the direction of the disturbance, she caught a glimpse of an exquisite woman with flowing red hair that was wildly whipping around in the wind. The woman was pointing in Jaiden's direction, and when her piercing green eyes landed, Jaiden's heart skipped a beat. Another attractive woman was chastising her. Jaiden wondered if they were a couple. A third woman stood close, looking embarrassed.

"Shh, don't make a scene. I see her," the woman with wavy blonde hair said.

Jaiden craned her head to see who they might be talking about. There were a few tourists wandering about the large novelty shop at the end of the dock. She grinned as she began to weave a tale in her head. She'd make all of the women lesbians including the tourists meandering through the shop. In her private fantasy, all the women were part of a covert organization designed to rid the world of misogynist pigs. She began to chuckle, and when she looked up again, the stunning woman with red hair had a cocky smile on her face. *Oh please let her be a single lesbian looking for a good time.*

Who was Jaiden kidding? She'd never had a single one-night stand in all her life.

†

"She's cute in that slightly stiff, academic way, huh?" Imara was looking directly at the woman with dark tousled hair sitting on the dock. Even though her petite form suggested a potential frailty, Imara sensed the power within. More than anything, it was Jaiden's eyes that acted like a tractor beam. Describing the color was nearly impossible; they weren't quite violet, nor a lighter shade closer to lilac. Her face was neither handsome nor delicate. *Could a person have an intelligent face?* Crisp angles met soft, full lips that weren't red or pink—another color Imara couldn't describe. Jaiden was beautiful in that unconventional manner, because all her seemingly incongruent features blended nicely together for a complete picture.

"Do you have to call attention to yourself? Isn't it enough you have that flaming red hair that shines a neon light on us all? I'm sure she saw you pointing at her," Elle grumbled.

"So. She'll think nothing of it when we introduce ourselves."

"Can't you cast a spell to have her come to The Enchanted Page II when we open for business? I doubt we'll need to introduce ourselves. She's an avid reader, isn't she? Please tell me you've done your homework with this one and haven't merely settled on her good looks to determine she's one of the chosen?"

"You two better decide how you're going to do whatever you plan on doing, because she's walking this way," Tanya said.

†

Elle glanced at the woman and wondered how Imara had chosen this one. She certainly didn't appear to lack confidence. Usually, the chosen were women in great need of an adventure to help bring them out of their shell and show them life was more than the four walls of their cubicle at work or their bland residence.

"Hi, do you need help? Maybe a recommendation on somewhere to eat? Looking for a particular gift?"

"That is mighty hospitable of you, but no, we're in the process of opening a bookstore in that empty space next to Mystic Crystal," Imara said.

Under her breath, Elle whispered, "Mighty hospitable. What? Are you from Texas?"

Elle felt a pinch to her arm as Imara hissed, "Shh."

The woman raised an eyebrow. "Looks like we'll be neighbors. I own Mystic Crystal and operate the store in the summer months only. The town closes up in the fall when most of the tourists leave, which works out well for me. I'm a teacher."

"Oh, how noble," Imara gushed.

Elle had never seen her old pal act this ridiculous, and she wondered if maybe this woman wasn't some kind of witch herself who had cast a love spell on Imara.

The woman stuck out her hand to Imara. "I'm Jaiden. I suppose you could shorten that to Jai, but no one has ever really done that before. Although I think I'd like a nickname." She smiled warmly.

"Jai it is." Imara clasped the woman's hand in both of hers, adding an extra layer of intimacy to the handshake. "Oh, these are my colleagues Elle and Tanya."

Elle and Tanya each shook Jai's hand more formally.

"Sorry, which one is Elle, and which is Tanya?"

"The attractive one is Tanya, and the one who looks constipated is Elle."

"Funny. You know you're the only one to bring out that look. Quite odd, since you're the one who's full of shit," Elle quipped.

20

Tanya laughed. "She is kinda right about that. I've mostly only seen Elle's fun-loving side. This is a whole new experience for me."

Jai looked between Elle and Tanya and asked, "Are you two together?"

Tanya smiled, and Elle stroked her arm. "We are," Elle proudly announced.

Imara shrugged. "I guess there is no accounting for taste."

"You know, I wouldn't mind a recommendation on a place to eat. The trip over was rather long, and I'm beyond starved," Tanya declared.

Elle didn't believe Tanya was as hungry as she stated and saw the tactic as a way to stop Elle and Imara from continuing their barbs at one another. She decided that wasn't a bad idea. Maybe Imara would settle if they all had a nice meal together.

"What kind of food are you in the mood for? Fancy or casual?"

Elle looked at Tanya, hoping she would weigh in.

"Casual I think," Tanya said.

"Fancy," Imara said at the same time.

"Hmm, Mo's Taphouse does have some decent food and it's casual, but they'll treat you like shit there. I've been a local for ten years now, and they've only recently started to smile at me. Tourists always receive their typical disdain. Oystercatcher is our fancy restaurant, and they have marvelous food. Knead & Feed is right on Main Street, and that's one of my favorite places to have lunch. Who doesn't like a bakery with a lunch menu?"

"Will you join us? I hate being a third wheel, and you'll certainly improve the ambiance no matter where we decide to go." Imara was laying on the charm, and Elle nearly gagged at her blatant flirtation.

21

Jai blushed. "Um, I can't. I've already been away from the store too long."

"Perhaps you can show me—us—around later. Dinner?"

"God, I'm sorry I agreed to go to a movie with a friend. I really wanted to see the new Wonder Woman film and well…beggars can't be choosers in this town."

"A date?" Imara asked.

"Ugh no, bite your tongue. A colleague. I'll probably regret saying yes. Franklin is as thick as a person can get when it comes to picking up on the rules of love and attraction. No matter how many times I tell him I am not interested in men, he doesn't seem to get the concept of a lesbian."

Imara grinned. "I like a woman who knows exactly what she is, and is not, attracted to."

"Perhaps I'll see you around, considering we're neighbors." Jai frowned. "Not to be Jaded Jaiden, but I do hope your bookstore does well. Lately, e-books are all the rage and have pushed the small bookshops out of business." Her face turned red as she held up her tablet. "I suppose I'm one of the culprits."

"Oh, don't you worry about us. Our books are special," Imara declared.

Elle jabbed her elbow in Imara's side.

"Ouch," Imara cried out.

Tanya chuckled but kept quiet.

Jai adopted a quizzical expression. "Oh, do tell."

Elle answered quickly before Imara opened her big mouth and sent the poor woman for the hills. "You'll have to come visit the store and see for yourself."

"I'll definitely do that. I don't always buy e-books. Sometimes I like to feel the paper. This island loses power in the winter a fair amount. That necessitates going back to pioneer days and paperbacks."

"Wonderful." Imara clapped her hands.

"Um, sorry to cut this conversation short, but I really do need to get back to my store."

"It was very nice to meet you, Jai," Tanya politely offered.

"Yeah, we need to have some lunch and sign the papers to make it all official. We plan on opening in a couple of days," Imara said.

Jai lifted her eyebrow. "Wow, that's fast. How in the world will you manage to pull that off?"

"Magic and sorcery." Imara grinned.

Jai waved her hand and smiled as she walked away. She turned her head once after leaving. Elle had to admit her smile was warm and friendly as she looked back. She could understand how Imara was intrigued with the woman. Jai exuded a kind of quiet intelligence and strength similar to Tanya. If she hadn't met Tanya, the temptation to bestow her own magic might have occurred.

†

The island was so different from Moses Lake. Tanya was enjoying the warm but not overly hot temperature, along with the slight breeze. She squinted against the sun's reflection on the water. She'd left her sunglasses in the car. All around her was green, and she could see the mountains off in the distance. Most of the snow had melted, but that didn't stop the view from impacting her sense of peace. The plan to spend the summer on the island was looking more appealing to her, as long as she could control the bickering between Imara and Elle. The constant jabs between the two were beginning to wear on her.

"Why'd you tell her about the magic in our books? You can be so…so…insufferable," Elle huffed.

"Um, hon, to be fair, I do believe you hinted at the magic when I first came into your store," Tanya said.

Imara responded with a full belly laugh. "Busted. Oh, I do like you, Tanya. What are you doing with Miss Stuffy Pants here?"

Uh oh, Tanya knew that look. She'd made a critical error. Even though her statement had been factual, she should have kept her mouth shut. "Sorry," she mumbled.

Elle stalked away in the direction of the center of town.

"Whoops. I believe your girlfriend is pissed at both of us now," Imara said.

"I wish you two would stop your idiotic posturing and unhelpful jabs. Elle offered to join forces with you. Why can't you be more...uh...supportive? For whatever reason, you seem to bring out the worst in Elle, and frankly, I'm exhausted by it."

Imara sighed and looked down. "I miss her," she whispered.

"Well you sure don't act like it."

"I screwed up and don't know how to apologize. Elle was my best friend. We've always needled each other a little, because it was fun for both of us, but you're right. Lately, our banter has an edge to it that never existed before."

"Why don't you try having an honest conversation with her? Tell her how you feel. Own up to whatever you did to cause this rift and then move on. If you really need Elle to bestow the magic on Jai, you'd better get everything settled now."

"Um...I don't exactly need Elle for the magic. That might have been a ruse so I could fix this little communication problem we're having. I actually need—"

"Oh brother, I said have an honest conversation." Tanya shook her head.

"Okay. We should hurry before she decides to send us both into a dark and dreary book."

"She wouldn't do that, would she?"

Imara shrugged. "Don't be too sure. She's got a bad temper. She won't send us into something dangerous. She'll do worse and propel us into the most tedious book she can find. She knows how much I hate boring stories. She learned from the best...Bea."

†

Elle couldn't remember the last time she'd felt so much anger. Anger wasn't her only emotion. She was feeling betrayed. Her biggest nightmare might happen again. Imara would swoop in and charm Tanya. Elle would lose the only woman she'd ever truly loved. Misty was an infatuation. At the time she'd thought it was love. It wasn't. The youthful crush wasn't anywhere near the depth of feeling she had for Tanya.

She wasn't sure where she was headed. Maybe she'd go to that tavern that treated their customers like shit and get herself a drink, or three. Her strides were long as she quickly made her way down the dock.

"Elle, wait," Tanya yelled.

Elle was tempted to slow down, but her pride got in the way. She continued on her track and almost bumped into the brick wall that magically appeared in front of her. She'd ignored the low and distant rumbling of Imara's voice conjuring the spell. She should have figured Imara would pull out her magic.

Elle pivoted on her heels and glared at Imara. "What the fuck, Imara?"

Imara held out her hands in a gesture of acquiescence. "Well...what did you expect? You wouldn't slow down."

25

"Please, honey. Will you speak with Imara and settle your past hurts? I'll take a walk, while the two of you talk and resolve this old grudge with one another, once and for all," Tanya pleaded.

"She's impossible and according to her, never wrong," Elle whined.

"No, I was very wrong," Imara admitted.

Elle opened her mouth to speak and then promptly closed it.

"Wasn't expecting that, were you?" Imara offered her cocky grin.

Tanya and Imara finally closed the distance and stood in front of Elle. Tanya placed a gentle kiss on her lips. "I love you very much. Talk to her, please, for me."

Elle sighed. "You'd better remove the brick wall before someone bumps into it."

Imara waved her hand in the air. "Already done." She grinned.

Elle smiled despite her anger. "You're getting better. Much quicker."

Tanya turned away and slowly walked down the pier heading in the same direction that Jai had come from earlier.

"I really am sorry. I want to explain what happened. When you met Misty, I was afraid."

"Ha, you afraid."

Imara held up her hand. "Let me finish, please. You have such an annoying habit of interrupting people. At least that hasn't changed."

"Is this an apology?"

"Oh right, yeah, back to my explanation. Anyway, you started spending all your time with that little hussy. I wanted my best friend back. All of a sudden, it was Misty this and Misty that. Good old best friend Imara was left out in the cold. Besides, I knew she would hurt you. I couldn't let that happen, even though I do understand how overbearing that seems."

"Oh."

"Yeah, you hurt my feelings. I do have them, you know. I thought if I wooed the little tart away from you we'd go back to normal, like we always did when you got your puppy dog crushes and they didn't last. She really wasn't worth it. I swear. The way she talked about you made me so mad."

"But I told you. She was different."

"I know. No offense, but when you were younger, you weren't the best judge of character."

"Harumph."

"You weren't. Remember when you started buzzing around what's her name?" Imara gave Elle that arrogant, knowing look she'd always hated.

"Corinthia."

"Yeah, she was a piece of work. Tried to get you to steal my spells so she could further her career by combining book chants with spells."

"Isn't that what you're proposing? To combine our book magic with yours?"

"I'm not gonna steal your chants. You're giving them to me. Totally different." Imara waved her hand in the air. "Come on. You have to agree; she was a complete bitch."

"Okay, I'll admit a pretty face sometimes got in the way, but not with Tanya."

"Agreed. She's the first one with substance. You know, falling for people with no substance is a lot like living in godforsaken Forks, Washington."

"Forks?"

"Yeah, the rainiest place in the United States. I spent four miserable months there. I was hoping to find real vampires and shapeshifters, but that movie series totally lied. Besides,

I wanted to see what the big, flippin' deal was. I still can't understand why that author is moving there."

"What author?"

"The one who wrote the book I plan on plucking the perfect character from."

"Now who's naive? And what does Forks have to do with appreciating attractive lesbians?"

"Living in Forks is like being married to a beautiful woman who's always sick. Gorgeous location, but it rains all the time."

"That's horrible. Do you mean to say you would leave your wife if she got sick?"

"Figure of speech. Okay, how about I say who's always cranky instead? Better?"

Elle laughed. "I have missed your shallow ass."

"I am not shallow." Imara put her hands on her hips and glared.

"Yes you are. Chasing after beautiful women without substance is what you do."

"Maybe I've changed."

"Doubtful. A leopard does not change her spots."

"Jai has substance…" Imara shifted her feet.

"Busted. You're gonna make a play and chase after her. You're not here to offer her an adventure."

"Maybe I want my own Tanya. Do you blame me?"

"What's so special about Jai?"

"She has this kind of quiet confidence. When she teaches, there's magic. I swear she enchants her students. She makes a difference in those kid's lives, especially the vulnerable ones."

"Ah, so you've stalked her?" Elle said.

"Not any more than you stalked Tanya when you were deciding about her worthiness as one of the chosen," Imara defended.

"Touché. My advice is to go into this with pure motivation. Exercise a bit of altruism by thinking of her first. If something evolves, it will be as it should." Elle slung her arm over Imara's shoulder. "Come on, let's go find my girlfriend and see about some lunch. She'll appreciate the blood splatter missing from our clothes. This is gonna be fun."

"So you forgive me?" Imara asked.

Elle nodded. She had missed her best friend, who could liven up any adventure.

"How about I give some of my wise advice? You'd better make that girlfriend of yours your wife pretty soon."

"Hey, don't push your luck. I just forgave you." Elle narrowed her eyes.

"Just saying. She's a keeper."

"That she is and paws off. Now I really don't give a shit if you go after Jai, as long as you leave Tanya alone."

"I promise. Cross my heart and hope to keep it from my cauldron." Imara crossed her index finger over her heart.

CHAPTER THREE

Jaiden continued to look out the window of her shop hoping to catch a glimpse of the women she'd met earlier. She was beyond intrigued. Walking back to her stool, she sat heavily. *Damn, I had to extend an invitation to Franklin today.*

She began to daydream about having dinner with Imara. She didn't mind tagging along with the other couple. They were cute together and clearly besotted with one another. Although she did detect a bit of acrimony between Elle and Imara, and a hint of jealousy. She wondered if maybe Imara and Tanya had been an item at one time. Jaiden had a thousand questions.

Closing time was approaching, and she hadn't seen or heard any rustling in the empty store next to her own. She'd have to run home and get her car to drive to Oak Harbor. Coupeville didn't have a theater. The town was small, although they managed to have a cozy movie house in

Langley. Too bad Langley was farther away than Oak Harbor and didn't have the new movie she wanted to see. Clyde Theater in Langley served popcorn with real butter, not that fake crap made of questionable ingredients.

Jaiden locked the door to her store and began to walk home. She appreciated the peacefulness of the quaint town where she lived that allowed her to simply walk to work. As she strolled along the familiar path to her cottage, she felt like someone was watching her. It wasn't exactly an unwelcome feeling, but certainly fell into the category of unsettling. After she changed into a pair of jeans and a long-sleeved shirt, she climbed into her car. It was still light out and the sun beat down on her car making it uncomfortable inside. She would appreciate the warmer clothes in the air-conditioned theater. The island also cooled down considerably at night.

Jaiden made it to the theater with just enough time to buy some of the crappy popcorn with the butter-flavored oil she knew was horrible for her. The distinct smell of popcorn was always so much more appealing than the taste. At least she didn't imbibe in the Milk Duds. Sweets had a way of glomming onto her hips and ass. Thirty had been the magic number when she'd had to start increasing the amount of exercise she did to keep the pounds from attaching themselves to her petite frame. She accepted her small popcorn and grabbed several napkins from the dispenser.

Franklin rushed through the doors, breathing heavily as he bellied up to the counter. "I could have bought your popcorn. You didn't have to get your own. We could have gotten a big bucket and shared."

"This is not a date, Franklin."

"I know. But friends buy each other stuff," he said petulantly.

"I'll grab us some seats while you get your own bucket."

"Okay, I'll get a large in case you want more."

Jaiden groaned. This was going to be a long night. If Franklin was one of those who felt the need to engage in a running commentary while the movie was playing, she'd be tempted to grab his nuts and squeeze until he screamed like a little girl.

As she made her way down the aisle in the darkened theater, she saw the flowing red hair. *It can't be.* As if the woman with her two friends could hear Jaiden's thoughts, she turned around and grinned. Jaiden wracked her brain, trying to remember if she'd told the three women what movie she was seeing and which theater she was going to. She played the conversation in her mind. Yes, she'd revealed she wanted to see Wonder Woman and the only option was Oak Harbor, so this wasn't a huge surprise. Jaiden did wonder why the three women had decided to see the same movie.

At the same time Imara was beckoning Jaiden forward to join them, she heard Franklin rushing down the aisle. He slung his arm around her shoulder. "Who's that waving at you?"

Jaiden pushed his arm away. "The new owners of the bookstore next to my shop."

"Come join us," Imara whisper-called.

"Okay." Jaiden started to make her way down the row, squeezing past Tanya and Elle so she could sit on the other side of Imara. Franklin followed with a scowl on his face. When he stepped on Tanya's foot, she grimaced and stood to give him more room. Elle and Imara followed suit, and Jaiden thought she saw an evil glint in Imara's eye right before Franklin jumped and grunted in surprise as if someone had poked or pinched him. Jaiden stood in front of her seat motioning for Franklin to take the seat to her right.

Jaiden turned her head to meet Imara's twinkling green eyes. "Fancy meeting you here."

"When you mentioned the movie, I realized I hadn't seen it either and thought that would be a perfect thing to do tonight. You don't mind that we crashed your date?"

"It's not a date," Jaiden insisted.

"Maybe you should introduce me," Franklin peeved.

"Oh, right." Jaiden pointed to Imara first. "This is Imara, Elle, and Tanya."

Franklin tried to stretch his arm across Jaiden to offer his hand, but Imara only nodded and ignored the greeting. "Hi, I'm Franklin." His arm fell limply to his lap.

"I don't think Franklin is happy that you ran into us." Imara smirked.

"I don't imagine he is, but I'm glad," Jaiden answered.

"How about having a drink with us afterward?" Imara asked.

Even though Jaiden wanted to have a drink with the trio, she didn't wish to extend her time with Franklin. "Um, how about a rain check?"

Franklin settled back in his seat and smirked. "We can have a drink back at my place."

Through gritted teeth and a death glare at Franklin, Jaiden said, "Let me be clear that rain check does not apply to you. I am not having a drink with you, Franklin, neither at your apartment nor a tavern, not ever."

Franklin slouched in his seat. "I was being friendly."

When the lights went down and the movie previews started, Jaiden felt relieved and risked a glance at Imara, who was smiling like the cat who ate the canary.

†

Imara studied Jai while the movie played. She found the woman to her right more interesting than the movie. She had to give it to Franklin; he wasn't giving up. His hand snaked to Jai's thigh several times. Finally, after pushing his offending hand off her thigh three times, Jai pinched his hand. His audible *ouch* reverberated through the quiet theater.

Imara chuckled to herself, as Franklin kept digging a bigger hole for himself. She could see Jai's irritation build as he kept trying to engage her in conversation while the movie played. Imara was tempted to come to Jai's rescue with a short gag spell to cause Franklin to lose his voice, but she was sure Jai would hear her whisper the chant. She'd already muttered a very short spell earlier that caused a tiny shot of pain right up Franklin's ass. Tanya had heard and raised her eyebrow, but she didn't say a word.

The credits began to roll and their small group started to rustle around in their seats, preparing to exit the theater. Jai had her empty popcorn container and crushed water bottle in her hand. Imara watched Jai express her irritation when it was clear that Franklin was about to leave his garbage on the floor.

"Franklin, pick up your shit and take it to the garbage can," Jai directed.

"Why? They have people who clean up after every showing. That's what they get paid to do." Franklin pursed his lips together in an unattractive cross between a pout and sulkiness.

Jai gave him a quick shove and leaned over to pick up his mess.

Imara wanted to ask Elle to send Franklin into a book where he was part of a harem of women who had to serve some cruel master. He'd make an ugly woman for sure, but that would teach him. "I guess you're one of those men who

34

think women were put on this earth to serve you. I can think of a few ways to fix your viewpoint—"

"We should probably start heading out. It's getting late," Tanya interrupted.

"I am not like that. I'm a very enlightened guy. It's just that the workers here are paid to clean the theater. That's all."

Imara could almost see the steam coming off Jai. That was another thing about Jai that Imara admired. She could learn a few things from someone who treated wait staff and service workers with respect and kindness. That was the sign of a good person. Some days, Imara thought she did okay, and other times, she believed she had a long way to go.

Imara could tell Jai was about to explode. After spending the entire time dodging Franklin's overtures and pushing his roaming hand away, Imara was sure she hadn't enjoyed the movie. She hadn't seen a whole lot of the movie herself, because she'd been watching Jai. Imara had to admit parts of the movie were very appealing. Maybe she should suggest another viewing.

As the group shuffled out of the theater, Imara leaned in and whispered to Jai, "Seems like you weren't able to enjoy the movie. Would you like to come again tomorrow night and see it with me? I was also a little distracted."

A small smile graced Jai's lips. "I'd love to."

"Love to what?" Franklin butted in.

Imara brushed her hand over Jai's arm. "We'll connect tomorrow, okay?"

Jai nodded. The smile remained on her face until Franklin interjected himself into the conversation again.

"What'd I miss? What are you guys talking about?"

Jai tossed the garbage she'd picked up into the can. When she addressed Franklin, her smile was gone. "I'm heading out. I need to get home, because I plan on opening the store early tomorrow. I've got some inventory I need to rearrange." She turned toward Imara, Elle, and Tanya. "Hopefully, I'll see you tomorrow morning. If you need any help with your store, let me know. I'm sure I can spare a few moments when there is a lag in business. The noon hour is usually slow."

†

Imara watched Jai climb into her car and drive away. Franklin looked shell-shocked as she bowled past him without saying goodbye. She seemed to metaphorically swat him away like a fly. Imara was reveling in her good mood as she thought about the date she would have with Jai the next night. Her happy bubble burst when Elle grabbed her arm and turned her around.

"What the hell do you think you're doing?" Elle asked.

"Who me?" Imara chuckled.

"Is Jai going to be your chosen one or your next fling?"

Imara shrugged. "Why can't she be both? Tanya was," she retorted.

"Tanya was never a fling," Elle huffed.

"I don't understand why you're so upset. If my charms are directed toward Jai, they'll not be headed in Tanya's direction. I would think you'd be happy about that."

"I like her," Tanya said.

"Precisely. She's not like one of your witch bimbos. She's a nonmag. We aren't supposed to—"

"Are you seriously spouting the shit that Gordon used to lecture about not mixing with nonmags? Gordon and his cronies were total wankers. Did you know he managed to influence the warlocks with his poison? Some of them were starting to regurgitate the same crap."

"She's kinda right, hon," Tanya gently added.

Elle visibly deflated. "God, that's true. I have no idea where this is coming from. I guess I like her too and felt a bit protective. Are you sure you want to go 'through with giving her your brand of book adventure? You know how easy it is to fall in love with a main character who comes to life. They tend to ride the edge of perfection, even the ones that are written with flaws."

"True, but we're supposed to return them to inside the pages, because life on the outside is untenable for them. You know we only do this to jumpstart a better life for the chosen."

"This one doesn't seem to lack any confidence. Why her?"

"Because her lesson is a flawless lover does not exist. She must learn to look beyond the faults. I've picked out the perfect character for her. Her sense of social justice won't allow her to judge too harshly a person with a physical disability. She'll want to go out of her way to accept Dani. Besides, Dani is such a beloved character, I'd like to meet her in the flesh."

"Oh, Dani would be a hard person not to fall in love with," Tanya added.

"Hey now. Do I have to worry about the characters that this one"—Elle poked Imara—"brings to life, now?"

Tanya pecked Elle, as she lovingly stroked her cheek. "Never, you are better than any character in a book. Flaws and all."

"Flaws and all, huh? Well, at least I don't possess any flaws when it comes to bedroom acrobatics."

"No, you certainly don't..." Tanya laughed.

"La, la, la. I really don't want to hear all about that. Ick, imagining my best friend having sex is almost as bad as when I heard my mother with that male model. God, they were going at it for hours. I swear that left an indelible memory." Imara shuddered. "Why do you think I spent so much time at your place?"

"Oh my God. I remember that. The pharmaceutical industry should have tapped on your mother's door. Remember the potion she made that gave her lovers an eight-hour erection?" Elle laughed. "She didn't have to put warning labels on the tea she served them. I would have loved to be a fly on the wall when he swore to his doctor that he didn't have a prescription for Viagra. I'll bet the warlocks had a fit about that. She always did prefer nonmags for her boy toys."

"That's because the warlocks knew how to counteract her potions. They weren't as much fun, according to Mom. She did date a few warlocks. I'm still friends with one of them. He was a good guy. I'll never understand why he went out with her. We've stayed close over the years, even after Mom was a total shit to him. As a matter of fact, I was a little lost last year, and he let me stay with him on the island. That's how I became interested in Jai as the next chosen one. I saw her one day and started following her."

"How is Serafina?"

"Still trying to perfect her fountain of youth cream. You know how Mom hates wrinkles."

"Does it actually work? I might need some soon," Tanya said.

"No you don't, honey. Your skin is beautiful." Elle brushed her fingers across Tanya's cheek.

"Oh aren't you two precious? Amazingly, it does. She's been able to peddle her wares in Japan of all places. I have to admit she looks good for almost sixty, but then so does Bea, and she doesn't put any crap on her skin or go to the witches for anti-aging spells that don't work very well and sometimes cause side effects."

"Like warts. I wasn't exactly telling tales when I taunted Imara with that vaginal wart crack. I know witches don't get vaginal warts, but your run-of-the-mill wart, those are abundant on the older witches."

Imara nodded. "Unfortunately, yes, with big long hairs protruding from the middle."

"Why do they do it then?" Tanya asked.

"Because every once in a while, they hit pay dirt and it works," Imara explained.

"Oh, I guess I'll pass on your mother's cream," Tanya said.

"Personally, I prefer to grow old gracefully with my partner rocking in a chair next to me."

"You two are giving me a toothache."

"You're jealous," Elle taunted.

"Damn straight I am. Well not straight, but yeah, I'd like what you two have," Imara said earnestly.

"We should head back to the inn, we have a long day ahead of us tomorrow. It seems as though you've attracted too much attention. We'll have to set up the store without the assistance of anyone's magic, because she'll no doubt pop in to check on us."

Tanya quirked her eyebrow. "You've been holding out on me. I thought book magicians possessed very limited magic. You never told me you could inject sorcery into manual labor."

Elle shrugged. "Book witches often take the easy way and can perform all kinds of enchantments. Book witches or magicians aren't supposed to venture into the fringes, but Imara and I never paid much attention to the rules. Her fault, because she always sweet-talked me into trying to broaden my horizons."

Imara slung her arm around Elle. "No, we didn't adhere to those stupid conventions, did we? Welcome back, Elle. There's my best friend."

"I don't mean to be the one to interject a bit of practicality into the situation, but don't you think we should start looking for a more permanent place to stay until we remodel the upstairs apartment? I didn't realize how much the place needs attention. I can't very well leave Tolstoy on his own, even if my neighbor says she'll take care of him while we're on this mission, and I'd prefer not to keep using your favored mode of transportation."

"Makes you a little nauseous, huh?" Imara asked. She didn't really enjoy the way book magicians got around either. It was never a smooth journey and nausea always followed. Fast but uncomfortable was not her style. Slow and deliciously naughty was more her speed in everything. "Tolstoy is your adorable kitty, right?"

Tanya smiled. "Yes."

"Too bad the book magician has snagged you. You would have made a wonderful book witch. We are prone to travel with our familiars." Imara grimaced. "And they are never dogs. Only cats. Dogs are such disgusting drooling beasts. I mean, come on, they eat my familiars' excrement and consider it a treat. I once entertained a nonmag who brought her drooling mastiff, and he headed straight for the litter box. Ugh. And she used to let him lick her face. Double ugh. I put an anti-love spell on her. Instead of drawing her in, the spell acted like a repellent. Good riddance."

"Not all former nonmags are as charming as Tanya. Oh I mean, not all humbles."

†

40

For the first time in a very long dry spell, Jaiden was looking forward to going to her shop in the morning. During the movie, she could almost feel Imara's enchanting green eyes on her. She could see Imara watching her in the periphery but tossed aside the temptation to look. She'd been too busy battling Franklin's awkward advances. Half her time at the movie she'd spent pushing his roaming hand away. The other half she'd focused on desperately trying not to declare her lust for Imara. She didn't believe she was reading the signals wrong. Imara was interested, and Jaiden planned to take full advantage of that tomorrow evening after the movie. She really did want to see the movie; she'd missed more than half with Franklin's antics and her distraction over the exotic Imara sitting next to her.

Jaiden couldn't quite detect the perfume Imara wore, that is, if she was wearing any perfume. A sort of sweet and spicy scent wafted from Imara that was intoxicating to Jaiden's nostrils. She kept breathing in the scent, hoping to figure out what was in the unusual combination.

Settling back in her bed, Jaiden closed her eyes and imagined Imara straddling her as she nibbled her way over Jaiden's body. Jaiden clearly envisioned Imara's wild red hair falling loosely on her shoulders as she brought her lips close and absently flipped the heavy strands back out of the way. Those intense green eyes would drink in her naked form as Jaiden heaved under the barrage of slow kisses down her body.

Imara's tongue and fingers would expertly dance along her body until she begged for release. Her own hand traveled inside her underwear and found her wet lips. Too bad it was impossible to lick herself, or she might have tried to invent a new yoga pose. She'd have to be satisfied with the fantasy of Imara's tongue as it glided along her clit.

Tonight she wouldn't need to read a book to satisfy her craving. Jaiden's imagination was much better than the real thing or a book. This was a rare occasion when a real human being satisfied her hunger by assuming the lead role in her fantasy. When that happened, Jaiden always pursued her living fantasy. Unfortunately, none of them worked out. They hadn't lived up to what she imagined, and when a relationship progressed to the intimacy stage it all fell apart. She had a string of failed relationships to prove that. Physical intimacy was supposed to lead to emotional connection. When the bond didn't occur as prescribed, the arousal would diminish to nothing and her partner would catch on to the ruse.

Jaiden's fingers moved rapidly along her wet center, until she felt a familiar sensation overwhelm her body and cause a rapid succession of contractions. This orgasm rated highly amongst the many she'd given herself. As she settled back in her bed, calmer and ready to sleep, she let her mind wander to her last failed relationship. She cringed as she remembered that fateful night.

Ariana was pulling on her jeans as she directed her anger at Jaiden. "You might be the hottest lesbian on this godforsaken island, but I'm done. Good luck finding someone as perfect as the women in your damn books. No one has the kind of mind-blowing sex that you read about. This is real life, Jaiden, not some lesbian romance novel. It's messy, sometimes ugly, and most definitely imperfect like me, and believe it or not, like you. Call me when you're ready for a real relationship and you've decided to stop having fake orgasms."

"Okay, I admit that wasn't my best decision, but like you said, nobody's perfect," Jaiden defended.

"It's not just that…" Ariana's wounded look almost made Jaiden want to make it all better. She did love Ariana, who certainly was an exceptionally attractive woman. Ariana had everything going for her. She was intelligent, normally kind and easy going, sexy, and she shared Jaiden's politics. But something was missing. While she cared deeply for Ariana, she wasn't head over heels in love with her.

"What?"

"I want someone to look at me like I'm the only person in their sphere." Ariana's eyes brimmed with unshed tears. "Like I matter more than a handy companion to go to the movies and have dinner with," she added.

Ouch. "You deserve that. I can't argue. For what it's worth, I did wish it was me."

"But it's not. Hell, I might even have settled for you looking at me like I was the last meal on earth and you couldn't wait to devour me. I'd have settled for pure lust. Maybe not for the long term, but definitely longer than a year."

"One thing I'm absolutely positive about. My loss is some woman's very lucky find. You're amazing and someone will recognize that. You have no idea how sorry I am that I couldn't be the one."

"That's just it, Jaiden, I do understand how sorry you feel. You are that amazing person everyone falls in love with. I was just one of many and it pains me to leave you." Ariana took a big breath. "I can't bring myself to settle for someone who doesn't love me with equal fervor. I hope that someday you find what you're looking for."

So do I. Jaiden crawled out of bed and gently kissed Ariana on the lips.

"See you around, Jaiden." Ariana hurried out of the room still buttoning her shirt and wiping her eyes. Two weeks later, she moved to the east side of the state and took a teaching position in Ellensburg. Jaiden heard she'd started dating a very nice college professor and they'd moved in together. Jaiden was sure it was only a matter of time before they married. She'd felt a twinge of envy when she'd heard that but not because she wanted Ariana back. She simply wanted what they had. A loving, equal partnership where neither tipped the scales of love.

The unpleasant visit to the past caused Jaiden to toss and turn for the remainder of the night. She was sure she would wake up the next day with huge bags under her eyes. That was the last thing she wanted, considering she had a date with Imara and was sure to run into her during the course of the day.

CHAPTER FOUR

Imara was whistling as she pulled the books from the boxes. Although she was not too keen on the idea of stocking the shelves with all those boring nonmagical books, she knew that not everyone was suited to Elle's gifts. She wasn't exactly sure where Tanya fit into the equation. She'd heard Tanya could perform chants, and that alone was such a surprising development. She hadn't kept up with the book magicians after her falling out with Elle, so she wasn't sure what the Director of E-book Magic did. Could Tanya enchant e-books? Imara wondered if Tanya was skilled enough to bring the characters in e-books to life. That idea would need exploration at a later date. Imara needed to be on firmer ground with Elle before chumming up with Tanya.

Imara swayed to the music playing in the background. "I could do a small spell to have the books dance right onto the shelves along with the music…"

"No," Elle and Tanya said in unison.

"Aw come on, this is boring. I could be talking with the lovely Jai right now, instead of performing slave labor in this stuffy little store. We should simply fess up and tell her what we're really here for? From what I've heard, Tanya, you were amazingly blasé when you learned about book magic."

"We didn't have a whole lot of choice after Scrotumface sent her into a particularly dangerous book at a very unpleasant moment in the adventure."

Imara laughed. "Scrotumface, where did you come up with the colorful descriptor? Quite appropriate, but it doesn't really sound like you. If I remember correctly, you named Gordon many things, but Scrotumface wasn't one of them."

"Mom."

"Really? I would have guessed Aunt Clara."

"Mom was trying to curb her swearing. Aunt Clara did quite enjoy the creative words we came up with. I believe Mom started with poopbiscuit and the words sort of snowballed from there. Tanya contributed helicopter instead of hell, and yours truly added donkeyhole and then Scrotumface. I kind of prefer them now."

"Come on, Elle, you can't really want to shelve these books the hard way, can you? So what if she sees us. I'll bet she'll take the news like a pro. I get the sense she's something special too and wouldn't react badly to the realization her storefront neighbors are a magician, a witch, and whatever Tanya is. Have you figured that one out yet? The rumors are rampant, you know."

Tanya frowned. "I'm not sure I'm comfortable being the talk of the magical or mystical world."

Imara waved her hand in the air. "Oh, it's all good. Everyone is kind of jealous. They wanted to be the one to find a hybrid."

"That's worse than nonmag. You do know how offensive that is to refer to me as a hybrid."

46

"Sorry. I guess I never thought of it. What's your suggestion? The magical and nonmagical worlds are full of labels. It's how we easily categorize things. You're never going to get away from that."

"God, you two really are cut from the same cloth, aren't you? Do I need to bring out my argument about how those same labels can be so divisive?"

Imara raised her eyebrow. "Hmm. Maybe I need a little education, so I don't step in a turdbasket and then put that same foot in my mouth. I don't wish to offend Jai when we do come clean. Because, you know, we are going to have to explain why she's the chosen one when I bring that character to life. Witches don't have the luxury of keeping people completely in the dark. That tactic has never worked. The nonmagical world can believe they are dreaming when sent into a book adventure, but not when a living, breathing man, or woman stands before them."

Pop

"Turdbasket, good one," Bea said.

"Mom, how come you popped in?" Elle asked.

"Just want to check and see how my girls are doing."

Imara narrowed her eyes. She was a master at detecting any amount of deception and she'd been around her second mom long enough to know she was hiding the truth. "Don't give me a load of crap. Something is up."

Bea sighed. "Okay, I might have heard a rumor on the magical airwaves."

"What rumor?" Imara asked.

"Vlad heard about the two of you mending fences and your special interest in a nonmag. Sorry, Tanya, chantfree is really a horrible label..."

Tanya threw her hands in the air. "I give up."

"Try humble, I think that has a better ring to it," Elle said.

47

"Um, I think that's an existing adjective, or I suppose it could be a verb, not a noun." Bea shook her head. "Anyway, he is planning to make an appearance."

Imara saw Elle's eyes travel to the front window and go wide. "Um…"

Imara looked at the shadow taking shape outside their store. Vladimir Ambus's dark form emerged from the mist. Vlad was the most powerful warlock, leading several large covens of various specialties beyond the moderate numbers in the book witch covens. He'd tried to assimilate the coven Imara associated herself with. They had staunchly refused to join, knowing his lust for power and dark magic knew no bounds. The small coven wanted no part of his evil ways. Imara hadn't wanted to join any coven, preferring to freelance, but after the row with Elle, she'd felt a little lost and alone. She remained on the fringes of this particular coven.

Vlad's midnight-black coat whipped in the wind, matching the inky black of his eyes and hair, which seemed to turn impossibly darker. This black was the epitome of the absence of light. His slicked-back hair revealed a prominent widow's peak, and a goatee intensified his strong chin. *Does he think he's Bela Lugosi?* Vlad was handsome; she had to give him that. He had the classic chiseled features along with full wide lips that at times revealed a charming smile complete with a row of white, even teeth.

Vlad didn't suck blood from his victims. He sucked the life and joy out of those misfortunate enough to be around him. At least Imara thought his victims were random. Maybe they weren't.

"Shit. Fuck," Imara muttered. This recent development called for a few choice swear words, not the colorful versions Bea and Elle preferred to use.

The door to the shop opened, and a frosty chill filled the air.

†

Vlad's velvety smooth voice was hypnotic to Tanya. She sensed the others did not want him to enter their airspace, but Tanya couldn't help herself; she was enthralled, despite the fact she was a lesbian and madly in love with Elle.

"Imara, it is so good to see you again. It has been too long. Elle, Bea, likewise. Are you all using Serafina's new cream? None of you look a day older than twenty-five. Of course, I've not had the pleasure of spending much time with any of you lately. Something I hope to correct." Tanya thought his smile was charming, even though his row of blinding, white teeth somehow registered as evil.

Imara looked like she was choking on his declaration. She heard Imara whisper a short chant.

Bring the Addict up to speed, share my memory of his greed.

Tanya landed inside Imara's head. Acute thoughts played out the memory like a short film, and Tanya felt Imara's emotions. The last time they'd had a visit from Vlad, he had tried a spell or two to coerce Imara into his fold by sucking the life energy out of Elle and Bea.

Imara, Elle, and Bea were leaning on the counter in Bea's bookstore, laughing together over a funny story. An oppressive fog seeped under the door. There was a slight burning smell, almost like the remnants of a forest fire, but this wasn't smoke; it was more of cold density to the air. Imara shivered and saw the same effect on Elle and Bea.

Vlad slithered into the store and raised his arms. Imara cried out, as her "adoptive" mother and her best friend began gasping for air. Hands flew to their throats as if to remove the foreign substance impeding their airways.

"I can reverse the spell, but only if you join me," Vlad declared. He offered to unwind his spell on Elle and Bea in exchange for Imara's loyalty.

A reflexive reaction from Imara sliced through the evil manifestation. Imara had managed a blocking spell at the last moment, before doing the unthinkable and agreeing to join his coven. She wasn't sure how she was able to block the powerful Vlad. She likened it to the adrenaline rush that empowers a mother to lift a car when their child is in danger. She doubted she'd ever be able to repeat the monumental feat.

The dark cloud hovered all around Vlad as he realized his spell had bounced off the brick wall and landed with a thud at his feet. He had promised they would meet again.

Every few months, Vlad would attempt to charm Imara into submission because he no longer had the leverage of performing his dark magic on those most near and dear to her. Elle, Bea, and even Aunt Clara were the closest thing to family she ever had in her life, since Serafina had not been much of a mother to her. Vlad had never much interested himself with Serafina, other than a short-lived tryst, believing she was somehow defective because of her preference for sexual liaisons with mere mortals.

Shaken from the minimovie, Tanya heard the silky voice again. "Imara, you must introduce me to your new friend. I've heard many wonderful things about this delectable

50

creature." He turned his dark eyes on Tanya. "You are the famed nonmag called the book addict?"

Tanya felt a small tug and stuck out her hand. "Hello, I'm Tanya." Miraculously, she did not feel the need to lecture Vlad about his use of the label nonmag nor his reference to her as the book addict.

Vlad kissed her hand with a dramatic flair, reminiscent of old-world charm. "Positively delighted to meet you, Tanya. I am Vladimir Ambus, at your humble service. I am an old friend of Imara, Elle, and Bea. I don't mind labels." He winked. "I am what is known as a sorcerer or warlock. I also do not specialize, as does my dear friend, Imara. My power is broad and all-encompassing to include the many mystical possibilities of this world we all live in."

Elle grabbed Tanya's arm and roughly pulled her close in an overly protective embrace. "What the hell do you want, Vlad? You're no friend of mine, and I am confident you are no friend of my mother or Imara, either."

"Tsk, tsk, tsk. I truly thought a few more years on the planet would have taught you more manners, since it is clear your mother was never able to impart that necessary respect for your elders and betters. I won't teach a lesson here, because frankly, you're not worth my efforts."

"And you fear I would counteract the spell and embarrass you," Imara muttered.

Tanya was grateful for her extra-sensitive hearing. The anomaly had helped when they'd fought against Gordon. Apparently, Vlad had sensitive hearing as well.

"Your bravado, lovely Imara, will one day land you in hot water. Although I prefer not to use that tired old cauldron you mere witches prefer, my idea of hot water is a lake in the depths of hell. Don't test me."

"Then let me ask the question as respectfully as I can. We repeat, what business do you have on Whidbey Island?"

51

"Ah, direct as usual." His eyes swiveled from Elle to Imara. "Both of you. I've been made aware of a very special individual that resides on this tiny island. Honestly, I was quite surprised. Whidbey seems relatively insignificant, but this person does intrigue me. I believe you may have made her acquaintance. I'd be amenable to working together and almost wasting my vast talents to perform a spell that is clearly beneath me to bring a character to life for her. I believe her name is Jaiden. She is quite beautiful. Don't you agree?" Vlad smiled.

Tanya felt a small shiver when Vlad smiled.

"We don't need your assistance, Vlad, but I appreciate the offer," Imara said through gritted teeth.

"Perhaps not, but I'd like to stay for a while to see how everything evolves. Just in case." Vlad's long, black coat lashed about his body, his exit as dramatic as his entrance. "I'll be in touch, ladies." Vlad's parting comment seemed to create an air of peril.

†

Imara was speechless as Vlad made his exit and seemed to suck all the positive vibes from the shop. She sat down heavily on the stool she conjured for the store.

"Holy poopbiscuits! I do not want to be on Vlad's radar. He scares me a lot more than Gordon ever did," Elle exclaimed.

"Holy poopbiscuits? Try Holy Fuck. Sorry Bea, but we are in deep shit. And not to be too critical, but did you have to poke the warlock with your snarky question and comment?" Imara asked.

"You asked him the same thing," Elle defended. "Besides he turned his evil intent in Tanya's direction. It was pure instinct to protect her. You need to do something, Imara."

"I know, I know," Imara acknowledged. She wondered if pulling their resources together, the four of them could fight Vlad. Usually power came in multiples of three, or five with the strength of the pentagon. She worried four was not the correct number.

"He didn't seem so bad to me," Tanya interjected.

"Imara, fix Tanya. That slimy scrotumface put a spell on her." Elle pulled Tanya tight against her body.

"He did no such thing," Tanya argued.

"Oh, he most certainly did," Bea chimed in.

Imara took Tanya's hand in hers and chanted.

Undo the enchantment spell,
Never let it land again
Tanya, now and forever,
Remains my protected friend.
Endeavor to break my spell
And forever rot in hell.

Tanya's eyes cleared. "What just happened?"

"Vlad put a charming spell on you, and I reversed it with a little bit of flair. If he tries that one again, a nasty little surprise will await him. He won't. He's smart enough to recognize I wouldn't let him get away with it. Although, he may not completely realize how much I've learned over the last few years. I've evolved quite a bit. Enough to make it very uncomfortable for him; at least for a short duration until he manages to find an antidote."

"But…I didn't hear him chant," Tanya said in confusion.

"You wouldn't. He has mastered the skill of uttering chants in his mind. Unless you can read minds, you won't hear his spells. I've almost found the answer to that dilemma.

I can sense a spell, but I don't hear the exact words. I'm in the process of perfecting that potion so that I will."

"I want to drink that potion when it's ready. I'd like to know what's coming at us," Elle declared.

"Me too," Bea and Tanya said together.

"It's not ready for testing on anyone other than myself. I don't want to subject anyone else to any nasty side effects."

"I'll take my chances," Elle said.

"Me too," Tanya and Bea chimed in.

Imara laughed. "I think there is an echo in the room."

The tinkle of the bell interrupted their conversation, and when Imara saw Jai step inside a warm feeling flooded her soul.

†

Jaiden had listened to the music and the rustling around next door and tamped down her urge to run right over. She'd had to stop herself from rushing a few customers, without patiently explaining the purpose for each crystal. Jaiden had a knack for pinpointing the perfect match but only after spending a good deal of time with each person. It wasn't unusual for her to talk with a customer for an hour or more.

Finally, the morning rush had abated, and she was free to check on her new friends. She'd seen the mysterious man approach their store, then linger outside of hers. She'd felt his presence hovering outside her four walls. Something was a little amiss about him. The minute she'd caught a glimpse of him leaving the other store, she'd placed her strongest protection crystals near the front door. Two crystal formations of black tourmaline and smoky quartz were not for sale. She'd meditated on the two rock displays for the specific purpose of transmuting negative energy.

When she opened the door to The Enchanted Page II, she felt like she'd interrupted something important. The question she'd had about the new sign and when they had a chance to hang it fell off her radar, as she looked at four alarmed faces.

"That man can't have been the health inspector. You aren't selling any food. He didn't look like a fire inspector either. I happen to know them," Jaiden noted.

"No, he wasn't either. An old acquaintance..." Imara answered.

"No offense, but the guy gives me the creeps. His whole aura screamed negative energy. I pushed a few of my favorite crystals near the door in case he abandoned his whole lingering routine and came inside."

"He was hanging around your store?" Imara's voice squeaked.

Jaiden thought that was an interesting reaction coming from the normally unflappable woman who held a hint of arrogance about her. Imara's cockiness was barely within the acceptable limits of what Jaiden was normally attracted to. Perhaps arrogance was the wrong word. Confidence on steroids might be more appropriate.

Jaiden blushed as she realized she would have to admit to paying close attention to the happenings at The Enchanted Page II. They might think *she* was some creepy stalker. "Yeah, I saw him go into your store. When he came out, he sort of hovered on the other side of my door. The urge to keep him away warred with an impulse to invite him in. When I picked up my favorite crystal display, it became clear I did not want him coming into my store. Thankfully he didn't."

All four women seemed to expel a collective sigh of relief, and Jaiden quirked her eyebrow in response.

"He isn't a friend of any of us. Not a nice man doesn't begin to cover it. I'd recommend staying clear of Vlad," Elle declared.

Imara's tone was almost pleading, "Please, get one of us, preferably me, if he tries to approach you. I'm better equipped to deal with him than Elle, Bea, or Tanya."

"Bea?" Jaiden asked.

"That would be me, dear." The attractive woman held out her hand. "You must be Jai. It's a pleasure to meet you. I do hope you will help keep this one"—she pointed to Imara— "out of trouble. If you do that, she won't rope my daughter into any hairbrained schemes."

Jaiden wasn't sure why she was letting all of these new friends, and now this older woman, call her Jai, but it felt right.

"You know you've missed me, Bea."

"I have, but I have not missed all the commotion you tended to cause." Bea smiled warmly at Imara and the color seemed to return to her face.

"Are you planning to grab some lunch today? I was going to head to Knead & Feed. Would you like to join me?" Jaiden offered.

"You two go ahead, and we'll finish setting up the store. You can bring us back something. You remember what I like, right?" Elle asked.

"Yeah, roast beef if they have it. What about you two? Bea, do you still like pastrami or turkey?"

"Yes dear, either one will do."

"Tanya?"

"Turkey or vegetarian, please. I'm not much of a meat eater," Tanya responded.

As Jaiden and Imara left the store, Jaiden thought she heard Tanya whisper to Elle, "That was sweet of you, honey."

Elle murmured back, "I have my moments. They are kinda cute together."

CHAPTER FIVE

Although the threat of Vlad was looming over her, Imara was enjoying her stroll with Jai. Clearly, people grossly exaggerated the island's reputation for constant rain. Since they'd arrived, not one drop of precipitation had fallen. As they came to a set of wood stairs leading to Knead & Feed, Jai paused and leaned on the wooden rail. She sighed, as she looked out on the water.

"I love this view. I never tire of it. For me, the water has such healing properties. I don't think there is a more perfect place in the world to live than Whidbey Island. In the famous words of Charlton Heston, you'll have to pry my cold dead hands from this place before I would ever leave." Jai chuckled.

"You don't seem to be a person who would support the NRA."

"Oh, I'm not. I own a crystal shop for God's sake. I would be considered one of those flower-toting, flaky hippies, who chant make love not war. But I do read, you know. Keep your enemies close and always know what shit they are spouting."

Imara laughed. "You are quite the dichotomy, Jai. A teacher who owns a crystal shop. How did you find your way to the New Age movement?"

"Mom was quite the hippy. She was a devout Wiccan, who danced naked under the light of a full moon. Every solstice. Although, that is a misconception perpetuated by writers and artists. Not all people who practice the Wiccan religion dance naked, and not all people who dance naked under the full moon are Wiccans. I think the naked dancing part is a personal preference. Anyway, as far back as I can remember, the crystals my mother strategically placed around the house fascinated me. I'm sure I slobbered all over the rocks."

"Didn't you cut your mouth on the crystals when you were gnawing them as a baby?"

Imara was fascinated with Jai's early memories. Yes, there was definitely something special about Jai.

Jai's face scrunched up in confusion. "No, I guess I never did. Crystals have only ever been my friend. No matter how sharp the edges, I've never cut myself on one. I remember falling once, when I was a toddler and a little unstable on my feet. I landed on this spectacular amethyst cluster that must have cost my mother a mint. It was huge. Not a scratch or bruise to show for my clumsiness. I remember my mother looking at me strangely but never saying a word. It was almost as if she were scared that if she said something, the marks would suddenly appear. Huh? Strange that I remember that. I couldn't have been more than two. But I clearly remember her panicked expression, and that was after she'd checked me for injuries."

Imara cataloged this piece of information. She wondered if Jai could be a powerful witch and not know it. A lot of women thought they were witches because they practiced the Wiccan rituals, but that didn't make it so. The opposite was also true, and in fact, more common. Real witches rarely adhered to the Wiccan religion. She'd often heard her mother scoff at the notion that being a real witch was tied to a particular religion. Her mother railed against organized religion of any kind, even those religions considered on the fringe by the very vocal evangelical Christians who did not recognize any teachings beside their own.

"Are you ready to descend the stairs? The delicious aroma wafting from below is making my stomach growl. I smell cinnamon rolls. Even though breakfast has long passed, I'm getting one. I love how it is perfectly acceptable to eat dessert at breakfast. I'll get a sandwich too and maybe add a cookie, because I'll bet they bake them here."

"Oh, they do and they are scrumptious."

†

Imara watched the young girl with the cleft lip rush to the counter when she saw Jai walk into Knead & Feed. Her shining brown eyes and matching smile screamed adoration as she greeted Jai. "Hi, Miss Cartright. The usual? Want me to add some extra pickles for you? The cookies just came out of the oven too," she gushed.

Another teen poked his head out of the back kitchen and enthusiastically greeted Jai. "Hey, Miss Cartright."

Imara leaned in and whispered, "Fan club? Someone is crushing on you."

Jai chuckled and gave Imara a small push before returning her attention to the young girl. "That would be great, Sallie. I have some hungry friends to order for as well.

Can you add two turkey and cranberry specials and a roast beef?" Jai turned to Imara. "Everything is good here, what's your pleasure?"

"Well, my pleasure might not reside between two pieces of bread," Imara answered in a low voice that only Jai could hear. "I'll have the roast beef as well."

"Okay." Sallie smiled brightly. "The cookies are your favorite, Miss Cartright. I made the batch myself."

"Well, by all means, toss in a dozen for us." Jai dug into her pocket and pulled out a couple of twenties.

Imara pushed her hand aside. "Let me pay, please."

Jai grinned. "Okay, I won't argue. This time."

"Hon, could you please throw in a couple of those decadent cinnamon rolls? I have it on good authority they are to die for." Imara winked at the young girl who blushed. "We'll take everything to go, please."

After Imara paid Sallie, Jai pulled them to the side to allow other customers a chance to order. They took one of the empty tables to wait on their food.

"So, Sallie's one of your students, huh? She's clearly besotted with you. I never had an infatuation with any of my teachers. Of course none of them looked like you. It seems like more than a simple crush on a teacher. She positively lit up when you walked in. Like you're her own personal heroine. What's the story?"

"Sallie's father is in the military. When they first moved here, Sallie went to the high school in Oak Harbor. That city is very different from Coupeville. The kids were especially cruel. Our school has a more robust antibullying program." Jai shrugged. "I might have been the one to start the program. Her mother caught wind of it, and they moved here so she could switch schools. The father is no longer in the picture. They split when he learned about the nature of some of the bullying Sallie endured. The kids didn't limit their bullying to her physical appearance."

"Let me guess. Sallie's a lesbian."

"Maybe. When she was in my honors English course, I took a special interest in Sallie. I had to tease her out of her shell. She's very bright and had some questions about her sexuality. I'm a safe person to talk to. I don't hide that I'm a lesbian. She's a good kid and has blossomed in this school. When I first met Sallie, I honestly thought she was a suicide risk. That's how horrible it got for her."

Imara wished she'd had a teacher take a special interest in her when she was younger. If Bea hadn't taken her under her wing, Imara was sure she'd be right beside Vlad, doing God knows what to innocent people. Teachers could have such a positive impact on young men and women. She didn't know why she'd never realized what a noble profession teaching could be. Kids were impressionable. They could absorb messages of hate, bigotry, and cruelty, or love, compassion, and acceptance.

"I'll bet you've made a positive impact on many young lives. I'm glad there's someone like you teaching kids. You've got some serious magic going for you. I've never seen anyone so...um...never mind."

Jai looked at her curiously. "Thanks. Some days I feel I really make a difference and other days..."

"Your order's ready Miss Cartright," Sallie called out. "I put some extra cookies in the bag for you to snack on later."

"You're an angel," Jai answered.

The young girl was all right, but in Imara's humble opinion, Jai was the real angel.

†

Books were flying through the air, alphabetizing themselves by author, and landing on the shelves, while Elle pointed to sections in the store. By far, the largest area was the lesbian section. There were enough gay and lesbian titles to give each their own section. The bisexual, queer, transgender, or others that fell into a new and emerging category were grouped together.

"How come you said no to Imara when she wanted to shelve the books with magic? You weren't exactly honest with your explanation." Tanya frowned.

Elle grinned. "Sorry, I didn't want to show my hand, so to speak. It's just that Imara is a spoiled rotten witch who needs to appreciate the value of hard work and not always have magic as her solution to everything."

"I thought you two patched things up," Bea said.

"We did, but I think she could benefit from some good, old-fashioned restraint to avoid a propensity toward laziness. Book magicians are bad enough when we take the easy way. Book witches are far worse. Don't you think?"

"I don't know about that. That age-old rivalry is fraught with peril. Seems like we fall into the same trap as nonmagicians. Demonizing another is never useful. Thinking another group is so different from your own tends to plant the seeds of judgment, which then leads to discrimination and treating others poorly," Bea explained.

"I couldn't agree more. Well said, Bea." Tanya ducked as a flying book almost hit her in the head.

"Oh sorry, honey. I guess I'd better slow down the speed of the books."

"By the way, how did you learn this trick? I didn't realize book magicians could do much else besides put magic into books, transport themselves and others from one location to another, and neutralize the wall ears." Tanya sat on a stool out of the path of the flying books.

"Aunt Clara keeps going to these out of the way places where they've mastered some very interesting tricks. Imara is not the only one who has a plethora of maneuvers up her sleeve."

"Be careful, honey, Imara might try to convince you to convert and join a coven with her or start her own," Bea teased.

Elle's wheels began to turn. "I know you're teasing me, but Mom, I might consider that offer if it's genuine. Sidell is not getting any younger. You know as well as I do, if he leaves the council, Fay will no longer have a majority. They will regress and all our hard-fought rights will go by the wayside. We'll be relegated to apprentice status again and become second-class citizens. At least some of the book witches have fought back and created their own covens that want nothing to do with Vlad."

Bea's expression turned dark. "But for how long? His power is growing. He only needs one more very powerful witch to tip the balance. I believe that is what he's looking for. There is more to Jai than meets the eye."

"Do you think it's time to fill her in?" Tanya asked. "You provided me the full scoop when you realized I was in danger. Don't you think we owe it to her to do the same?"

Elle grabbed her own chin and contemplated Tanya's question. "Maybe? Imara still thinks she should bring a character to life. Even if Jai is more than meets the eye, she has a valuable lesson to learn. A bit like you, my love." Elle leaned over and kissed Tanya.

"Jai doesn't seem to lack any confidence," Tanya stated.

"It's not confidence she needs. It's the acceptance of imperfection. A far more challenging lesson to learn. We ought to have Imara bring her character to life first. Then we can explain the challenges we will face in the coming weeks with Vlad slinking around."

"I don't know. I'm a big proponent of honesty. Subterfuge has never worked very well, in my humble opinion," Tanya added.

"We have far bigger problems than when to bring Jai into the loop. I don't think Imara can fight Vlad on her own. The magical grapevine has consistently reported on his growing power and massive following. We need to figure out a way to shore up support for Imara and not leave her hanging on a limb to fight him all on her own."

"What about hiding inside various books? We could all pop into an adventure when we want to avoid him. Not being in the same space makes it hard for him to activate his spells. Warlocks can't pop into books without book magicians handing them the magical books," Elle suggested.

"Maybe that would work. I heard a rumor he has an inside person working with him—a book wizard who desires power himself and has decided to join forces. If that's the case, he'll simply use that donkeyhole to follow us." Bea folded her arms around herself in what Elle thought was a protective gesture. The realization that her mother was very worried hit Elle hard.

"E-book magic," Tanya declared.

"What?" Elle asked.

"I'm the only one that has mastered injecting magic into e-books. If I work on limiting the magic to certain specific devices, we can bounce from book to book with a single tablet or e-reader. He'll never be able to follow us because the e-books will allow a more fluid and faster transition from book to book."

"Brilliant. I love you, Tanya. That could really work," Elle praised.

"It could." Bea smiled and seemed to visibly relax.

†

Jaiden and Imara meandered down the sidewalk back to The Enchanted Page II carrying several bags with the lunches they'd ordered. They'd added a selection of chips to their purchase, but it was the scent of sugar and cinnamon that leaked from one of the bags Imara carried.

Jaiden had been tempted to buy her own had but recently made a deal with herself to indulge only once a week. The processed flour, sugar, and butter were definitely not on the healthy end of the scale. Most of the time, she tried to eat well. *Everything in moderation.*

Normally, she would pass judgment on those who overindulged. For some reason, she saw Imara's double purchase as living life to its fullest instead of putting too much crap in one's body. Judgment and criticism. These were her greatest flaws. Jaiden knew she tended to become overly critical of the women she was most interested in dating. Self-awareness was not her downfall. The flaw was subtle. She didn't actually voice those criticisms. That would be rude, and Jaiden was rarely impolite. Unfortunately, she was unable to control her disapproving looks. Jaiden dated intelligent and insightful women. They always knew, regardless of whether she gave voice to any objections or criticisms.

Jaiden wished she could meet the few heroines in her books whose imperfections were physical. Her opinions regarding the social conventions around beauty might help her with this major flaw. Those imperfections would never register with her. Surely she wouldn't judge those women too harshly. She believed falling in love with a woman confined to a wheelchair or one that was unattractive by most societal standards might be easier. Thus far, no one like that had come along to sweep her off her feet, and she'd continued to date beautiful women whom she nitpicked to death in her head.

"You seem awfully introspective," Imara noted.

"I'm trying to figure out why I'm so harsh and critical of those I'm attracted to. My mother is the most loving, gracious woman on the planet. Not only did she accept her lovers, shortcomings and all, but rather seemed to relish in their fallibility. She's the epitome of nonjudgmental, and she drilled that into me from an early age," Jaiden answered honestly.

"Lovers?"

"Mmhmm. She had many over the years. Just when I would begin to get used to one, they would leave. None seemed to stick around longer than a year or two. Gender made absolutely no difference. Both left my mother heartbroken, looking again for love in all the wrong places."

"I see."

"You have a knowing look on your face."

"Well, I'm no armchair psychologist, but maybe those revolving lovers are the root of your harsh critique of potential partners."

Jaiden found herself in front of The Enchanted Page II and breathed a sigh of relief that she could redirect the conversation. She looked at the sign again and wondered when the women had managed to hang it.

"I didn't notice the sign this morning when I opened my store, and I also didn't see anyone hanging from a ladder. How did you manage to escape my eagle eye?"

Imara winked. "Magic."

Jaiden pulled open the door, and her mouth hung wide open as she looked at hundreds of books flying in the air. When she blinked, books and empty boxes littered the floor, almost as if they'd fallen on the ground haphazardly.

Elle coughed. "You're back."

"Did I…um…" Jaiden shook her head. Obviously, she had been hallucinating. Maybe the magic comment had put some ridiculous picture in her head.

Imara narrowed her eyes. "I'll expect you to reconsider my idea for shelving these books. The disorganization is blatantly clear." She pointed to the floor.

"Busted," Tanya muttered.

Jaiden raised an eyebrow and saw the surprised look on Tanya's face. "I have excellent hearing."

"Good to know," Tanya answered.

"Do you need some help? No offense, but it looks a lot worse than before we left to pick up lunch. It won't kill me to keep my store closed for the remainder of the afternoon."

"Don't worry about us. I have an idea on how to get all these books shelved in no time. I'm sure Elle will agree with me now. Won't you Elle? She shoo-shooed my idea this morning, but as you can see, I don't think she'll object to it now. Clearly her way is not working."

"Shoo-shooed. That's a new one. I like it better than poo-pooed. Ick. Think about the connotations around that figure of speech." Jaiden shuddered. "Well, if you're sure you can handle it."

"I'll come get you when we're done, and we can grab some dinner before the movie. How does that sound? You haven't forgotten, have you?" Imara asked.

"Oh no. I am so pissed at Franklin, the octopus, for causing me to miss most of the movie."

Imara laughed. "I did notice his roaming hands. It must have seemed like he had eight for the multiple times you needed to push them away."

"Ugh, don't remind me. I had fantasies all last night about chopping them off."

"Really? You didn't dream about me and what my hands could do?" Imara joked.

Ignoring the question, Jaiden headed for the door. "I'll leave you ladies to it then."

Jaiden could hear Imara chuckling as she left the store.

†

Imara had caught them red-handed, taking the easy way as she had suggested earlier. She surprised herself by her lack of irritation over the whole matter. Sure, she would poke Elle about it, but she wasn't at all angry. She supposed it was due to her time with Jai as they relaxed into their walk. Jai had a way of smoothing her sharp edges.

"Well?" Elle asked.

"Well, what?" Imara grinned.

"When are you going to let me have it for using a tiny bit of magic to shelve all these books? I thought for sure we were going to get an earful from you versus that dopey grin you have on your face. If I didn't know any better, I'd say the wicked-witch wanderer is in luuurve."

"She is a rather fascinating chosen one." Imara lifted her arm in the air and chanted.

Give these books a little direction,
let them find an appropriate section.
Vanish the need to supervise,
make sure they fly counterclockwise.

Hundreds of books rose from the tangled mess on the floor and began to move in a counterclockwise pattern, as they found their way to the meticulously labeled shelves.

"How come she doesn't have to utter the chant three times?" Tanya asked.

"Because *I* am a book witch," Imara haughtily replied.

"There's the book bitch we all know and love," Elle taunted.

"Careful, Elle, your jealousy is showing."

"Ha, I'll take consistency and quality over flash in the pants with unwelcome side effects any day of the week."

"Now you know that doesn't happen very often. You book magicians always embellish the stories when things go wrong. I seem to remember a whole lot of side effects when you jumped into books or didn't pay enough attention to the stories before sending a chosen one on an adventure."

"Oh for poop's sake, will you two stop already," Bea interjected.

Elle narrowed her eyes. "You know, you never really told us why we're needed anyway. You can bring characters to life with your hands tied behind your back. What gives? Why enlist a lowly book magician?"

"The character I need to bring to life is in those modern e-books, and I don't know how to get her out. Both paperbacks are currently out of print. Honestly, none of the book witches have figured out the newfangled technology. I hate to admit this, but most of us are stuck in our old ways. Truth be told, we wish we had our own Director of E-book Magic."

"You didn't mention that…" Tanya said.

Elle lifted her eyebrow and looked curiously at Tanya.

"Well, I didn't get a chance to answer you honestly before. It's still true that part of the reason I came here was to mend fences with Elle. But yes, the other reason is I need your help, Tanya."

Elle pulled Tanya close to her. "Apparently, you two have already had a conversation about Imara's motives for coming to us. Imara, don't even think about recruiting her to your motley crew."

"I swear that was never my intention. Cross my heart and hope to wither." Imara swiped her finger over her heart and then twirled it in the air. "I only wanted to borrow her expertise. Besides, I don't exactly have a coven of my own, yet. I'm still interviewing and haven't made my final selections. I also honestly wanted to reconnect with you, Elle."

"Bullpoop. You are such a con artist. I'll bet you've been solo for quite some time because you pissed off too many witches."

"Did not."

"Did too."

Tanya began shaking her head. "Best friends should bring out the best in each other, not infantile behavior akin to our current president. I am surprised how quickly the two of you devolve."

"She started it." Both Elle and Imara pointed at the other.

"I'm happy to help," Tanya said.

"Remember, I've picked out the character named Dani. She's the brilliant scientist who uses forearm crutches, because the Russian mob shot her. It's a minor detail that in the second book she has a sort-of girlfriend. In the first story, she has no love interest until the end, unless you count the back story. But that character dies, so we can work with it."

"Right, yes, I love those books. Great choice. I would love to meet Dani in the flesh. That sounds like a wonderful choice for Jai. She'd really feel like a heel for not accepting that imperfection. The author lives here in Washington State." Tanya bounced on her toes in excitement.

"Precisely," Imara answered. "We can work on bringing her to life tomorrow. Tonight I'd like to enjoy the movie with Jai. Too bad she isn't the shy, insecure type, or I'd be tempted to bring Wonder Woman to life. Yummy."

"The characters are for the chosen, not for your personal pleasure," Elle chastised.

"I know, but a little eye candy never hurt any witch that I know."

Tanya frowned. "I had to struggle with the ethics of simply propelling unsuspecting people into books, regardless of the good intent. There's a new policy that requires book magicians to give the chosen ones a choice rather than make the decision for them. I don't quite know how to consider the morality of springing a character in a book onto an oblivious chosen one."

"I guess we've never really considered the ethos of what we do. I know I have the best of intentions. Jai really needs this lesson in order to move forward and clear the way to love. I suppose that old human saying, 'the road to hell is paved by good intentions,' is apropos. You're not going to help me unless I ask her permission, are you? I don't know which person to seek permission from. Jai or Dani?"

"Good question," Elle added. "I suppose Jai, because she's the only one that's real."

"True, but after I do my thing, they certainly feel real enough. About a year ago, I brought this character, Lara, to life. Boy was she pissed at me. I suppose she wasn't the best choice anyway, seeing as how she was a two-timing bitch. In my defense, she was very charming. After I explained things, she was on board. The new rules for book magicians might not apply so easily to book witches. Do characters have civil rights? I suppose you won't help me unless I get permission from both, huh?"

Tanya shook her head. "It's kind of a personal rule of mine. I never liked people making decisions for me that were for my own good. The insinuation there is that I'm not intelligent enough to make my own choices in life or love. It was a darn good thing I fell madly in love with Elle, or I would have been royally pissed at her.

"If characters become flesh and blood, they have the same rights as we do. What happens to the story if you remove the character? Won't that change the tale? I keep thinking about that old Christmas movie, *It's a Wonderful Life*." Tanya placed a finger on her lips.

"I'm not familiar with old movies, I prefer the new ones. The women are far more scantily clad." Imara smirked.

"Here's a quick summary. A man contemplates taking his own life. An angel shows this guy what a loss it would be if he'd never been born. This also makes me think about those sci-fi movies where you aren't supposed to mess with history during a time travel episode, lest you make matters worse. Although, they eventually got it right in *Back to The Future*. God, I love that old movie." Tanya sighed.

"Pfft, it's only a book," Imara scoffed. "Besides, I don't pull the character from every single copy of the book, just one."

Tanya looked aghast. "Oh no, when we send the chosen into the e-books, the same thing could happen. We wouldn't mess up one adventure, we'd affect thousands."

Elle rubbed circles on Tanya's back. "I think you're being a little dramatic, hon. Most of the books we inject magic into are lesfic. The reality is that more than a thousand books sold isn't common except for the big names."

"Readers depend on those books," Tanya insisted.

"It isn't at all common for the books to change when we send someone inside. You know as well as I do that nonmagicians can't alter the trajectory of the book. They're just along for the ride. They become one character and get to experience the excitement in the story," Elle defended.

"Maybe, but have we really thought out the consequences of pulling characters out of e-books?"

"Just because we haven't quite worked out the ethics doesn't mean we should stop doing what we're doing. So much good comes from our work. Don't you think it would be a shame to stop?" Elle asked.

"I'm not suggesting we stop, simply pause and consider all angles before forging ahead. With immense power comes great responsibility. I don't intend to ever forget that." Tanya shifted and began looking around the shop. "Wow." She pointed to the shelves. "Will you look at that? We were so engrossed in this philosophical discussion we didn't notice all the books are in their proper places. Too bad we haven't come to any logical conclusions."

"Something about asking a character's permission seems wrong to me. I still insist they aren't real. A fair compromise is coming clean to Jai." Imara put her hands on her hips in defiance.

"I honestly think you shouldn't pull her from an e-book, too much could go wrong, but I won't make a fuss if you decide to bring her to life from one of the paperbacks. There must be some used ones we can find. That way you'll only effect one book."

"Your girlfriend is as stubborn as you, Elle. I believe you've met your match. I still would like you all to stick around. We have that little problem of Vlad taking too much of an interest in Jai." Imara sent a small prayer they would agree to stick by her. She didn't want to let on how unnerved she was about Vlad and needed all the support she could get. The gossip and news about the powerful warlock had not escaped her ears.

"We'll be there for you, promise," Elle said solemnly. Tanya and Bea both shook their heads in what Imara hoped was 100 percent agreement.

"Thanks." She only hoped she wasn't putting her friends in great danger. Elle and Bea were important to her, and so was Tanya. She couldn't bear to lose any of them to Vlad's dark forces.

†

Vlad leaned back in the antique chair in his room, swirling the red liquid in his wine glass. It gave him great pleasure to stay at the very inn the trio had chosen for their temporary lodgings. He reveled in the fact that his blocking spell had completely masked how close he was to them. He was growing tired of the insufferable book wizard, but if he wanted to create a little havoc and continue to put a wedge between book magicians and book witches, the sniveling creature would have to do. Perhaps, someday, all of them would bow to his greatness.

Nothing would stop him when he had a powerful protector by his side. The scales would finally tip in his favor, once and for all. He grew weary of the small advances his brother had made on those weak souls who were destined to join him.

"Make the necessary arrangements, involve the nonmag if you have to. I see the darkness in his soul. He should be an easy person to convert." Vlad's gaze drilled a hole into the rotund wizard's eyes.

"I am looking forward to seeing Elle and Tanya again. I owe them so much." The wizard's sneer added to his grotesque physical appearance.

Vlad found it distasteful to surround himself with wizards, witches, or magicians who did not meet his standards for a pleasing appearance. He'd have to consider changing this wizard's outer shell if he decided to keep him around. He wasn't sure if the effort to cast a spell was worth it for such an inferior creature.

"Zelda and the Sanguine have been a burr in my magical ass for far too long. They should have called that sickeningly sweet do-gooder's sect the Saccharine. My brother and his little whore have stolen from me for the last time. Imara choosing Jaiden has my brother's fingerprints all over it. I am not surprised, since he took such a shining to Serafina's promising offspring. Ah, Serafina was one of the better ones to play with. Such a pleasurable fuck that one was." Vlad flicked his wrist. "Big brother doesn't know how this fits perfectly into my plan. I'll capture two little love birds with one powerful spell."

"What makes those two so special?" the wizard asked.

"Never you mind about that. I have my own score to settle. You must never lose sight of the end goal. Need I remind you how a chosen one got the better of you?" Vlad warned.

"Our power will be unimaginable when the wizards and warlocks combine to once again take control. I shall be honored to share in the glory." The wizard lifted his glass of wine in the air.

Vlad inclined his head in agreement, but laughed inside at the absurdity of this lowly wizard believing he would in any way share even a tiny portion of the power. Once Vlad had exhausted his usefulness, he would swat him away like the tiny gnat he was. Toying with the wizard was almost as much fun as amusing himself with the trio. Of course, the ignorant wizard couldn't know why Jaiden was of special interest to Vlad. He decided a movie tonight was the perfect form of entertainment. He wondered about Jaiden and Imara. Would he be able to bring one into his fold and not the other?

CHAPTER SIX

Jaiden didn't know Imara very well. After all, she'd only met her yesterday. But she seemed uncharacteristically jittery tonight. A woman who appeared to have something important on her mind replaced her light and flirtatious manner.

"I was rather enjoying the overconfident flirt. Where did she go?" Jaiden asked, as they stood in line waiting to purchase movie tickets.

Imara's eyes darted around the open area outside of each theater showing the various movies. "Huh?" she asked distractedly.

"Are you looking for your next date?"

"What? No!"

"You seem a little preoccupied tonight. You keep looking around like the FBI is after you because you're on their ten-most-wanted list."

Imara laughed. "Good one. I'm sorry. I swear, I'll fill you in after the movie. That is, if you agree to have a nightcap with me."

"Yes! She's back."

Imara's intense, green eyes focused on the amethyst crystal Jaiden always wore around her neck, and she reached out to touch it. The crystal laid against Jaiden's chest, mere inches from the indentation of her cleavage. Imara's finger lingered, then shifted a few inches downward before she removed her hand.

"Do you always wear that necklace? I hadn't noticed before, but did you know the color of the crystal is almost an exact match to the color of your eyes? I don't believe I've ever seen anything so alluring. It isn't exactly Elizabeth Taylor violet, it's subtler than that. Unusual."

"Hmm, convenient line to justify your fleeting touch a hair above my breast. You definitely have your mojo back." Jaiden purposely ignored the comment about her eyes. She'd heard something similar from every woman she'd dated and didn't wish to place Imara in that same category of exes.

Imara grinned, then her expression turned serious. "Don't take it off, ever."

"Is this about your creepy...uh...I don't know what to call that guy, Vlad. You never explained his relationship to you. I don't think he followed us to the movie, but I did notice him slinking around Mo's, while we had dinner." Jaiden snapped her fingers. "That's it. You really are a fugitive, and he's an FBI agent," she declared as she tried to lighten things up.

"I wish. The FBI I can handle. In fact, those badass-butch types in the FBI can be quite delightful."

Jaiden quirked her eyebrow. "Really? That's your type. I would not have guessed that."

"I don't have a type. I enjoy women in all their various forms. Short or tall, athletic or allergic to exercise, thin or of generous proportions. All of them fit my criteria. The only thing I'm a sucker for is a confident, intelligent woman. I suspect that is my type. Witty conversation is quite the aphrodisiac for me. I call it intellectual intercourse."

"Ew intercourse sounds so clinical. What about sapient sex? I couldn't find an appropriate word that starts with the letter F, to go with fucking."

Imara laughed. "I do love a woman who can weave fuck into a sentence and still exhibit perspicacious judgment."

"Oh, now you're just trying to one up me, because I managed to use sapient in my sentence. English teachers are an obnoxious bunch." Jaiden stepped up to the counter and pulled a twenty from her pocket. "Two for *Wonder Woman*, please."

"Hey, wait a minute, I asked you. Please let me pay," Imara insisted.

"Nope. You paid for lunch and dinner, despite my objections. I suppose I was as distracted as you when I saw Vlad the bad slithering around Mo's."

Imara clenched her jaw.

Jaiden moved her hand to Imara's face and caressed the area where she saw tightness. "You really ought to come see me at my shop. I have a few crystals sure to chase away the negative energy that is certain to wreak havoc on those beautiful teeth. Grinding is never a good thing."

"Vlad the bad. Now that has a nice ring to it." Imara's smile seemed forced. "All right, you can pay for the movie tickets, but I'll get the popcorn and candy. That's my last and final offer." Imara moved around the corner to the concessions stand and joined the queue.

"No candy for me. I'll just steal some of the popcorn from the jumbo container you need to get for both of us. I'll be disappointed if you can't put away as much popcorn after dinner as I can. There is no such thing as being too full when popcorn is on the table." Jaiden grinned.

"Water or soda?"

"Water of course. Too much soda is terrible for you," Jaiden replied.

"Says the woman who wants a jumbo bucket of popcorn with, I presume, a huge amount of that crap that passes for butter."

"I know. I do wish this movie was at the Clyde Theater in Langley. At least they use real butter."

"Oh, I'd like to visit there. I haven't had popcorn with real butter in ages." Imara turned to the young woman behind the counter. "We'll take a jumbo with butter. Put some of that artery clogger in the middle of the bucket, please. Oh, and two waters. We'd like to attempt to push the fat globules through our system somehow."

"Water may be helpful to cleanse your system, but don't expect a miracle. I don't believe it has any impact on arteries. We need red wine for that."

Imara took the bucket of popcorn from the clerk and handed one of the waters to Jaiden. "Does that mean you are accepting my invitation for a nightcap? You know, purely to clear out those clogged arteries."

Jaiden chuckled. "You had me at 'I swear I'll fill you in after the movie.' Who knew your cloak and dagger routine would be such a turn on."

Imara made a fist and pumped it into the air. "Yes! It works every time." She waved Jaiden ahead of her, and they made their way into the dark theater.

Jaiden felt Imara stiffen beside her before she saw the black coat and the obsidian, slicked back hair of the man she knew was Vlad. He was sitting in the last row, and when they passed, she could feel his eyes burrowing into the backs of their heads.

On instinct, Jaiden touched the crystal that lay on her chest. She gathered the charm in her hand and squeezed, feeling the positive energy emanate from deep within the small talisman. Jaiden sensed Imara needed to put as much distance between herself and Vlad, so she kept walking down the aisle until they reached the front row of the theater.

After they found two empty chairs, Jaiden set her water in the drink container built into the seats and grabbed Imara's hand, bringing it to her chest and the powerful crystal. "Let me share the energy. I can feel the negative air vibrating in this theater."

After Imara's hand enclosed the amethyst, Jaiden put her own hand over top. The warmth spread through her body, and she suspected that energy made its way into Imara's as well.

"We can leave if you want," Jaiden offered.

Imara kept her hand wrapped around the stone. "Wow, this is amazing. No, I do believe there is enough power and protection with your stone and...I refuse to let him intimidate me."

"Good, but will you be able to enjoy the movie without distraction?"

"No."

Jaiden frowned. "Honestly, we can go."

Imara grinned. "Oh the distraction won't be from Vlad the bad, it'll be from my insane need to catch glimpses of you all night."

As the lights dimmed and the previews began, Jaiden tried to control her guffaw at Imara's last comment.

†

Imara felt the power of the talisman around Jai's neck when the heat penetrated her hand and spread throughout her body. This small measure of assurance was all she needed to relax and ignore Vlad's presence in the back of the theater. She could sense how the new barriers had momentarily stymied him. She was sure he had not expected this obstacle.

Although she had teased with Jai about being distracted as she sat near, the movie completely suckered Imara into the plot. She would have preferred them to completely shoot the movie on the Amazon's secret island location without any interference from the outside world. But she supposed there wouldn't be much of an action adventure if that occurred. Still, was it really necessary to have Diana Prince fall for the cocky, male spy? Imara could have done without that part of the story. His assistant would have been a better choice. At least the assistant was a bit quirky and funny.

As the lights started to brighten and the credits rolled on, Imara stretched her back. "With the exception of a few minor flaws, that was a very enjoyable movie."

"Chris Pine?"

"How did you guess? I suppose he is an above-average specimen for a man, but I would have preferred a different pairing. Too bad they couldn't find a badass woman pilot. Although, I would have been unhappier if they killed her off. Television shows seem to be doing that a lot lately with lesbian characters. Just when we all start putting our faith into the entertainment industry, they have to yank the rug from under us and say, 'psych.' Maybe someday I'll toss a spell their way to let them know how displeased I am."

Jai stood and began walking toward the exit. "A spell? You sound a lot like my mother. Although she is more of a pacifist. Meditation, chanting, and crystals were all designed to rid the space around her of negative energy. Never once did I hear her advocate for something that would threaten or cause harm to another person or life. No matter how small or seemingly insignificant. Mom wouldn't even swat at a mosquito. I make up for it. Those nasty little bastards piss me off. Most bugs, and especially the flying variety, have suffered my wrath on occasion. Cockroaches are right up there with the winged pests." Jai grinned.

"I like it. An evil streak will come in handy. Never underestimate the power of an imperfect vigilante. Sometimes it's okay to fight fire with fire. Nice guys and gals unfortunately do finish last on occasion, and there is nothing wrong with a healthy dose of confidence coupled with a pinch of revenge."

"Hmm, I guess I've been attracted to the wrong kind of imperfection. I usually feel bad for judging the do-gooders too harshly and have nitpicked the loveliest women. Each rivaled my mother with how nice they were. Time to look for a woman with low morals and a hint of wickedness. You seem to fit that to a T."

Imara and Jai reached the back of the theater and had almost made it through the doors when Vlad stood, nodded, and walked toward the exit. Imara slowed her breathing and whispered a short chant.

Create a healthy space between us,
time alone to talk a plus.
If Vlad so much as looks our way,
my evil streak comes out to play

At this point Imara didn't care if Jai heard her chant. The important thing was to provide some time to give Jai a full explanation. At least that was her intent. She felt and smelled Vlad's foul breath on her neck as he whispered in her ear. "Nice try, Imara. A seven on a ten-point scale. I'll bust open your spell in less time than it takes for you to say my name," he warned.

Jai turned in Vlad's direction and glared at him. She stuck her hand in her pocket and brought forth a small smoky quartz. She took Imara's hand, slowly opening her fingers, and placed the rock in her palm. "A gift. I can drill a hole in this tomorrow and add a chain if you'd like."

Vlad hissed and took a step back, allowing the two women to exit and put a fair amount of distance between them.

Imara looked at Jai appreciatively, as she closed her hand around the gift and decided it couldn't hurt to have a necklace made out of this apparently strong item that clearly kept negative energy from coming too close. She wondered how long that would last, before Vlad had a way to counteract the effects. It seemed like he was always finding ways to fight everything she threw at him. Her energies were waning, having to battle him by herself. She brightened as she realized Elle, Tanya, Bea, and her surprisingly competent new friend were all there to lend a hand and provide the strength needed to get him to back off once and for all.

"Thank you," Imara responded. Even though Jai didn't know it, that thank you was for far more than the crystal.

"He's like a leech, huh. What are leeches, by the way? They aren't aquatic bugs, are they?"

"No, more like annelid worms with suckers on both ends. Very efficient parasites. An apt description of Vlad."

"I'm an English teacher, not a scientist. Although I read a lot, I've never come across the word, annelid."

"Segmented. You know, like earthworms. I believe leeches and earthworms are cousins. Now that I think about it, calling Vlad a leech is an insult to leeches. Sometimes they can be very useful. Certain toads, worms, and other properties from various living things are quite essential to healing potions and other…well let's just say the oddest ingredients make the best potions."

"Potions, huh? I really cannot wait to get back to your place and have that cocktail," Jai said.

"About that. Not that I don't enjoy hanging out with Tanya and Elle, but we have temporary lodging at the Captain Whidbey Inn. The food is great, but I was hoping for a more private and cozier location to spill my guts. Besides, you would appreciate being in your own territory. A familiar location when listening to somewhat unbelievable information is helpful."

"We'd better stop at the store then, because I don't have much along the lines of libations. An old, partially consumed bottle of chardonnay is about it. I haven't had much along the lines of company lately. Not since Ariana left in a huff."

"I'd be happy to pick something up. Are you hankering for a fancy, blended drink or a simple bottle of wine?"

"Let's go with something in between. I'd kill for a good mojito right about now. Fresh ingredients are the key, but they aren't too difficult to make. We can also select a few bottles of wine. It never hurts to have a stash for future occasions when wine might be a better option."

"Done. I don't really know that drink, but the Internet is my friend. I'm so pleased at how advanced you all have become. It's almost like magic. Tiny little boxes that spit out all kinds of information. I must admit to being completely fascinated with tablets and smartphones. Although Tanya is more of an expert in that arena. That's why I decided to brave the bitch-slapping from Elle. I suppose an equally good reason was because I missed my best friend. I knew that eventually she'd get over her anger. The little misunderstanding happened eons ago…Elle sure can hold a grudge."

"Now that's a story I am looking forward to hearing. It sounds rather juicy. There must have been another woman involved. Usually that's what causes all the lesbian drama." Jai placed her finger on her chin. "In my case, another woman was never the issue. I guess I'm talented enough to cause a great deal of ire without the introduction of a third party. It's my special sauce." Jai grinned.

"So I've heard," Imara muttered too low for Jai to hear.

"What's that?"

"Oh nothing," Imara answered innocently.

†

Jaiden pulled her car into the gravel driveway that led to her cedar bungalow. Her home was so far back into the wooded area, it wasn't visible from the main road. Earlier, they'd walked down the road that wound around the local park, adjacent to the small cluster of stores on Main Street. She turned the knob to her front door. In Coupeville, she'd never gotten in the habit of locking her door. People didn't bother on the island, even though things had changed a bit over the years, with the advent of drug use. Habits were hard to break.

"You don't lock your door?" Imara asked incredulously.

"It's Coupeville. No one locks their doors. I've never been robbed. Unless you live on the island, it's not apparent there are houses tucked this far back in the woods. I'm fortunate to have found this little gem. It's close to work, yet nestled in the trees. I even have a small view of the water through the break in the tree line. I've strategically placed a couple of chairs on the deck for maximum viewing. The water is only one advantage to living here. I've got a pair of eagles who nest in the tall tree less than fifty feet away from the house."

She beckoned for Imara to follow her into the open-style living room and kitchen that led to a wraparound deck, where two wooden Adirondack chairs and a small table sat facing the water. Jaiden often wondered why she'd bought the second chair. She rarely had need of the forlorn extra; having the pair only served as a reminder to Jaiden of how often her partners didn't pass muster.

Jaiden set the bag with the bottles of wine on the kitchen counter, while Imara looked around. Opening her refrigerator, she placed two bottles of white inside. Imara's eyes seemed to roam around the room, taking in every detail. Jaiden wondered if she was somehow categorizing the information for later use. She casually strolled to Jaiden's built-in bookcase and began studying the titles. She let her fingers graze against a few of the book spines.

"I'm very relieved to see you have such a large collection of paperbacks and some very old hardbacks. Your collection is impressive and diverse," Imara noted.

"I am an English teacher," Jaiden answered as if that were the only explanation needed.

"Yes, I'm very aware of that. I suppose the e-book craze has not completely taken over the world. I guess I expected that some of the older novels would be in hardback or paperback, but there are a fair number of new titles. I thought I saw you reading on a tablet."

"Paperbacks are making a comeback. Besides, the island loses power a lot in the winter. Paperbacks come in handy. I try to spread my money out and buy both. I'll admit, the e-book craze has fed the beast within me." Jaiden stood next to Imara and studied her collection. The floor-to-ceiling bookcase covered an entire wall. She supposed it did hold an impressive number of books.

Imara turned to face Jaiden and quirked her eyebrow. "Beast?"

"Yes, I have an insatiable need. I've been known to devour three to four books a week. More in the summer months."

Imara nodded and plucked a book from the shelf with her free hand. She still had the grocery bag with all the supplies for mojitos hanging on her left arm. "Do you mind?" she asked, as she set down the bag and flipped open the pages to the book.

"No, of course not. Why don't I bring the other bag into the kitchen and start on the drinks, while you peruse the pages of that book? It's a lesbian favorite. Ass-kicking women, the Russian mob, and a host of cool inventions. A very fun story with memorable characters." Jaiden began to lean down to pick up the bag.

"Um hmm, so I've heard," Imara absently answered before closing the book, gently stopping Jaiden's hand, and snatching the bag before Jaiden had time to retrieve it from the floor.

The fleeting touches that Imara blessed Jaiden with were driving her crazy. Although Imara was a beautiful, witty woman whom Jaiden was wildly attracted to, something was definitely off about her. *Stop that, stop that right now. Already you're picking away on the first date. There won't be any flesh on her bones after you're done with her.*

Jaiden considered whether this was a date. Sure, Imara had been flirting with her since they met and had asked her to dinner and a movie, but thus far she hadn't made any other typical date moves. No hand holding or stolen kisses. There had been numerous opportunities. Other than when she'd touched her necklace, she'd not made any overtures.

Jaiden was startled from her musings when Imara took charge. "I'm going to root around in your kitchen and make the best mojito you've ever had, while you head to the deck and star gaze."

"Bossy much? This is my house, you know. I should be the one preparing the drinks and playing perfect host."

"Nonsense. I forced you into this. Go. Sit." Imara pointed to the wooden deck.

Jaiden smiled and opened her closet door to retrieve a light jacket. When the sun went down, the island cooled; it could turn chilly quickly. "Shall I grab a jacket for you?"

Imara nodded, as she began pulling drawers open and emptying the bags from the grocery store that they had stopped at prior to driving back to Coupeville. Jaiden pulled another coat from the closet and opened the door leading to the deck. She sat on one of the chairs and zipped her jacket up to her chin to block the chill of the evening from penetrating her body. She couldn't resist turning her head to see what Imara was up to.

Imara already had two glasses on the counter and was cutting the fresh limes in half on a cutting board. The book she'd pulled from the shelf lay on the counter, along with a smartphone. She was absently scrolling on the tiny device. Jaiden assumed Imara was looking for mojito recipes. She could hear Imara humming, as she worked and swayed to the melody she was creating. Forget marching to the beat of your own drum. Jaiden chuckled as she imagined a new quote apropos to Imara. She was dancing to the melody of her own making. Mischievous, green eyes captured her own, and Imara grinned, not bothering to stop her dancing.

Along with the humming Jaiden thought she heard Imara singing a tune, or perhaps it was some sort of melodic chant. She couldn't quite hear the words. Jaiden had excellent hearing, but the wind outside had picked up and was somehow distorting the sounds on the inside of the house.

Imara found the chopsticks and was pushing on the fresh mint in the glass, stirring gently and muddling at the same time. Jaiden thought this was an extremely targeted way to

89

crush the mint. If the mixologist did not know what they were doing, the muddling process could seriously ruin the perfect mojito. Abusing the small veins of the mint leaves would release the bitter and earthy chlorophyll instead of the herb's fresh flavor. Jaiden silently gave Imara two points for her interesting approach. Imara brought her nose close to the glass, took a deep breath, and nodded. After sniffing her concoction, she added the rest of the liquid and began stirring again.

Jaiden turned around to look at the water, then leaned back in her chair and breathed in the smell of fresh pine. She was looking forward to what she suspected would indeed be the perfect mojito. When she heard the door open and Imara entered the deck with two cocktails in her hand, Jaiden turned her head again and accepted one of the glasses.

Imara sat in the chair next to Jaiden and lifted her glass in the air. "To new adventures."

Jaiden touched her glass against Imara's and took a small sip. She smacked her lips. "Divine. I need to learn your special technique."

"I'm a master with potions."

"That's an unusual way to describe a cocktail."

"Basic principles of mixology. It's all the same."

"Were you a mixologist in college or at some point in your career? I know nothing about you. I just realized that. You know all the essentials about me, probably more than I care for, and I know absolutely zilch about you. Remember, you promised to fill me in if I had cocktails with you. Here we are. Start filling, missy."

Imara's lips curled into a smile. "Right. Yes. A promise is a promise...I am a book witch. No college required for that occupation."

Jaiden's head tipped back as she laughed loudly. "Good one. I suppose the next thing you'll say is that Vlad is a vampire and wants to make you his eternal mate."

"He does fit the stereotype, I suppose. But no, Vlad is a warlock. A very powerful one, with many covens in his fold. I'm not joking. I bring characters to life. Elle and Bea are book magicians. A completely different sort, but with similar skills. Tanya, well…she's a kind of hybrid. I think. A nonmag who has somehow developed skills as a book magician."

Jaiden looked left and right. "How in the hell did they even manage to put a camera out here without someone noticing?"

"What?"

"You know for the punking show that Ashton Kutcher used to be a part of or *Candid Camera.* Or maybe there's a new reality show I'm not aware of. I don't really keep up with the latest trends. Perhaps they have something brand new like selfie sylloge."

"Hmm, that's a bit of a stretch on the word sylloge. I suppose a collection of gossip kind of fits, but I'd go with selfie scandal or selfie scuttlebutt. Don't you think? Has a better ring to it. And I suspect this generation would understand those words a whole lot better."

"You're redirecting. Is that part of the gig?"

Imara sighed. "I rather hoped you would take this much better, sort of the same way that Tanya did. I suppose in all fairness, Tanya did witness the wall ears. So perhaps that convinced her."

"Oh, my, God. You're serious, or rather seriously unwell."

"Well shit, this is the one time I wished I was a book magician. They do have that neat trick of transporting themselves from one place to another. I suppose I'll have to try my go-to chant for a small demonstration. Or…I could bring Dani forth right here and now." Imara nodded. "Yes, that's what I'll do. I did hope to get to know you a bit better before bringing Dani to life, but desperate times call for desperate measures." Imara waved her hand. "Drink up, Jai, you're going to need it."

Jaiden took a big gulp of her mojito and sputtered when some of the liquid went down the wrong section of her throat. She coughed and managed to say, "Wrong pipe."

"You can speak, so I don't suppose you need the Heimlich. Just let me know when you're ready." Imara sat patiently sipping her drink.

Jaiden's coughing began to subside.

Imara stood and abruptly left the deck. She walked into Jaiden's house and returned with a paperback in her hand. She set it on the ground in front of her and sat back in her chair.

"Here we go."

Jai is ready for a new adventure;
bring the egghead for her pleasure.
Make the trip as smooth as can be.
Even though I failed the introduction,
the teacher grows with this lesson.
Make Dani's flaws the perfect key.

Imara reached into her jeans pocket and produced a small vial that she proceeded to open. She winked as she sprinkled something on top of the book. "My special potion. I use it to stabilize the journey and the character. Sometimes they destabilize and leave too quickly, or the opposite happens and they are relegated to our world for all eternity. Neither is a very good option."

Jaiden blinked several times when an attractive young woman in forearm crutches slowly took shape on the exact spot Imara had sprinkled whatever liquid was stored in the tiny, glass container. Her last words before she blacked out were, "Holy shit."

†

Imara looked at Jai's crumpled form in the chair and the broken mojito glass on the deck. "Well damn, that didn't go quite as expected."

Dani was leaning heavily on her crutches with a wild-eyed look. "What? Where?"

Imara stood and offered Dani her chair. "Sit," she directed.

"Who...um...who are you? Is she okay?" Dani pointed to Jai.

Imara pursed her lips. "I certainly hope so. I think she's a bit overwhelmed by your sudden appearance."

"That's a good place to start. How did I get here, wherever here is?" Dani asked. "And here I thought the technology Toni and I've been working on was cutting edge," she said in an apparent afterthought.

Imara held up her hand. "Hang on. Let me check on Jai." She barely made contact with Jai's forehead, as she gently brushed her hair aside. She lingered a fraction of a second after Jai stirred.

Jai looked in her eyes, and Imara saw a combination of fear and awe. "I guess I'd better open my chakras. My mother would say I need to breathe in the energy and avoid being so damn narrow-minded." She turned her head to Dani sitting in the chair beside her. "You've done a good job matching her physical appearance with how I envisioned her when I read the two novels."

"Thanks. I'm rather proud of that myself. I've been told I do an outstanding job of bringing characters to life, matching their physical appearance exactly to the version my chosen one has in their minds," Imara responded.

Dani cleared her throat. "Look. I don't need you two whack jobs talking about me as if I'm not here and not making any sense on top of it."

"Oh, right. I guess I need to fill you in, Dani." Imara twirled her finger in the air.

Explanations require a seat;
pop one in nice and neat.
A temporary chair will do just fine;
make it from this lovely pine.

A third chair appeared several feet behind Imara in a similar style to the Adirondack chairs Dani and Jai sat on.

"That's some kind of optical illusion, right? I should know. I create them for the...never mind." Dani shut her mouth and looked as though she was gluing it closed so she wouldn't reveal state secrets.

"We know all about your talented inventions, Dani. Although they're only the figment of a very imaginative author. You don't need to censor yourself." Imara pulled the chair close and sat. "I didn't wish to loom over you as I explained everything. You know, having a clever inventor come to life might actually benefit us. Vlad is definitely a pain in my ass right now, at the very least. Worst case scenario..." She shuddered. "He might choose to blackmail me by threatening to do unspeakable things to one or both of you."

"If I'm following this very odd conversation, you're telling me I'm not real. I'm just some character in a book.

While I commend your flair for creating a very compelling illusion, I have important work to do. I'm needed in the lab. So if you'll please loan me a cell phone, I'll call my buddies to come pick me up."

Imara sighed. "This is the worst part of my job." She patted Dani's hand. "It's such a blow to a character to learn they aren't real. Sometimes it helps when I tell them an author has a sequel planned. Unfortunately, I have it on good authority, no sequel in the works. The author adamantly rejects writing a third book. So…you don't really have any important work to do. She might consider a few follow-up short stories. That's the best you can hope for, Dani. Would you like me to intercede and have this author write one entirely about you? I think it's only fair since I did drag you into this world without your permission, like Tanya seems to insist upon. Oops—"

"Oops? What now? I didn't think things could be worse," Jai interrupted.

"Well…I sorta agreed to obtain your permission, and I didn't exactly do that. You didn't believe me. So what was I supposed to do? Tanya is Zen by nature, but she does have a little fire in her when she's passionate about something. This is one of those details. I don't like raising her ire."

"I am not a character in a book." Dani jutted her chin out.

"Jai, do you mind pulling up either *Asset Management* or *The Organization* on your tablet?" Imara pointed to the ground. "I'm sorry for ruining your book. It's unavoidable if I wish to ensure a close match. I suppose I could try to flip through the mangled pages, but I believe the tablet will be more compelling. Dani here, needs some proof of her own."

"I don't think that's a very good idea."

"Trust me. It is. I've found it works better when I yank the bandage off. Chinese water torture and the trickle approach is far less acceptable."

Jai slowly made her way back inside. Imara watched her fluid movements and marveled at her grace, despite the shocking events of the evening. She wished Jai was not a chosen one. She would have liked to get to know her outside what she believed was expected of her. There was definitely something more to Jai than met the eye. Her gaze followed Jai all the way inside, before she reluctantly turned her attention to Dani.

Imara took this gift of alone time with Dani to provide a concise explanation. "I'll be brief, then we can talk again at a later time. I've breathed life into you for a specific reason. Jai needs a very important lesson, and you are just the woman to give it to her. The dichotomy of your physical imperfections, but otherwise nearly flawless character is an ideal blend of what she needs. The plan is for Jai to fall in love with you and finally realize perfection does not exist in a suitable partner. You will, of course, offer your irresistible charm to achieve the necessary results."

"Are you out of your fucking mind? First you insult me, then you basically tell me I have no say in this little matchmaking adventure. For the record I still do not buy into this whole 'you're a character in a book' malarkey. Toni may give Sophie shit, but she's never played a trick on me. We don't have that kind of relationship."

Imara frowned. "Perhaps I chose the wrong character, but you seemed to be the one least entangled with another. Your physical disability definitely works to my advantage with this particular chosen one."

"Stop saying I'm a character." Dani snaked out her hand and pinched Imara on the arm.

"Ouch," Imara cried out.

"Doesn't feel like I'm some imaginary being, does it?" Dani shot Imara a smug smile.

The door opened to the deck, and Jai held the tablet in her hands. "Do I have to separate the two of you? You aren't playing very nice with one another."

Dani looked at Imara. "Teacher?"

Imara nodded. "English, yes. They do all have that teacher voice, huh?"

"Well, it does seem like the two of you earned my teacher voice. When adults act like children, it simply sneaks out." Jai handed the tablet to Imara. She crossed her arms and remained standing. "There, have at it. For the record, I still think this is a bad idea. Worse than spring break in Mexico and the worm at the bottom of a bottle of tequila."

Imara flipped open the cover to the tablet. After pressing the button at the bottom she ordered, "Password please."

Jai grabbed the tablet and used her thumb to access the screen, then handed it back to Imara. "The app is on the first page. Scroll until you find the two books you're looking for."

"Thanks." After Imara had opened one of the books where Dani was a character, she touched the magnifying glass to activate the search feature and typed in Dani's name. She handed the tablet to Dani. "Take a look for yourself."

"Well fuck me. I can't believe Toni would do this to me. How in the world did she manage to come up with this elaborate plan? She is an ingenious little shit, but we don't do this to each other. If she put some long-acting drug in me as a test, I'm going to fucking kill her." Dani shoved the tablet back into Imara's hands.

Imara tried to hand the tablet back to Jai, who shook her head. Imara sighed, set the tablet on the table, and picked up the mangled paperback. She began shuffling through the pages. Her eyes scanned the book looking for the spot where Dani appears. She pointed to the page and gave the book to Dani. "How much more evidence do you need?"

"Oh please, creating books that parallel my life with information Toni has complete access to is child's play. Toni is off the charts in the intelligence arena. I haven't quite worked out the whys, but I suspect she is testing a new gadget or something and didn't want to poison the results. She probably needs my true reaction. Yeah, that's it. She couldn't tell me, and I'm the only one she trusts besides herself to be the guinea pig. Of course she couldn't test this ruse out on herself."

Jai sat next to Dani and grabbed her hand. "Hon, if this is all a ruse, I've entered an alternative universe, and my world is the one that isn't real, because I only know you as a character in a book. Toni is simply another character. Unbelievable as this may seem to you, I think Imara is telling the truth. That is my book and my tablet. I've read both stories. So have a lot of other lesbians, who by the way, have asked for another in the series with you as the lead."

Dani blinked twice. "I'm not real? But I feel real." She picked up a piece of the glass that littered the deck from Jai's drink. Before Imara could stop her, she brought the sharp point to her arm and created a large gash. Dark, red blood began to flow from the self-inflicted wound.

"Would a character in a book bleed?"

"Shit!" Jai jumped from her chair and ran inside.

Imara hadn't intended for anyone to spill blood. Bringing a character to life was supposed to help a person. Imara tried to see the positive impact of Dani's dramatic gesture. Maybe this turn of events wouldn't be so bad in the long run. The two of them could bond over their mutual hate for how she'd handled the situation. She couldn't help feeling disheartened by that. Jai's opinion of her meant more than she wanted to admit. Frozen, Imara stared at Dani's dripping arm, wondering how it all went sideways. Maybe Vlad's sudden appearance was the culprit. She needed to control this situation because her attention was required elsewhere. She would make her apologies and return to Elle, Bea, and Tanya. Hopefully, Tanya would forgive her minor indiscretions. They needed to learn what Vlad was up to. *This has his slimy prints all over it.*

Soon enough, Jai had returned with a massive first aid kit and a scathing glance in Imara's vicinity.

†

Jaiden was not happy at all. When she returned she let Imara know with a look that could have annihilated the entire population of the United States. Dani looked so small and dismal, sitting on the deck chair with her crutches neatly set to the side. A small river of blood was congealing on Jaiden's deck.

She quickly opened a bottle of hydrogen peroxide and generously dosed the cut. She let the bubbles subside, before tearing open a large package of sterile gauze and pressing it to the wound.

"Please don't do anything rash again. I promise we'll navigate this whole strange...um...I don't know what to call this. It isn't an adventure, really. Anyway, we'll do it together, seeing as how we are both targets of a crazy person. Unfortunately, a whack job as you so eloquently put it, who appears to possess an interesting skill set."

"Right about now, I feel more lost than when I was shot and had to learn how to walk again." Trusting blue eyes fluttered upward to look directly at Jaiden. They turned a stormy gray before she directed her next statement at Imara. "If you're so talented and I'm just a character, why did you bring me to life as a cripple? Can't you simply wave a magic wand or something and make the pain in my body go away?"

"It doesn't work that way. You can only arrive in the state you were in during a specific location in the book. The writer never allowed you to recover completely. Don't put that on me. Blame the author. At least I didn't bring you to life right after your unfortunate tangle with the mob. I tried to pick a moment that offered you the optimal mobility."

"Well bully for you. Give the witch a medal."

"No need to be so snarky. Listen, I'll be the first to admit that I haven't handled everything in the best possible fashion, but I honestly think something else is going on here. My bet is that Vlad has somehow interjected his nastiness into the mix. I swear I've never had this kind of negative reaction before. A little surprise at first, yes, but both the chosen one and whomever I picked to bring to life were delighted with the outcome."

"Who is Vlad? And what the hell does he have to do with anything? If he's some new Russian mob boss, Char and Maggie will want information on him."

"I don't think Vlad is Russian, and he tops the creep scale. Honestly, he's probably far worse than the Russian mob, and that's saying a lot. Leonid surpassed all known metrics in the bastard category," Jaiden answered.

Imara adopted a very conciliatory tone. "The plan was to explain to Jai who I was and what I intended to do for her. But then I saw the book on her shelf. It seemed like the right thing to do at the time. Originally, I thought I needed Tanya and Elle's help, until I realized Jai had a paperback collection. I don't quite know what to do, except excuse myself and bring in the reinforcements. Unfortunately, I believe things are going to get a lot worse before they get better. I'm really sorry."

Jaiden sensed Imara's bewilderment. She suspected Imara probably hadn't experienced many, if any, failures in her life. "Go find out what new hell Vlad is about to rain on us. I'll take care of Dani. Do you think it's safe to go to the store tomorrow? Or should you bring your reinforcements back here in the morning?"

"Actually, your store provides some powerful protections against negative energy and The Enchanted Page II might have some resources at their disposal as well. I sure would love it if the trio of book magicians were able to send Vlad into a particularly depressing or dangerous book and let him try to deal with that alternate reality." Imara walked to the front door. "I'll just let myself out and walk to the inn."

"I can drive you back if you want. It won't take long."

"No, better take care of Dani. The fresh air will do me good."

CHAPTER SEVEN

The one trick she'd always envied when it came to book magicians, was their ability to transport themselves to a new location in a matter of seconds. She'd experienced the nauseating side effects when Elle used to escort her when they were younger. Today, she thought it was worth it. Even though she'd said the fresh air would do her good, she was rethinking the late-night walk back to the inn. She couldn't see anyone, but she certainly felt like eyes tracked her every move.

Imara supposed that feeling was something akin to the wall ears that used to pop out all over the place when the book wizards took over the Magicians' Council and placed restrictions on the female book magicians. The wall ears were the wizards' clever way of monitoring a magician's every move. It used to creep her out when they wiggled. The way the current attorney general's ears stuck out of his head reminded her of the wizards' tools. Those intrusive ears were worse than any modern listening device employed by the FBI or CIA. She might have to pick Elle's brain about the chant she used to vanquish those pesky ears.

After knocking on the door to Tanya and Elle's room, she tried to explain what had happened. Imara swore she could see steam coming out of Elle's ears. In all the years she'd known Elle, she'd never seen such a voracity in her reaction. It seemed so out of proportion.

Seeing Bea lounging in the room worried Imara. It was rather late for a social visit. She wondered if they'd called upon Bea because they were afraid Imara might act impetuously. Of course, she had, but that was beside the point. She hated the fact that Elle didn't trust her to handle the situation with finesse.

"You left! How could you be so irresponsible?" Elle exclaimed.

"It wasn't like I had a lot of choice. I smell a big, fat, black, slicked-back-hair rat. Dani picking up a piece of glass and cutting her arm is completely out of character," Imara defended.

"Okay. Everyone calm down. We need to work together, not apart. Or worse, clawing at each other's throats. I know you two have history, but I thought that was all water under the bridge. It's not like you to hold a grudge, Elle. It seems Dani is not the only one operating far outside their character. In the past several days, there is a definite change in the air. I'm not saying this to hurt you, Elle, but that fun-loving side of you has suddenly taken a vacation. You've been moody, jealous, and kind of a rule stickler. That's not you," Tanya said.

"Vlad," everyone said in unison.

Imara pinched the bridge of her nose. "He's got to be doing something from a distance. That's new. I wonder how far his reach goes. Or maybe he has someone working for him that we wouldn't notice. Have you seen anyone hanging around more than usual?"

"Could that science teacher, Franklin, be a part of all this? He seemed so...well...nerdy. I know I shouldn't talk," Tanya interjected.

Imara whipped her head toward Tanya. "He was only there the first night at the movie."

"No, I've seen him loitering around the store. I thought he was merely a love-sick puppy. You know, trying to get Jai's attention. I'm a bit like him. Jane Q public doesn't normally notice people like us. We fade into the background. I suppose it takes a nerd to notice a fellow nerd."

"You are nothing like Franklin. He was beyond repugnant," Elle noted.

"Maybe, but none of you noticed him hovering on the other side of the street today."

"Hmm. I'll bet Vlad promised him Jai for his obedient service. What I can't figure is why Vlad needs anyone to step into the mix. He usually prefers a more personal touch when trying to convince someone to join his vast spider web of covens. He won't keep his promise, either. He'll definitely want Jai for himself. Still, things aren't adding up. He's toying with us. The minor alteration to our personalities is kid's play. He has something else in mind. I know for a fact his powers are ten times what they were when we went nose to nose several years ago."

"I agree. From what I hear on the magical grapevine, he's like a cat. He likes to play with his prey before eating them," Bea said.

Tanya's eyes grew wide. "He doesn't actually eat people, does he?"

"No dear. Simply a figure of speech."

"So, what's the plan?" Elle asked.

"I don't have one." Imara wouldn't meet Elle's eyes. Fury she could handle, disappointment was a whole other kettle of fish.

"You don't have one?" Elle's voice climbed an octave and the surprise and fear intermingled. "You always have a plan."

That was another thing out of character for Elle. She was fearless.

"I don't enjoy admitting this, but I believe a small spell has managed to infiltrate my defenses as well. I haven't much acted like myself over the last few days. I've had bouts of insecurity, and you know that is definitely not normal."

"It's like the real me comes and goes. I know exactly what you mean. The changes aren't constant. More like fleeting moments here and there. Sometimes they linger and other times they dissipate quickly," Elle added.

"Exactly! I know I can sometimes be an ass, but…I don't know if that has anything to do with Vlad toying with us or something else that might be disrupting his spells. We need to find out if we have something working to our advantage that we don't know about. Maybe we've had some dumb luck. It certainly feels like we're flickering light bulbs, and I sure don't want to end up burnt out before my time." Imara decided she should sit. They might be in for a long evening of trying to unravel the mystery.

"What about that potion you've been working on to try to hear his spells so we aren't going into this blind?" Elle asked.

"I've already ingested a vial. I don't think it's working in the way I envisioned. Maybe that's what's causing the intermittent changes. At least it's having some positive effect."

"I don't think that's the reason. You're the only one who drank the potion. It must be something else. Perhaps Jai's store and her powerful crystals are providing a barrier that causes the flickering you've described," Bea offered.

"Elle, have you noticed any changes in how I act or react?" Tanya asked.

Elle tilted her head. "No. Actually I haven't."

"What about Jai? Imara, have you studied her enough to know whether she's acting strange or not?" Tanya leaned forward in her chair.

"I don't think so," Imara answered.

"So, we have two book magicians and one book witch acting strange, but neither one of the nonmagical sorts have been affected," Tanya observed. "I think that means something."

"Wait. Are you saying Mom is acting strange, too? What about your abilities? You're not exactly devoid of magic."

"I don't think I fall strictly into the same category as book magicians or book witches. And yeah, no offense, but Bea is usually not as assertive. I've heard her take the two of you to task a few times. She also popped in and chastised you for interrupting her...uh...intimate time with her husband." Tanya's face turned a deep shade of red.

"That doesn't make sense. Why would Vlad suddenly make me more assertive? Wouldn't he wish to reduce my confidence?" Bea asked.

"Maybe he thought you'd turn aggressive and that would drive another wedge between us. Or maybe he enjoys the chaos. Perhaps another attempt to simply play with his prey. I don't know. I *am* perplexed by everything and that's causing all my wires to cross, which in turn shuts down any ideas for attempting to deal with the slimy bastard. We'll have to depend on the nonmags to think clearly for us all. I need a drink. I never got a chance to finish mine and it was damn good if I do say so myself." Imara popped up from her chair and looked around. "Do you have any alcohol stashed in this room?"

When Imara saw the strange looks shared between her friends, she plopped back on her chair. "I'm doing it again, huh? Not quite acting appropriate."

Tanya and Elle nodded.

"Dani is not a book witch or book magician. Why is she affected by Vlad?" Tanya asked astutely.

"Probably because she's a recipient of book magic. I suspect Vlad or his delegate has only poisoned anyone possessing the magic, or the direct result of that magic. I don't have all the answers, like why Tanya is completely unaffected. Perhaps her hybrid status is the reason, or maybe she's just special in more ways than one," Imara answered.

Elle nodded and kissed Tanya's cheek. "That she is."

"So I guess we better involve Jai. Elle, I know that sometimes Aunt Clara is a little eccentric, but she knows about certain things from her many travels you or Bea might not be aware of. You should transport Imara to wherever Aunt Clara is spending time these days. Maybe try my dad's place first," Tanya said.

"I think I know where she is," Elle answered.

"Aunt Clara popped in earlier to say hello to Imara. She was willing to join us before the two of you started scratching each other's eyes out. Now that you're not as testy with one another, I'm sure she'd be willing to give you some ideas. Plus, with you putting some distance between Vlad and yourselves, that might help with some clarity. If I had to make a guess, I would say Vlad has been following you for some time now, Imara. He can't transport himself without the help of another book magician, right?" Bea asked.

"I don't think so. Hard to say. He's elevated his maneuvering to a whole new level. Before today, I would say no way would he mix with a book magician. No offense, but he sees book magicians as beneath him," Imara answered.

"What about the male variety? Book wizards. Does he feel the same way about them? I'm guessing he doesn't look at directing Franklin in the same manner because he retains total control," Elle said.

"That makes sense. Who knows? A powerful book wizard who offers something he needs might sway him to at least pretend he is an equal. He's a snake, though. When the wizard is no longer needed, he'll discard him like yesterday's newspaper." Imara leaned forward in her chair.

"I guess we'll have to take the chance you can make the trip without a witch's version of wall ears hovering over you. I'll go see Jai and try to smooth things over. Well later, after she's had a chance to cool down and we pick Aunt Clara's brain." Imara sighed.

"What shall I do?" Bea asked.

"Why don't you go back to your husband? You still have a lot of years to make up for. If a nasty wizard separated me from the love of my life for over twenty years, I wouldn't want to leave her side. Imara was right when she said five might be the magic number, not six. For whatever reason, my gut tells me Dani is needed as the fifth person," Tanya suggested.

"She's just a character in a book," Imara insisted.

"I don't think so. When you brought her to life, reality sprouted another green shoot. I'd work on treating her as an equal partner of this new team we're forming," Tanya advised.

"Ooh. A team. Like *The Avengers*. Can we have a cool name, too?" Elle's eyes lit up.

"Magical Mercenaries. Or how about, Fiery Five," Imara suggested.

Tanya chuckled. "You keep working on that."

"I will. Come on, Elle, let's go find Aunt Clara." Imara took Elle's arm.

"Let me know if you need me for anything and keep me informed, especially if Vlad ratchets up the danger. I am not without my own resources. I'll bet Fay, Oren, and maybe even Brendan will want to help. Brendan is always up for an adventure. Ah, youth. Tootles." Bea gave the group a little wave, then left in a swirl of mist.

†

Jaiden was definitely out of her element as she considered how to deal with Dani. She was a teacher, not a psychologist. The initial first aid was easy. Dealing with emotions wasn't as straightforward, especially when Imara had added a mystical element to the equation. Jaiden wasn't sure mystical was the right word to use in this situation, but she couldn't think of an alternative.

She tried to imagine how Dani was feeling. Her world completely turned on its side. Dani had to feel like she was spinning uncontrollably in a washing machine, drowning in confusion about who and what she was, along with being tossed around like a puppet on a set of strings.

"Come on, let's go inside. It's getting nippy out here. I know you're old enough for alcohol. How about if I open a bottle of wine. White or red?"

"Would you think less of me if I said I'm not really a wine kind of gal?"

"No, of course not. I don't think I ever read about your preferences. If I did, I've forgotten. Sorry. Beer?" Jaiden stood.

"No. Not a beer drinker, either." Dani grabbed her silver crutches and winced when one pushed against her bandage.

Jaiden wasn't sure whether to help her inside or not. She felt like she knew enough about Dani to surmise she was fiercely independent and wouldn't look too kindly on an offer of assistance.

Dani screwed up her face. "You know. I don't really know what kind of alcohol I like. I'm not sure why I said I wasn't a wine or beer drinker. Interesting. What I do know is that alcohol and navigating new territory with these walking sticks probably don't mix. I don't want to embarrass myself by tumbling down a flight of stairs because I've discovered I can't hold my liquor."

"I seriously doubt one glass of wine will affect your fine motor skills that much. Live a little. I'd rather not drink the entire bottle myself. I sure wouldn't mind the company. It's been an eventful day."

Dani hesitated, picked up the mangled book, and moved inside. "White then. It's what my sister usually drinks."

Jaiden wanted her to feel at ease. "Look, my goal tonight is to make you feel as comfortable as possible in my home. I'm not a great hostess, so if you could settle in wherever suits you. We'll talk some more over a bottle of wine. I'd appreciate it if you wouldn't try to prove you're real again. I can't imagine what else you might choose to do to make your point."

Dani looked down at her feet and shifted on her crutches. "I'm sorry. I don't even know why I did that. An odd compulsion came over me. I immediately regretted my actions, but of course it was too late to rewind."

"Please, get comfortable on one of the chairs or the sofa. Prop your legs on the table or nestle into the leather recliner if you want. Anything you need to do to relax." After tossing the book onto the coffee table, Jaiden headed for her kitchen and pulled out a bottle of white from the refrigerator. She watched, as Dani chose her modern European recliner. It was a favorite of Jaiden's when she decided to pick a good book and read.

Dani carefully set the silver sticks to the side of the chair and seemed to settle. She watched in silence, as Jaiden opened the bottle of wine and filled two glasses. Her inquisitive blue eyes appeared to have unanswered questions. Finally, she broke the silence. "How many?"

Jaiden brought over the wine and handed one of the glasses to Dani before sitting on the couch adjacent to the chair. "How many what?"

"How many books am I in? Do you think I could read them?"

"Um, sure. Two and a half," Jaiden answered.

"Two and a half?" Dani smiled.

Jaiden thought she had a very nice smile. "Yeah. I don't think the Thanksgiving short story is considered a whole book." She pointed to the glass of wine and took a sip.

Dani brought the glass to her lips and tipped it back just enough to consume a very small quantity.

"Well, what do you think?"

"Um, it's okay, I guess."

"Wine is an acquired taste. Sometimes it's better with dinner because certain wines enhance the flavors of particular culinary dishes. I should introduce you to pairings. You might appreciate your first foray into wine much better with dinner."

Dani took a larger sip. "It's growing on me." She paused before asking, "I'm not a main character, am I? Certainly they wouldn't make a half-cripple the heroine."

"Oh, you'd be surprised. This particular author likes to write about unlikely heroines. You're a prominent character in the story, but no, not one of the main characters."

"So I'm a sidekick?"

"Sort of. If it makes a difference, you are a fan favorite, and we all kept sending the author notes about you having your own story."

"You too? I mean have you sent requests to the author to feature me in a book?" Dani asked shyly.

"I have," Jaiden answered honestly.

"Oh. Did you ever think that maybe we're in a book right now and you're simply a character?"

Jaiden squirmed in her chair. "Okay, that was very effective at helping me walk in your shoes. I don't like thinking I might not be real. For the record, I don't buy it. You are very real to many people. Who knows what constitutes reality and what comprises fantasy?"

"That would be intensely convoluted, huh? A story about a character bringing another character to life." Dani laughed.

"The unknown is a scary thing, but science is funny like that. What we know today could be completely wrong. I've always thought if I can dream it, it's possible. That's how we were able to fly to the moon. Do you think most of the world thought that possible 200 years ago? I think not."

"Exactly! Toni and I feel the same way about our inventions. Maggie and the rest of the gang don't ever treat us like our prototypes are crazy. In fact, they argue over who will be the one to try out something new." Dani's voice became animated, and Jaiden liked seeing the joy that seemed to spread like a wildfire.

"For the record, I believe you are very important to either the events in this real world or some make-believe story."

"At least in this story I get to be part of the action. Except for when I was an undercover agent and subsequently shot, I've always been behind the scenes. Sometimes I'm jealous of my colleagues who get to be in the thick of things. Even if some parts of the mission Char, Sophie, Ronda, and Val have had to endure are truly frightening, I feel like I'm on the outside looking in and trying to join the cozy group. My badass fighting days are over." Dani sighed.

"Here's to making you the heroine for a change." Jaiden lifted her glass and met Dani's as they toasted.

"Thanks, you're very sweet." Dani took a small sip. "Okay this is definitely growing on me. Who knows? Maybe I'll develop a real hankering for the stuff." She laughed.

Jaiden didn't know what to make of Dani's comment. She didn't particularly believe she was sweet. Most of her exes would call her overly critical. She needed to shift the conversation. "I don't know if this is some weird, alternate universe we're occupying, but I feel the negative energy from the man they call Vlad. I sure would like your perspective on him."

"What do you know about this man?" Dani asked.

"Not much. Apparently, he's not a vampire. He looks like one to me."

"Funny. First I'm a character in a book and now you suggest that vampires exist."

Jaiden chuckled and shrugged. "I don't know if vampires exist or not. I wouldn't eliminate that as a possibility. If characters in books can come to life and bleed on my deck, well then…"

"Okay, so you've told me what he's not, but not what he is. Sounds like he's magical in some way."

"Yeah. Imara said he's a very powerful warlock. It appears as though he has been following her or me. I'm not really sure which. At first I thought he was following Imara, because she knows him, but my gut says that might not be the case."

"Interesting. Do you have books on warlocks we can read up on?"

"No, not really my cup of tea. I prefer lesbian romance." Jaiden felt her face flush with embarrassment. She wasn't sure why she would feel self-conscious about that, but it seemed a frivolous thing to admit to, especially to a virtual genius.

"Um, I better give you some information about the reason for my existence. Imara brought me to life as a...shit, I don't know how to say this without it sounding arrogant or positively archaic."

Jaiden lifted her brow. "Just spit it out."

"I'm supposed to be a love interest for you. Something about teaching you a lesson. I know that sounds preposterous, but somehow I'm expected to get you to fall in love with me. Apparently, my physical challenges are key to the lesson. Something about imperfection. If I wasn't so shocked by the whole book character thing, I would have latched onto her insensitive comments." Dani looked away, and Jaiden thought she appeared suddenly very uncomfortable.

"When did you learn this crucial piece of information that Imara failed to share with me?" Jaiden was profoundly irritated that Imara had not only decided to meddle in her love life, but she hadn't said one word to Jaiden about this unhinged plan of hers.

"Um sorry, she briefly filled me in when you came into the house to retrieve the tablet."

Jaiden didn't want to play into Imara's seriously warped plan, but she also didn't want Dani to feel inferior. Her feelings seemed to bounce all over the place. If she were honest with herself, both Imara and Dani piqued her interest. They were attractive, interesting women whom she would normally pursue. These were not your run-of-the-mill circumstances. She needed to tread very lightly.

"Aren't you involved with Candy? You don't strike me as the cheating sort."

"I'm not. And thank you for treating me like a real person and not some figment of your imagination. I don't live a normal life. Candy's never been to the compound and well…"

"She thinks you have something major to hide and that's affected your relationship."

"Yeah. A big understatement. I've thought all along I wasn't being fair to her, but Maggie wasn't too keen on me letting her into our very tight security. Not being able to share everything was a relationship killer. I tried not to blame Maggie, especially after her brush with death. Things got so crazy there at the end, and I wasn't able to talk to Char about it when she took the reins. By then it was too late. I was spending so much time in the lab, and I couldn't reveal the biggest part of my life. It was inevitable for us to go our separate ways."

Jaiden smacked her hand on the chair. "Oh my God. This is important."

"What?"

"Nowhere in any of the books or short stories does it say anything about your breakup with Candy. If you're just a character, you'd stick closely to the script in the book. Either the magic is evolving or…"

"I'm not really a character?"

"Your guess is as good as mine. We need to talk to Imara. If you don't mind, can we pursue this tomorrow after I track down Imara? The mental gymnastics we're engaging in are very tiring."

"Um, I don't have anything to wear. I don't even have a toothbrush. By the way, where are we? I mean what's our location?"

"Coupeville, Washington."

"As in Washington State?"

Jaiden nodded. "Uh huh."

"I thought it rains all the time here. By the looks of the stars in the sky, it's a cloudless night."

"The amount of rain is grossly exaggerated. The locals don't correct that misconception, because we don't want hordes of people to move here. You'll keep our secret, won't you?" Jaiden winked.

"Obviously, I'm good at keeping secrets. Covert organization. Remember?"

"Right. Okay, you can be trusted." Jaiden chuckled and looked appraisingly over Dani's body. "You look like you'll fit into my clothes. Are shorts and a t-shirt okay with you? I can also rustle up a new toothbrush. Tomorrow, you can peruse my closet and find something to wear. I don't have tons of money. I am, after all, a lowly teacher. So, it's only fair that Imara takes you shopping and sets you up with a new wardrobe."

"There's a part of me that wants to travel to the East Coast to make sure the compound doesn't exist. I have plenty of money. I suppose I could simply jump onto the Internet and search for my bank account."

"Tomorrow. We'll do that tomorrow. Okay?" Jaiden stood and waited for Dani to follow her to the guest bedroom.

†

Imara was impressed with the location. Even though the distance made the trip a little rough for her, the view was breathtaking. They'd landed on powdery white sand, so fine it reminded her of caster sugar but softer. If a magician combined sugar and baby powder, the result would be this beach. The palm trees swayed in the light breeze, as they looked out on the bluest water Imara had seen in a long time.

Whidbey Island was pretty, but the beauty of the Puget Sound did not compare at all to this paradise.

"How do you know Clara is here?" Imara brushed off the sand, as she stood and tried to quell the rising bile. Several deep breaths managed to settle her stomach. She wasn't looking forward to the trip back to Whidbey.

"She mentioned that Frank, Tanya's father, always wanted to fish for Marlin. I think that's why we used him as a test." Elle seemed unfazed by the journey and was removing her own batch of sand.

"Test? I have no idea what you're talking about."

"We were trying to decide who we could get to test the e-book magic. It was so new. Who better to test the new magic on? Frank was enamored with Ernest Hemingway. So, we sent him into *The Old Man and the Sea*. Aunt Clara and Frank took a shining to each other, and they've been dating ever since. Cairns, Australia is one of the premiere places to fish for Marlin. The Gold Coast is also a favorite place for Aunt Clara to visit. She can't resist a beautiful, sandy beach." Elle pointed down the beach. "There she is."

A tousled head of salt-and-pepper hair turned in their direction, and Clara gave a tiny wave. She looked relaxed, and her lazy eye appeared to be behaving itself today. Imara marveled at how she could look like an attractive, middle-aged woman one minute, and the next moment a frantic bag lady. Today she was beaming. It appeared as though the glow of love surrounded her. Imara smiled when she saw the fancy drink with the tiny umbrella sitting on the sand next to Clara's chair.

"Hello, girls. It's good to see you two have kissed and made up. Well, not literally. I know Elle is with Tanya. You know what I mean." She waved her hand in the air and took a sip from her drink.

"It's okay, Aunt Clara, we understand."

"Sorry about not joining you on your mission, but I was waiting for you two to duke it out and clear the air. Besides, when I learned Frank wanted to try his hand at the real thing—you know, fishing for Marlin—I couldn't resist popping us to Australia. What brings you to paradise?"

"Clara, you are looking particularly good today. Must be love. Or maybe it's lust." Imara cackled.

"Definitely lust." Clara grinned. "So, it must be important for you to brave the nausea. What can I do to help?"

"You've been all around the globe. What can you teach us that might come in handy? I get a bad feeling all of a sudden. Vlad's power is growing, and somehow he's managed to get others to do his bidding. Nonmagicians who might even have low-level powers. We're not really sure about that. Maybe his spells or potions have long-distance impact."

"You give yourself too little credit. Vlad may puff out his chest and pretend to have more pull than he actually has. Otherwise, he wouldn't be after you. I'm certain you can hold your own against him."

"I'm not worried about myself. I'm worried about Jai."

"And Dani. Don't forget about Dani," Elle reminded.

"She's a character. She doesn't need protection."

"You're jealous," Elle stated.

"I am not."

"Why'd you bring her here if you wanted Jai for yourself?"

"Because she needs the lesson. The way to love is cluttered. Dani will clear the path to allow love inside. After that occurs, Dani will be returned to her book and…"

"That's cold. Get someone to do the hard work and then you'll swoop in when the berries are ripe for the picking. Careful, Imara, you know what they say about the best-laid plans. Besides, I agree with Tanya, I don't think Dani is merely a character in a book. Something tells me the magic has shifted. Maybe that's Vlad. Maybe it's something else. Regardless, you have to stop being your naturally arrogant self and treat her as an equal. Otherwise, I believe you'll be putting Jai in greater danger," Elle gently chastised.

"I'm afraid Elle is correct. I've always believed the characters book witches bring to life may be a whole lot more than meets the eye. If the right circumstances present themselves, fantasy could very well become an eternal reality. Book witches have the same level of responsibility to their chosen as book magicians. You must always be able to locate Jai no matter where she is, wherever Vlad may choose to send her. Let me teach you the location spell. If possible, three people must recite the spell together for the optimal effect."

"That's great. A location spell in our arsenal is a wonderful tool to have. What about chant blocks or healing potions? I know you have a group of book magicians and book witches you hang with who don't give a rip about this chill that has developed between the two groups." Elle lowered herself to the ground and sat cross-legged in the sand facing her aunt.

"The witches sure know how to party sometimes. I rather like the old rituals of dancing naked in front of a full moon. I almost have Frank talked into joining me for one of the shindigs held during summer solstice. He's still pondering that. He insists I don't want to see his aging, white behind."

"So, have you learned anything useful from them?" Elle asked.

A wry grin blossomed on Clara's face. "Well, I learned how to make a very tasty mai tai." She lifted her glass in the air. "Care to join me in a drink? I have some mixed up in that cooler over there."

119

Imara laughed. "Rain check. I think Elle meant regarding how to counteract Vlad and whatever he has up his grimy sleeve."

"Grimy sleeve? As I recall, Vlad is normally impeccably dressed. He does tend to prefer that very depressing monochrome of black, and could certainly benefit from a splash of color, but I've never seen him dirty."

"Figure of speech and you know that, you old cougar. Come on give us some good stuff to use."

Clara looked right and left. "What I've learned can be very dangerous in the wrong hands. I'm not sure how safe it is to…"

"It's not like there are any walls out here," Elle insisted.

"No there aren't wall ears to worry about." Clara nodded toward some large conch shells on the beach. "Not only do they collect the sounds of the ocean, but I've heard some very resourceful witches have used them inappropriately. Why do you think I find remote places to shelter and relax?"

"I know you have chants to put a bubble of protection around you. We should go back to your room, where you can eliminate any prying ears and seashells. Then will you tell us what you know?"

"Very well, but these spells and chants are not without a certain amount of risk. Backfires are common."

"We'll take our chances." Imara looked at Elle for confirmation and she nodded.

†

Plop! Plop!

"God, I hate the reentry. Haven't you learned to smooth things out a little more?" Imara stood and rubbed her behind. Tanya thought she looked slightly green. The trip must have been a rough one, because Elle looked a tad ill herself.

"It's the time change. Australia is on the other end of the world, you know," Elle defended.

Tanya yawned. "You two were gone longer than expected. Did Aunt Clara provide some assistance?"

"She did. Everyone thinks she's an eccentric old lady, but wherever she goes, she soaks up the information like an enormous sponge. That woman never forgets a thing. She told us about three doozies. A stronger protection chant, a location chant, and a character chant." Elle crossed the small space and crawled on the bed to sit next to Tanya, who was propped against the headboard reading a book.

Tanya missed curling up with Tolstoy, and she hoped they would be able to get the loft fixed up quickly so she could bring him to the island. She wasn't sure what they would do with her condo, if they decided to remain on the island permanently. Staying at the inn was not an option for the long term. It was expensive, cramped, and Tanya felt like a criminal as she considered breaking the rules to bring Tolstoy back. Elle had assured her money wasn't an issue, but Tanya still felt bad about her possible foray into crime.

Tanya set her book on the nightstand. "I know what a protection chant is, but can you tell me a little more about the other two?"

Imara sat in the old wingback chair, crossed her legs, and leaned back. "I've heard rumors about the character chant, but I've never seen anyone perform the magic. Probably because Clara says it backfires a fair amount of the time."

"That doesn't really tell me what it is."

"Oh, right. Apparently it's the opposite of a book witch's primary directive. We bring characters to life for our chosen. The character chant turns people into characters."

"How is that different from what a book magician does? Elle transported me into a book, and I became one of the characters. Why is that such a big deal?" Tanya asked.

121

Imara had a glint in her eye. "Because we call upon the author to create a brand new story and whomever we choose is written into the book, locked inside for all eternity. They cease being real. They become a permanent fantasy."

"That sounded relatively simple to me, but then Aunt Clara explained how many authors are unpredictable with their stories. Other individuals who are in the periphery can be caught in their net of intrigue," Elle added.

"Bugger. If what you are saying is true, that means we all could cease to exist except as characters in a book. I don't like the sound of that," Tanya exclaimed.

"Yeah, me neither." Elle reached over and grabbed Tanya's hand.

Imara waved her hand in the air. "We'll only use it as a last resort. Besides, I can counteract the chant and bring you back to life. That's what I do best."

"How are you going to do that if you get swept into the net?" Tanya asked.

Imara frowned. "I don't know, but surely I won't lose my powers. She also hinted that, with a tiny variation, we could send people into other mediums, like paintings or prints. Maybe those chants have less side effects."

"I hope the location chant is not as dangerous," Tanya said.

"No, it's not. Someone should have already taught me that one. It seems a very basic spell that is beneficial to both book witches and book magicians. I wonder why we haven't ever learned it before now," Imara pondered.

"Because we never needed it until Scrotumface and Donkeyhole came along to mess with us," Elle snarled.

"Most of the time, I can sense the distress of my chosen one. I suspect that is the same for book magicians, but we can't locate them with refined accuracy. Clara says this chant will nearly put you on top of your chosen one. As close to

122

the action as one can get without actually overtaking their body," Imara explained.

Tanya nodded. "I suppose that would have come in handy when you arrived to save my behind the first time. Did you have to do some speculation on where you would find me in the book?"

"I did, but Gordon was not at all creative, so the location was relatively easy to surmise. Vlad is a lot more cunning than Gordon ever was."

Tanya yawned again. "Thanks for the update. No offense, but it's getting late and a good night's rest will do us all a world of good."

"Don't stay up half the night having sex. We all need to be sharp tomorrow," Imara teased as she left the room.

Elle nuzzled against Tanya and kissed her neck. "I'll be more alert after we've rocked each other's world half the night."

Tanya giggled. "Since I'm already considering a reign of crime by bringing Tolstoy to the inn. Why the heck not?" She pushed Elle down on the bed and straddled her. "Tonight I get to have my way with you first."

"Fine by me." Elle reached up to bring Tanya's lips to her own.

After breaking from the passionate lip-lock, both began frantically removing their clothes and tossing them aside. Tanya rocked against Elle, who responded with a loud moan. She started her descent down Elle's stomach and then parted her legs and settled in between. When Tanya reached Elle's wet center and delved inside with two fingers, her tongue started to make small, precise circles on Elle's clit. Elle cried out, "Oh Goddess, yes, just like that."

Bang, bang, bang.

"I can hear you," Imara called through the wall of the adjoining room.

Elle giggled. "I guess I should be a tad bit quieter."

"Darn, I like when you're vocal. I suppose, unless we want company at an inopportune moment, quieter is better. Can you control yourself?" Tanya lifted her head and looked mischievously into Elle's eyes.

"You aren't going to make it easy for me are you?"

"Nope." Tanya dived back into her sweet treasure. She loved when Elle was in the throes of passion. The way her body arched, how she cried out, and the expression on her face during climax created the most beautiful image Tanya had ever seen. Tanya's life was infinitely better with Elle at her side. Great sex was only one reason why.

CHAPTER EIGHT

The sunlight had barely filtered through the windows, when Jaiden heard the clip-clop of Dani's forearm crutches on the tile floor in the kitchen. She scrambled out of bed and went to her bathroom to finger comb her hair. The attempt to flatten certain places where her hair stood up in disarray was mildly successful. After a quick brushing of her teeth, she headed to the kitchen.

Dani was peering into one of the cabinets. Her crutches were propped against one wall. Shutting the cabinet, she quickly moved to the next one and exclaimed. "Aha, there you are, you naughty coffee. Trying to hide from me, are you? I guess you don't like that scorching water hitting your delicate grinds."

Jaiden laughed at the adorable monologue. "Hmm, I suppose you think coffee has feelings."

Dani turned around and grinned. "Are you a coffee drinker? I thought making a pot was the least I could do for you. As for coffee having feelings, stranger things have occurred."

"I would think the grinder would hurt even more than the scorching water. Before they even get to the grinder, they're plucked from their cozy nests and roasted in an oven. That can't be pleasant."

"Cozy nests? I like it. Would the branches of trees be considered a cozy nest?"

"Absolutely. If you're going to talk about adding boiling water to coffee grinds, I get to start at the very beginning."

"Hmm. Do you think they fall on the ground like Freddy the leaf in that children's book? Maybe the little beans are shivering in the cold and embrace their ultimate demise."

Jaiden threw her head back and laughed. "Did you sleep okay?"

"I did. Thanks for asking. No horrible nightmares. Only pleasant dreams."

"Do tell." Jaiden arched her eyebrow.

Dani blushed and avoided the question. "So, do you like your coffee strong or weak? Or perhaps you'd like some tea. I haven't found your tea stash yet."

"Coffee please. I do live in the Northwest. Entrance into this special club means drinking coffee with a kick versus the wussy stuff I imagine y'all drink on the East Coast."

"Not since Starbucks took over. We've been acclimated to the virtues of a good, strong cup of coffee."

"Perfect. Are you a fan of breakfast or does breaking eggs also cause a moral dilemma for you?"

"Honestly, I can take or leave breakfast. If something is put in front of me, I won't reject food in the morning. Sometimes I'll simply grab a few pieces of fruit or yogurt."

Knock, knock, knock.

Jaiden looked at the clock on the stove. "It's awfully early for visitors. I thought we were supposed to meet the trio at the store."

"Maybe they found out something and needed to update us pronto." Dani shuddered.

Jaiden felt the sudden shift in the density of energy around her. A choking feeling threatened to close her airways, which soon evolved into feeling as though the walls were closing in around her. "Something isn't right."

"Then don't open the door," Dani warned. "I've learned to trust my gut. If yours is screaming danger, there's a reason for it."

"I'll just grab one of the crystals in the windowsill." After putting one of the rocks in her hand and touching her necklace, she opened the front door.

"Franklin?"

A wide-eyed Franklin appeared frantic just outside the door. He looked rather greenish and likely to hurl any moment. Standing next to him was a portly man with thinning, gray hair and a close-cropped beard. The man's beady eyes reminded Jaiden of a shark's—dead. Jaiden immediately sensed evil.

"You're in grave danger, Jaiden. I know this sounds crazy, and I wouldn't have believed it myself, but Gordon convinced me with this transport trick. It's…it's like Star Trek come to life. He literally beamed us here from my place. I'm a man of science and this defies every scientific theory I know, but here we are."

Just as Jaiden motioned for them to come inside, Dani exclaimed, "Don't invite them in."

"Jaiden, you know I would never hurt you, and I won't let anyone else harm you either," Franklin said in earnest.

The hurt look on his face convinced Jaiden. "Well come on in and tell me what the hell you're talking about." She placed the crystal back on the windowsill and followed them into the main seating area of her great room.

Dani's eyes narrowed to tiny slits. She grabbed her forearm crutches and struggled to make her way into the living room.

Franklin sat on the couch. He looked at the overweight man with the mean eyes, who simply nodded. "This is Gordon, he's a book wizard. I don't even know where to begin. Do you know a man called Vladimir Ambus?"

"If you mean a man who has a penchant for black clothing and looks like he could play Dracula in the movies, yeah, I've seen him. He's been skulking around. A bit like you, Franklin."

"I didn't like the looks of the guy, so I've been watching out for you ever since I saw him outside your store."

"And what were you doing hanging outside my store in the first place?"

"It's a free country. I do live in Coupeville, you know. There aren't many places to go during the day."

"Right. Just get on with your story."

"You don't seem surprised about me telling you Gordon is a book wizard. How come?" Franklin looked perplexed. "I would think that sounds as equally crazy to you as it did to me. I mean, I know you have a crystal shop and believe in all that mystical crap, but book wizards?"

"Let's just say my mind is amenable to many different possibilities and my eyes are continually opened to the magical world we live in. You're a man of science. I'm more inclined to accept the unbelievable. Although I have to admit, lately, that envelope was pushed much further than ever before."

"This Vlad person is very bad news. He's a powerful warlock. Gordon says he can protect both of you by sending you into this novel. Well, uh… He'd send you into it Jaiden."

128

He looked at Dani. "He'd send you back where you came from." His eyes shifted to the book on the coffee table. He pointed to the mangled paperback. "That's the one. Vlad can't follow you there. You'll be protected by these super women in the book."

"My friends and my sister," Dani filled in.

"Yes, exactly. Those women that own that new store next to yours are book magicians and a book witch. They aren't your friends, Jaiden. Gordon says they are reckless and working alongside Vlad."

"I seriously doubt that. I've told you before, Franklin. I am never going to be interested in you. This ruse is over the top. Even for you. I'm not sure where you collected all this information. Maybe you overheard some conversations you shouldn't have by hanging around The Enchanted Page II."

"I swear, Jaiden, this isn't about us. Vlad wants to enslave you along with that tall redhead who was making eyes at you during the movie. He's promised you to her once she joins him. These are not the fun-loving Wiccans you're used to," Franklin said with conviction.

Jaiden crossed her arms and glared at Franklin. "There is no us. Nice try, Franklin."

"I know it sounds unbelievable. I can barely wrap my arms around what Gordon told me. Show them, Gordon."

"Very well, Franklin. If you insist. We must protect the ladies." Gordon picked up the book on the coffee table.

Jaiden didn't have time to react and wasn't sure what she could do to stop him from chanting when she recognized the evil glint in his eyes.

Franklin ripped the crystal from her neck.

Send these ladies into this book,
a place no witch will think to look.

No need for them to touch a page,
they will arrive at center stage.

Gordon spoke the chant three times.

†

Imara's eyes popped open, and she glanced at the clock to her right. Seven thirty in the morning. That was far too early for the panic she sensed coming from...*Oh, shit, Jai and Dani.* She jumped out of bed, not bothering to put on clothes, and ran to Elle and Tanya's room. She pounded on the door. *This is all my fault.*

Tanya was scratching her head when she opened the door in a fluffy, white robe. "What the..." Tanya took a step back and averted her eyes. "Hon, you'd better come quick and bring the other robe."

"Jesus, Imara, where's the fire? You couldn't bother to get dressed. I've seen you naked before, but my girlfriend hasn't. She tends to be a bit more modest than me."

"No time. Jai and Dani are in trouble. Please, take us to Jai's house pronto. We don't have a moment to spare," Imara exclaimed as she put on the robe.

"Take my hand. You too, Tanya." Elle grabbed Tanya and Imara's hands, and Imara felt the familiar tug.

†

The journey was remarkably smooth, but Imara didn't have time to ponder why.

Standing in the center of the great room where she had mixed the mojitos the prior evening, Imara looked around. "Jai, Dani. Where are you?"

A glint caught her eye. Sunlight peeking through the window captured the reflection of Jai's protection crystal.

Elle saw where she was looking and touched Imara's arm. "We'll find her, don't worry. We can use the location spell. You can't go traipsing around without clothes, though. Go root around in Jai's drawers and find something to wear. Hurry."

Imara nodded and felt tears form in her eyes. She went quickly to Jai's bedroom and tore open the drawers. A selection of khaki shorts, a lilac sports bra, and a black t-shirt would do nicely. She slipped into a pair of tennis shoes, reciting a quick spell to enable the clothes and shoes to fit her larger size.

She walked back out to the living room, and Elle nodded her approval. Imara would never be able to forgive herself if something happened to Jai or Dani. Neither of them deserved the danger she had brought their way. What she'd done was unforgiveable. Her cockiness had caused this whole damn situation. She was beginning to think there was something to the notion that Dani was a living, breathing, human being. "Jai's necklace might not have protected her, but it sure will help us locate her." She pocketed the necklace.

Tanya craned her neck and pointed to something sticking out of the wall.

Wall ears? Elle mouthed.

Tanya nodded, and Elle's face filled with confusion.

Tanya began searching the drawers in the kitchen until she found some paper and a pen. She began scribbling and handed the paper to Elle. Imara looked over Elle's shoulder and read, *Do the chant that Aunt Clara taught you.*

Nosy ears have no place,
on the walls in any space.

131

Make them all disappear;
we won't stand for coerced fear.

Nosy ears have no place,
on the walls in any space.
Make them all disappear;
we won't stand for coerced fear.

Nosy ears have no place,
on the walls in any space.
Make them all disappear;
we won't stand for coerced fear.

"Okay, what the hell is going on? I thought the wall ears were banned when Fay took over as Grand Magician," Imara asked.

"Something smells rotten in Coupeville. I'm betting one of the book wizards is helping Vlad, but which one?" Elle asked.

"I thought it was something smells rotten in Denmark?" Tanya interjected.

"We aren't in Denmark," Elle answered.

"Focus, people. Sheesh. We have a real problem here."

"Sorry," Tanya and Elle said in stereo.

"We don't have time to figure out which one of the wizards is being a total asswipe."

"Donkeywipe," Tanya corrected.

"Whatever." Imara glared. "Come on, Elle, we need to all say the location chant together. I need you both with me. I don't know what we'll come across when we find them, and reinforcements are necessary. It might be dangerous. Besides, Clara said it works best if there are three people behind the chant. That whole power of three thing."

"I'm in," Tanya replied.

"Me too. I'd never let Tanya walk into a dangerous situation alone. Well, I'd do the same for you, but Tanya is my first priority. Do you think it matters that we aren't witches?"

"I guess we'll find out." Imara grabbed the paper and neatly wrote out the spell for Tanya's benefit.

If the chosen is exposed
to a place that's undisclosed,
time to visit this location,
well before we feel vexation.
Make the flight a peaceful trip,
even at a hasty clip.

"Hey, those last two phrases weren't part of what Aunt Clara told us," Elle said.

Imara glared. "I added them. I don't particularly enjoy this mode of transportation. It can't hurt to add a teensy request. We don't know what's on the other end of this trip, and I'd rather not feel the effects of motion sickness. That won't serve any useful purpose if we have to come out fighting."

"Good point," Tanya said.

"Maybe, but those added verses could weaken the spell. I don't like messing with what is tried and true."

"Nothing is tried and true. Clara said this spell doesn't always work anyway. The degree of precision is a bit of a crapshoot, she warned. Even though it is the most effective spell in her arsenal for locating a chosen. I say it's worth the risk if we land without the accompanying side effects."

"All right. We need to say it together, but thankfully only once. Witches' spells don't require us to chant in threes," Elle said.

"Are you ready?" Imara held out the paper at an angle so all three of them could see.

†

"Shit, don't move," Dani yelled out.

Jaiden looked around and saw the pattern of red laser beams. Something felt vaguely familiar about her surroundings. Someone yelled, "Fuck, we're screwed."

"What the hell—" Jaiden exclaimed.

"Welcome to my world," Dani said.

Jaiden heard the low rumbling of another voice. She hadn't caught the first part of the command, but she clearly heard the woman order, "Toni, clear these lasers, now."

Panic hadn't yet set in.

"Got it, I'll work on the other traps. Go, go."

Jaiden assumed the response was Toni's and scrambled to a standing position. She held out her hand.

Dani grabbed the offered hand. She was wincing as she stood. "That's our cue to move. Come on. If I'm not mistaken, we have about three minutes before this place blows up."

Jaiden blinked twice. "You're serious."

"As a heart attack. No time to spare."

Jaiden slung her arm around Dani's waist and pulled Dani's arm around her neck. "Let me help you. You won't be able to move quickly enough if I don't."

"Okay. We need to find the others. There's a safe room somewhere. That's our only chance."

"I remember. It's in Leonid's bedroom, but the book didn't exactly provide a blueprint for this mansion. I have no idea which way to go." The panic started to consume Jaiden.

"If we head toward the commotion, we might run into the others."

"Good idea. I think it's this way." Jaiden pointed down the hallway, as a tall menacing woman rounded the corner. Two more women were on her heels, running as if the devil himself were chasing them.

"Dani, what are you doing here? And who the fuck are you?"

"No time to explain. We have to get to Leonid's bedroom." Dani turned her eyes toward one of the other women and shouted, "You need to get Toni. Now, Char."

"Yeah, we have about three and a half minutes before this place lights up. Toni won't have enough time to disable the bombs."

Char turned back and started running.

"Gina's here and knows where the shelter is. Just lead us to Leonid's bedroom. Trust me," Dani said.

"Okay, let's go. Ronda get on the other side of Dani and help her and whoever the hell that is." The woman pointed at Jaiden, and Jaiden felt her intensity. "You two pick Dani up and carry her if you have to."

"I can—" Dani was cut off.

"Pride has no place in survival." Ronda maneuvered herself on the other side of Dani. "Let's go. Time's a ticking."

Another woman pushed Jaiden aside and took her position on the other side of Dani. Jaiden wasn't about to get into a pissing match with the two women, who were now mostly carrying Dani as they followed the tall blonde.

The women made it to Leonid's bedroom quickly, and a petite, dark-haired woman Jaiden suspected was Gina nearly

135

ran into Val. The story was coming back to Jaiden. She believed she had all the characters straight in her head. Val was the one in control. Jaiden banked on the fact that in the story everyone made it out of the dilemma unharmed. She needed to make sure she followed this group down into the hole and out of harm's way. Maybe this was a fantasy, but it felt perfectly real. She wasn't about to take any chances.

"Where's the bomb shelter, Gina?" Val asked.

"This way. Follow me."

"We have to wait for Char and Toni," Val said.

Gina grabbed Val's hand and pulled. "No time. It's stuck. I tried to pry it open, but it wouldn't budge. I need your help. The shelter is in the walk-in closet. We have to hurry." Gina began to cry.

"Okay, honey, shhh. It'll be all right." Val halted their progress. "Ronda, you wait here for Char and Toni. Sophie and I will get this damn thing open," Val said.

"I can help," Jaiden offered.

"No," Val barked. "You help Dani."

Val and Sophie followed Gina into the bedroom, while Jaiden helped Dani to the edge of the closet. Jaiden peered inside. In the center of the small space was a brass wheel. Val dropped to her knees and grunted as she pulled. The wheel wouldn't move left or right. Nothing. Just like in the story, it wouldn't budge. Sophie dropped down on the other side.

"On three. One, two, three," Sophie counted.

As both women worked, the covering began to move a few inches. Droplets of sweat fell against the metal, as the threads on the secured entrance to the bomb shelter finally loosened and they managed to unscrew the lid.

"Sixty seconds, Val," Ronda called out.

Val and Sophie finally removed the heavy brass seal, and Val peered down into a dark tunnel.

"There's enough space to hold everyone," Jaiden announced.

"Shut the fuck up, I don't need your commentary," Val growled.

"Val, don't, please. Jai's a friend," Dani pleaded.

Toni and Char rounded the corner and skidded to a stop two feet from the hole.

"Go, go, go," Val barked. "Gina, you're first. Please don't argue. We don't have time."

Gina crawled into the dark hole. Val pointed to Dani. Jaiden helped her to the hole, hoping she had enough strength to climb down. She stepped aside to let the rest of the women follow Dani. Val's touch to her arm was surprisingly gentle, as she gestured for Jaiden to go ahead. Val was the last to find the stairs. She kept her feet anchored to them, dragged the heavy cover back over the hole, and screwed it tightly in place. Val had barely tightened the cover, when Jaiden heard and felt the vibrations from the blast. Val slumped against the cement stairs and ran her hand through her hair.

"I guess today wasn't a good day to die after all," Val murmured.

Jaiden stepped farther inside the shelter and allowed Gina to touch Val's leg. A cell phone illuminated the cramped bunker. Jaiden could see the love between the two women as they caught one another's eyes.

Val took Gina's hand, quickly scrambled down the stairs, and pulled her close. She held on for nearly a minute.

Tiny bursts of light from four other cell phones revealed the group of women huddled together in the ten-by-fifteen-foot cement box with reinforced steel. The crude space contained a few chairs and minimal supplies for survival.

"I don't think we need to hang out in this little rat hole too long, but maybe it would be prudent to stay a few minutes to make sure all the tremors subside. There might be some residual bomb that acts like a timed-release medication to catch the unsuspecting person in Leonid's insidious trap. I'm glad you had help finding the needle." Char's face had a freaky glow from the flashlight app on her smartphone.

"Anyone have a good ghost story?" Ronda asked.

"That is a really bad joke," Toni answered.

Char turned her penetrating gaze toward Gina. "Not that I'm ungrateful for your help, but what made you come back?" Char's glance traveled over to Jaiden, and she narrowed her eyes. "I'll get to you later. You too, Dani."

Gina looked perplexed and swung her eyes from Char to Dani, then Jaiden. "Dani…uh…I don't know how you got here and who this strange woman is…"

"I found a line of code that was out of place and banged on Gina's door. I thought she could help find the escape route. The rest of the story is too convoluted, and you probably won't believe a word I say anyway. If I hadn't seen a few things with my own eyes…Maybe I'm having a psychotic break or something, but if you see Jai here, I guess that's proof I'm not. Can we explore that craziness later?" Dani pleaded.

The shelter became eerily quiet, as all eyes turned to Jaiden. She was relieved when Sophie broke the silence and shifted the conversation back to the story's original script. Jaiden wondered if their appearance at a critical place in the book would make a difference to the novel. Maybe this was like time travel, and the slightest change could alter history in a very positive or very negative manner. The whole thing was giving her a headache.

"So what are your plans, now that you're a widower?" Sophie asked. "You sticking around? The compound isn't really a place to raise a kid."

Val glared at Sophie. "Shut up, Sophie."

Everyone grew silent as the seconds ticked away. Jaiden wanted to turn herself into a speck of dust in the musty bomb shelter.

†

Not bad. Not bad at all. Imara would have to remember those last two verses. She'd never travel with Elle or any other book magician without adding those lines. She didn't feel any of the familiar bile rising in her throat.

Elle swiveled her head around, quickly taking in her surroundings. "Any guesses as to where the hell we've landed?"

Tanya was smiling broadly. "That was the smoothest trip so far. Can we please use Imara's added lines to any future chants?"

"Sure, honey." Elle brushed Tanya's lips.

The sprawling mansion was a bit over the top for Imara's liking, but the grounds were certainly nice. The well-manicured lawn that led to a grove of trees almost lulled Imara into a sense of peace and tranquility. A large boom shattered the quiet and sent shards flying in every direction.

Imara instinctively jumped onto her two companions and covered their bodies, as the debris rained on top of them.

Let me be the hearty shield,
protect my friends on the battle field.

Imara lamented not being quick enough. She saw the trickle of blood coming from Tanya's head. Taking the brunt of the blast had also resulted in a very tender spot in the middle of her own back. Several more explosions occurred, before Imara believed it was safe to survey the damage. She crouched next to her colleagues. "Tanya, are you badly injured?"

Elle tenderly brushed hair away from Tanya's face. She whipped off her t-shirt and pressed it against the wound that was now clearly visible.

Tanya started to sit up, when Elle gently stopped her motion. "Just hang on. Don't get up yet. Not until you're sure you aren't going to pass out on me."

Tanya offered a weak smile. "I'm okay. Too bad we don't have a chant to stop the nausea after some idiot blows up a perfectly good house. I guess they wanted to redecorate. Their methods are a bit drastic, don't you think?" Tanya's grin grew more confident.

"I guess you're doing okay if you're joking about the big bang." Elle helped her sit up. "Are you still feeling nauseous or dizzy?"

"A little, but not as much."

"Imara, I'm not willing to take any chances here. I've got to get Tanya back to where she can get some medical attention. I'm really sorry to leave you in this mess to find Jai and Dani, but Tanya is my first priority."

"I understand. Go, but can you come back to get me after they patch her up?"

"Of course. I won't be long. Do you have anything I can use to locate you quickly?" Elle asked.

Imara reached in her pocket and pulled out Jai's necklace. "I'll be wherever Jai is because I'm going to find them."

Elle nodded and began her chant to take them back.

The time has come to take us back,
before the wizard's next attack.
Send us safely with my magic,

lest she faces something tragic.

Elle recited the chant three times, but nothing happened. Imara began to worry. Elle was a powerful book magician. If her chant did not allow them passage back to their own world, someone very formidable was blocking her.

"Shit, someone is preventing your return to the real world." Imara scanned her surroundings, looking for the source. Nothing seemed to stick out. She thought she saw movement in the trees, but it could have been the shadows playing tricks on her eyes.

"Now what?" Elle was glaring at Imara.

"We find Jai and Dani and get help from them. Maybe they'll have someone close we can flag down." Imara held out her hand for Jai's crystal and stuck it back in her pocket.

"Anyone know where we are?" Tanya asked.

"I don't think we're anywhere near Whidbey Island. If I had to venture a guess, I would say we're in Maryland, or maybe Virginia. Definitely East Coast." The lightbulb finally went off in Imara's head. "Aw, damn. We're in the second book in the series. If I'm not mistaken, this is the place in the book where Leonid set booby traps in and around his home. The stupid bastard blew his own mansion up in an effort to get the last word."

"Careful, Imara, you're starting to talk like these characters are real after all," Elle prodded.

Imara shrugged. "If you can't beat 'em, join 'em. Besides, the evidence seems to suggest I might be wrong about a few things."

Her cavalier attitude was short-lived. She suddenly realized Dani and Jai might not have survived the blast. "Son of a bitch," she screamed and catapulted upright. "We need to find them. Oh God, oh God, oh God. I'll never forgive myself if something has happened to either one. Who would do this? Who would send them into the book at this particular moment?"

"Don't panic yet. If I remember correctly, there's a bomb shelter. If you find the round, brass door that screws into the floor or something, you might find Jai and Dani. Hopefully the rest of the team of women pulled them inside. I don't think they'd ever let anything happen to Dani," Tanya soothed.

"God, I hope you're right." Imara was pacing.

"Hon, are you all right sitting here while we check it out?" Elle asked. "I don't like leaving you, but we need help."

"Yeah, I'm fine. Am I still bleeding?"

Elle pulled the shirt from Tanya's head. "Not as badly as before, but you'd better keep that pressed against your head. Hopefully, we can find the rescue team and get you some much needed medical attention. Your wound might not be life threatening, but stitches are definitely in your future. The sooner we find them, the sooner we can take care of that nasty gash."

"When you do locate them, I'm sure you'll give the ladies a thrill prancing around in your bra. Do be sure to remind them you aren't single."

Elle leaned in and kissed Tanya. "You never have to worry, love." She turned to Imara and said, "Come on we have a team of badass women to find."

Imara and Elle carefully made their way through the rubble inside the mansion. Elle pointed to a round brass plate like Tanya had described. Imara hurried to the doorway and tried to turn the hatch. She felt like she was opening the door to a submarine. Once the cover was completely unscrewed, she grunted as she tried to lift the heavy covering. Elle took the other side, and together they managed to remove the door and set it to the side. When they returned to peek inside the shelter, the barrel of a gun pressed against Imara's forehead.

"Who the fuck are you?" The angry voice came from a very sexy blonde.

"Um, you must be Val."

"You'd better move your ass to the side. I swear, if you so much as twitch a muscle, I'll put a bullet in your head without a second thought," Val warned.

"Okay, okay. We're friend, not foe."

"Val, don't shoot her," Dani called from inside. "That's Imara. While I have my issues with her, she does not deserve elimination."

"Then tell her to get the fuck out of my way. I don't like being crowded. After ten minutes in this hole, I need some space and fresh air."

Imara moved aside and let the women emerge from the shelter. She breathed a sigh of relief that Dani seemed unharmed, but she hadn't heard or seen Jai yet. "Is Jai with you?" she called down to Dani.

"Yeah, we're both fine," Dani answered.

Imara wanted to mention that Tanya was hurt, and they needed help, but Val seemed awful twitchy. She knew Val was the bat-shit crazy character who didn't mind eradicating threats and wouldn't lose a bit of sleep over it either.

Elle blurted out, "My girlfriend needs medical attention. Her head caught a piece of flying debris."

"You know this person too, Dani?" Imara suspected the challenge came from Char.

Dani shook her head. "Um no, I don't know her."

"I do. Please don't hurt them," Jai pleaded.

"Somebody better explain what the fuck is going on." Rigid posture. Scowl on her face. Imara nodded to herself as she identified Sophie, the ex-FBI agent.

"Tanya is completely innocent and has nothing to do with this whole mess. Please, we don't know exactly where we are or how to get to a medical facility," Elle implored. "She says she's okay, but she's the kind of person to downplay the extent of her injuries. I know you have a full medical facility in that underground complex of yours, and you have plenty of vehicles to take on a few more passengers."

Char gasped. "Dani! You didn't—"

"No, no, it's not like that. I would never. They read all about it."

"What!" Sophie exclaimed.

"Can't you transport us to their complex? Problem solved. We get that little matter of disbelief out of the way, and we don't have to beg these paranoid women to take us there." Imara had forgotten that someone was blocking their magic.

"Don't you think I would have done that if I could? We don't have the book with us, so it won't work. Once we're in a book, our only option is out, not a different place in the novel. Besides, how quickly you forget we don't even have that option right now," Elle explained. "Medical attention first, then we can worry about the other problem. Maybe Toni or Dani will have some ideas. Or perhaps it will take all five of us to manage to break his spell. I assume this is the work of Vlad."

"Maybe, or it could be a combined effort. Vlad and a powerful book wizard." Imara cringed when Val looked like she was about to smack her with her gun.

"What the hell are you freakazoids talking about? And who is Vlad? Jesus fucking Christ, please don't tell me there is already another Russian mob boss in place. I'm getting awfully tired of needing to eliminate the slimy bastards. Maggie was right. Even when we cut the head off, they grow another one," Val growled.

Gina touched Val's hand, and Val seemed to relax her hairspring half a coil.

Imara sighed. "I'll tell you, but I don't think it will go over too well. It's one thing to tell a single character they aren't real and quite another to tell a whole passel of you."

"What is she talking about?" Char directed her question to Dani.

"Okay, here's the crib-notes version." Imara chuckled and flashed a grin at Elle. "Get it? Crib notes?"

Elle whispered. "I don't think now is the time to make puns."

"So, short version. I'm a book witch, and I bring characters to life. You are all characters in a book. We entered said book and unfortunately have a front row seat to this story, because...well...we haven't quite figured out how Dani was sent back into her own story and why Jai went along for the ride. There has to be another book magician involved. Actually probably a book wizard is my guess. Sorry, sorry. I suppose it's not so easy to squish everything into a crib note. Elle here, is a book magician. Her specialty is sending the chosen into various books to truly experience the adventure. A far better form of entertainment than 3-D goggles. Any questions?"

"Have you gone off your meds or something?"

"Well, Ronda. You get a real charge out of playing with explosives, so don't throw stones at me." Imara chuckled. "Oh I am so good at this, spitting out puns right and left. Everyone has a little crazy in them, but I'm not making this up. Why don't you all ask yourselves how I know your names and everything about you? I read both damn books, that's how. If you don't want me spewing all your deep dark secrets, best not to antagonize me. I'm getting pretty damn tired of being everyone's little whipping girl, 'cause you can't handle the truth."

"I believe I'll shoot you and be done with it. Problem solved." Val waved her gun in the air.

"No don't, please. I want to find my way back home. If you shoot her..." Jai pleaded. "We will find our way back, won't we?"

Imara reached into her pocket as she crossed over to Jai. She laid the crystal necklace in Jai's hand. It was the only thing Imara could think of to still the rising panic. Jai accepted the offering with a weak smile on her face.

Dani looked at each of her sisters in The Organization, and Imara knew she was appealing to their tight history. "You're going to have to trust me. I assure you it will be safe to take them to the compound."

Ronda smirked as the group approached Tanya. "So that's where you left your shirt. Nice bra by the way. At least they weren't making up the fact that someone is injured. Cindy would have my ass if we left this woman sitting here, bleeding all over Leonid's tattered lawn. I trust Dani. We are in the business of helping women, and my vote is that these three seem to need a lot of help."

"We're not crazy, if that's what you're suggesting," Imara insisted.

"Riiiight," Sophie added.

CHAPTER NINE

The ride to the complex was uneventful, except for most of the team sneaking sideways glances at Imara and Elle. Tanya suspected Char and Sophie were dying to interrogate them but didn't quite know what to ask. None of the women seemed to consider Tanya a threat. She sighed. Once again, she was a throwaway player in this little drama. She still wondered how she'd managed to catch Elle's eye. Elle insisted she was special, but Tanya was never one to stick out in a crowd. She'd politely acknowledged all of the women but hadn't tried to engage in conversation or offer any explanation on their sudden arrival. It wasn't Tanya's place to do that. Besides, her head was throbbing and she wasn't in the mood for any lengthy conversation. She was glad none of the others were either.

When they reached the nondescript cabin, Tanya smiled. The place fit what she had envisioned when she'd read the book. She worried about Dani navigating the tunnel without her crutches. They came to a stop several feet from the cabin, presumably a safe location away from any explosives strategically placed on the perimeter. Char jumped from the car and hurried to the vehicle Dani had ridden in. She helped Dani to the cabin and Jai followed. Elle provided a solid body for Tanya to lean on as she wobbled along. Perhaps the chunk that landed on her head did more damage than she'd originally thought. The dizziness seemed to increase with every step.

"You okay?" Elle asked. "You're looking a bit peaked all of a sudden."

"I'll be fine." Tanya gritted through the pain of her pounding head.

Val stopped before the door that would lead them into the underground tunnels. "If anything, and I mean anything, bad happens as a result of leading you into the complex, I will personally make it my mission to hunt each and every one of you down. I don't have a problem slicing my enemies into tiny pieces to feed to the fishes."

"I'd rather you hunt down the bastard responsible for sending us into this little nightmare. Trust me, you all aren't exactly the best welcoming committee to this world. I would have preferred jumping into a nice romance instead," Imara wryly answered. "If I find Vlad, will you promise to feed him to the fish?"

Val shook her head. "Freak."

Soon they came to the infirmary, and a tall brunette with an air of authority met them. Tanya suspected the woman was Cindy, Ronda's lover and the nurse practitioner for The Organization.

"Okay who needs patching up now?" Cindy's eyes narrowed at Tanya. "Who is this?"

"I was caught in the flying debris from the explosion. A chunk of something hit my head. The blood flow has slowed, so I don't think I'm in any real danger," Tanya blurted out in an effort to assure Elle she was all right. "I'm Tanya, by the way. It's nice to meet you, Cindy."

Char, Toni, Val, Sophie, and Ronda all exchanged a look of disbelief.

"Oh, sorry. I probably shouldn't have done that." Tanya was feeling increasingly dizzy. She knew she was about to pass out.

"Do we need to jump through hurdles for you to give Tanya a few stitches? Geez, you'd think we were selling black-market babies. Don't you have an oath or something to adhere to?" Imara asked.

"I don't need a lecture from you about my duties." Cindy glared at Imara. "And I don't need details right now. Your pallor is of concern to me. Bring her to this bed. Right now. The rest of you, get the hell out of my infirmary. I don't need you gawking at the poor woman. You"—she pointed at Elle—"can stay, but everyone else is seriously irritating me. And don't go bugging anyone else in my care either."

The group of women grumbled but left the infirmary. Tanya could hear them grousing all the way down the hall. She heard someone say it was time for a pow wow in the conference room, where they could get some straight answers on what the hell was going on.

After Cindy directed Tanya to an open bed, she closed the privacy curtain. Her efficient but gentle hands irrigated and stitched the wound quickly, after numbing the area with an anesthetic. She caught Tanya's eyes. "Not that the women who brought you in aren't the absolute best, but I'm wondering how you managed to get caught up in their latest mission?"

"I…I…I'm not very good at explaining things. I'm relatively new to Elle's world, and I only met Imara a few days ago," Tanya stuttered.

Cindy laid her hand on Tanya's arm. "It's okay, hon." She turned her stern gaze in Elle's direction. "I presume you are Elle and the other cocky one is Imara. She'll fit right in. Although I'd hate to see her tangle with Char or the others. Each has their own particular buttons. Press one and who knows what will happen. I suppose I'd better find you a shirt to wear."

"Thank you. Other than knowing a lot about you and this Organization, we aren't able to prove who we are and what we're capable of. At least not until we do something about whatever is keeping us in your world," Elle explained.

"I'll stick to the medical side of things. This sounds like it might be more up Toni or Dani's alley. They're the techno and science geeks. I don't really need to know." Cindy began clearing the discarded gauze and other supplies. "Why don't you hang around here for a little while longer? I have another patient on the other side of that curtain. Please don't disturb her."

"Maggie, right? I suppose Antonio is still by her bedside. She'll be fine."

Cindy opened her mouth as if to speak, then promptly closed it and shook her head. "Never mind." Cindy pulled the curtain closed, and Tanya heard the clip of her heels across the floor. A door gently shut. Tanya assumed Cindy had gone into her office.

Tanya remembered Maggie was recovering from a serious gunshot wound, compliments of a tussle with Leonid, the same mob boss who'd blown his own house to smithereens hoping the women in The Organization would join him on his one-way ticket to hell.

The metal rings scraped across the rod, as the curtain around Maggie's bed was pulled back. Tanya wondered why Antonio would leave Maggie's side. She looked up and noticed Elle's face drain of color.

"Gordon!" Elle's voice was barely audible, as she pushed out his name in obvious surprise.

†

Gordon was supposed to be in a constant state of upheaval. They had banished him to a book where he would spend the rest of his days plagued by nonsensical thoughts and random images of terror for all eternity. Vlad must have found a way to release him from the private torture they'd managed to transport him into.

His evil grin broadened. "Oh no, my dear, I'm Antonio. I quite like jumping into this particular character. I have unlimited finances at my fingertips, a loyal cadre of men in my employ, and the support and resources of a very talented group of women. Vlad has helped me see the error of my ways. You women can be far more useful than I initially gave you credit for. He is quite keen to have both Jaiden and Imara join his ranks. I'll be rewarded handsomely for my efforts. As far as I'm concerned, living out my days in this book surrounded by an adoring woman, and others who give me the respect I deserve, would definitely satisfy my bargain with Vlad."

Remove the block it has no power;
return us to the former hour.

Remove the block it has no power;
return us to the former hour.

Remove the block it has no power;
return us to the former hour.

151

The chant was worth a try, but Gordon's maniacal laugh dashed Elle's hopes. "Pathetic attempt, my dear. You aren't going back until we achieve our ultimate goal."

Tanya tried to sit up and grabbed Elle's hand protectively. "Elle."

Elle kissed Tanya's forehead. "It'll be okay. He would have done something already if Vlad wanted us harmed."

"He has a big ax to grind with us."

Elle turned toward the creak of a door opening.

"Antonio? Do you know these women?" Cindy held a t-shirt in her hand and thrust the garment at Elle.

"Oh yes, we are old friends."

Cindy nodded. "That must be how they know so much about The Organization." Her face contorted. "I don't think Maggie will be pleased you've shared so much with outsiders. It's one thing to combine forces and quite another to bring others to the complex and share details."

Elle quickly pulled the borrowed t-shirt over her head. "Um, can I go to the conference room and update Imara on Tanya's condition? Tanya probably needs her rest anyway. Antonio, I'm sure you're eager to return to Maggie's side."

"Do give Imara my best. I am looking forward to meeting her. Oh and be sure to tell her Vlad says hello. He speaks so highly of her." Gordon slithered back behind the adjacent curtain.

Cindy pinpointed Elle with an intense gaze. "I may not know exactly what transpired in the last few hours, but I'm quite positive the two of you are not close friends. What the hell is going on?"

"I know you have no reason to trust me, but that man is not who he purports to be. We have an unbelievable tale to tell. Everyone here is in grave danger unless we find a way to rewind certain events. Please, there is no time. I've got to get back to Imara, Dani, and Jai. I must provide an update on the latest wrinkle." Elle had lowered her voice so only Cindy could hear her desperate pleas.

"I'm a skilled healer, but I'm also very intuitive. Right now, I trust you more than… I can't really put my finger on it, but that is not the Antonio I know. There was something off about him. Come on, I'll take you to the conference room."

"Good. Your instincts are spot on. Stay with them. Hopefully, you can also sense the purity of our motivations. We don't want any harm to come to any of the women here. Even Imara is coming around to the possibility our two realms may not be as different as she's always thought."

"I have no idea what you're talking about, but I'd like to get Ronda to watch over Tanya before I take you to the conference room. Give me a second. I'll call her down here."

Elle was grateful for the offer and thought Ronda was a good choice. Gordon certainly would not wish to tangle with someone who was inclined to shoot first and ask questions later. "Thanks."

Ronda appeared a few minutes later, and Elle thanked her for coming. Her presence set Elle at ease. Cindy conveyed her request in a low tone. Ronda caught on quickly and responded barely loud enough for Elle and Cindy to hear.

"I'm not doing this for you or your friend. I'm doing this for her"—she gestured with her head toward Cindy—"and for Maggie."

"Girlfriend," Elle corrected.

"I don't give a shit about the status of your love life." Ronda's voice elevated slightly in concert with what Elle thought was increasing irritation.

Cindy stroked her lover's arm. "Thanks, hon."

Elle was anxious to leave the room. Ronda had unsettled her, but she needed to bring Imara and Jai up to speed on the latest developments.

†

The most common expression that donned the faces of the women sitting around the conference table was a mixture of disbelief and amusement. The Organization's muscle revealed a touch of irritation along with their apparent skepticism. So far, none of the women were buying the story Imara shared with them. She supposed if she were in their shoes, she wouldn't welcome the information either. No person wanted to hear they didn't really exist beyond the pages of fiction. It certainly never mattered how good the book was or how impressively the author penned the character.

Ronda took a call and abruptly left. One less person whose preferred method of problem solving was guns or explosives was fine by Imara.

"Isn't there some demonstration you can provide that Vlad hasn't blocked?" Jai asked.

Imara considered Jai's question. It was a good one. There had to be something she could do, a simple spell to convince this group of naysayers. "Let me think, let me think. I don't have access to any raw materials for potions to assist with a spell, but perhaps I can render a simple chant he won't consider dangerous to his plans."

Val rolled her eyes and muttered, "Whackadoodle."

Gina gave her a look of warning.

Cindy and Elle rushed into the conference room. From the panicked look on Elle's face, something was seriously wrong. Imara hoped Tanya's health had not taken a turn for the worse.

Elle skidded to a stop at the end of the large conference table. "Gordon's adopted Antonio's character. He's the one helping Vlad."

"The asshat former Grand Wizard you and Tanya banished into that book?" Imara had always suspected Vlad was responsible for the odd disappearances of the more outspoken book magicians fighting for equal rights. She'd been impressed when she'd heard what Elle had done to the wizard.

"Yes. I don't know if Vlad isn't able to transport himself into the book, or if he doesn't want to get his hands dirty. I suspect you still have strong support amongst the book witches who don't wish to get involved with Vlad. They could easily turn on him if they suspect he's wronged you in any way. These women could be collateral damage in your war with Vlad."

"Agreed. We're wasting time trying to convince these women, but I'm out of ideas. Maybe Toni or Dani is the key to helping us. I never thought a character would someday be my savior." Imara pushed herself away from the table. The sudden movement reminded her of the sore spot on her back.

Although Jai seemed to notice Imara's wince, she kept quiet. Imara was glad for that. Their focus needed to remain on the important challenges that lay ahead.

"That's it. I'm done with these loonies. Sophie, go get Ronda and the one that Cindy patched up. We're escorting them to the closest bus depot. I don't even mind giving them a few thousand to get the hell out of our hair." She turned her impressive glare in Imara's direction. "If you so much as dip a toe on this property again, a tiny nick on the head won't be the only thing you'll have to worry about." Val stood and stepped toward Imara.

Stop her progress with a wall;
on her ass she will fall

Imara was sick and tired of Val's attitude and instinctively voiced her irritation with an impulsive chant. The invisible barrier Imara erected did its job. Val was sprawled on the floor. She reached up to touch the invisible brick wall, a needed barrier between Imara and a very pissed off operative.

"What the fuck is this?" Val jumped to a standing position and looked like a mime, as she patted and groped what she could feel but no one could see.

"I've been trying to tell you. These women are for real. I didn't like hearing I'm not flesh and blood either, but I saw the books with my own eyes," Dani said.

"Maybe they're simply talented illusionists. Dani, you should know science can allow the seemingly impossible and evolve to endless possibilities. Your illusions in our hovels are proof of that." Toni leaned forward and looked as though she was trying to figure out a complicated math problem.

"I'm not a book magician or a book witch. I'm a…what do you call us?" Jai asked.

"Nonmag," Imara and Elle answered together.

"Yes, right. Well, I don't think any one person has all the answers. Isn't it entirely possible that the characters authors create exist in some other realm and are as real as you or me? I'd like to think each one of us has some kind of gift to add to the equation. We should be working together. I've seen this Vlad person. He sets off more warning bells than any entity I've come across in my lifetime. Maybe that is what I bring to the team, my ability to sense his presence. We are playing into his hand by allowing any kind of divisiveness to get in the way. Working together may be our only option." Jai calmly clasped her hands together and sat back in her chair after delivering her perspective to the group.

Imara thought Jai had many more talents than simply sensing evil. She looked around the group of women who had expressed at best, amusement, and at worst, open hostility toward herself and Elle.

"I'm in." Toni was the first to state her position.

"Toni is the smartest person I know, besides Dani. If she's in, so am I. Besides, I know I need to work on my greatest weakness, which is trusting new people." Char looked lovingly at her partner, then gave Toni a fleeting kiss.

Everyone but Gina and Cindy followed suit with their willingness to join forces. Although, Imara sensed there was still a grudging acceptance from Val and Sophie. She wondered where Sophie's partner was. Maybe they would meet Kim later and could get her to help calm Sophie down. Gina kept Val human, but she remained quiet and watchful. Imara couldn't blame her. She'd read what Leonid had done to her and how she'd hidden on his grounds in fear for her life.

"I'm not sure at this point given my condition…" Gina placed her hand on her belly. "I don't think I'll be much help."

"Do you want me to take you to my room so you can get some rest?" Val's eyes softened for Gina.

Gina kissed her cheek. "No hon, you stay. I can find my way."

"I don't think I'm needed here either but for very different reasons. I'll head back to the infirmary and check on my patients. That's how I'll be more of a help." Cindy left the conference room with Gina.

After hearing everyone agree to work together, Imara took control of the group. "First order of business, find a way to send Gordon packing. I very much liked Antonio. It would be a pity if Gordon managed to retain use of his character to his own personal advantage. Besides, if we don't banish him to another book, everything in this book is at risk of changing, including the welfare of all the women in The Organization."

"I need to know more about how you manage to do what you both do. Then maybe Dani and I can think of ways to help. This could be fun." Toni rubbed her hands together with glee. "It's not very often we get to combine the mystical side of the world with science."

"I have an idea…" Imara grinned. "Hopefully, Tanya is recovered enough to help. Do you think Cindy would let us remove Tanya from the infirmary for a little strategy session? No offense, Elle, but we need that brain of hers to anticipate the next two moves. She's the chess player, not you."

†

Vlad's strength grew, as he sensed the distress of the women. He couldn't resist hiding in the thick copse of trees next to Leonid's mansion. He'd known they were smart enough to avoid permanent injury and, frankly, that wasn't his end game anyway. The more distress he caused, the more his power grew. He enjoyed the outpouring of negative energy. The Organization's hostile reaction to the newcomers was simply icing on the cake.

In exchange for the cushy arrangement Gordon now enjoyed, he was helping to sow the fertile ground for the final move. Checkmate. Soon Imara and Jaiden would beg to join Vlad's coven. They'd have no choice. In the meantime, Vlad would use the little gems Gordon provided to assist his movement in this book. Vlad rather enjoyed this time, as he continued to play with his prey. The chase was almost as satisfying as the capture.

He transported himself to the secret complex and carefully stepped amongst the traps Ronda had set to protect their main headquarters. He waited.

Vlad was almost ready to spring his final trap. Let them plan all they wanted, everything was going exactly as predicted. He'd even let them take care of Gordon for him. One less problem to deal with.

CHAPTER TEN

Cindy had reluctantly allowed Ronda to escort Tanya to join the group in the conference room. Ronda hurried back to watch over her lover and keep an eye on the fake Antonio.

Jaiden was enthralled with the way Imara had taken complete charge of the situation. Gone was any tentative approach to their dilemma. She supposed that some people would find Imara brash or arrogant, but Jaiden found the "imperfection" a major turn on. In fact, Jaiden found nothing about Imara to nitpick. She'd noticed how Imara had winced earlier and thought she'd be the kind of stoic person to keep an injury to herself. Imara didn't need Jaiden mothering her, so she avoided making that observation known to the others. Maybe she would ask Imara about it later.

If the craziness hadn't occurred in a whirlwind of activity, Jaiden would have been royally pissed about Imara using a book character brought to life to somehow teach her a lesson in love. That same arrogance did have the potential to create massive irritation, yet for some unknown reason, it didn't. Jaiden shook her head. She turned back to the group and Imara's commanding presence. The conciliatory tone seemed to go a long way with the skeptics.

"Look, in the past twenty-four hours, my whole perspective about what I do has changed. I realize I may not have all the answers. For one, everyone here seems so real. I'd always been taught that book witches were the only ones who could bring fantasy to life. Now I am reconsidering that notion. Perhaps there is an entirely new dimension within the pages of a book that is as real as our world." Imara stood as though lecturing to a class. Jaiden thought the move subtle yet effective. Tower over people to give a slight psychological advantage. Teachers stood in front of classrooms for that very reason. Sitting gave less advantage when needing to control the students.

"I can attest to that fact. What happened when Tanya, Oren, and I transported ourselves inside another book in an effort to trap Gordon, is proof our two worlds may not be as different as we believe. When Gordon shot Oren, the bullet ripped into his flesh and created an actual injury that still gives him problems," Elle said.

"So, what's your idea and how can we help?" Toni asked.

"Our first major hurdle is removing the chant or spell that is blocking us from returning to our world. I don't know if that is Vlad's or Gordon's, but I suspect it's Gordon pulling those strings. Otherwise Vlad wouldn't have bothered to wrench him from his banishment."

"That makes sense. Book magicians have more power inside an adventure. Witches and warlocks seem to possess greater skills outside the pages of a book. I'm amazed you were able to reclaim your go-to parlor hoax out of your bag of tricks," Elle said.

Imara shrugged. "I've been doing that one since I was five. It's second nature."

Tanya touched Elle's arm. "Elle, do you think we could use Gordon's own chant against him?"

Elle frowned. "I tried a chant to allow us to return to the time before we entered this book. It didn't work. He laughed in my face, remember?"

"There's an old trick that I'm sure Vlad put in place. Toni, you might understand this better than most. There is a way to create a continuous chant. I believe it works like computer code running in the background. Gordon doesn't have to say anything. The power of the chant simply runs in his head until Vlad decides to remove it. I suspect Vlad is waiting for us to feel desperation before he tries to make a deal. That's where you come in, Toni. You have nanobots that can burrow into someone, right?" Imara asked.

"Hmm, a computer code similar to what I developed for the e-books." Tanya rubbed her head as though in pain, and Jaiden wondered if Cindy would lecture them about removing her patient before she'd had a chance to fully recover.

Toni nodded excitedly. "I know where you're going with this. We can place whatever message we want into Gordon's head, and that will counteract whatever is causing your current dilemma."

"Exactly! Elle, what's that chant Tanya was talking about?" Imara asked.

"Stop the chant; it has no power. Instead, replace it with a cower."

"Nice. Poetic justice." Imara nodded.

"Wait. I don't want anything bad to happen to Antonio," Dani said.

"Oh, I hadn't considered that." Imara pulled her bottom lip inside, in what Jaiden considered an adorable gesture of contemplation. Adorable and sexy. "Well, it's only step one. We'll need to do something very quickly after that to expunge Gordon from Antonio's body. Any ideas?"

"Can't we banish him again to another book?" Elle asked.

"I don't think it will stick. Vlad will simply pull him out again." Imara sat and sagged in her chair. "Besides, I'm coming to believe that permanently taking over a character's persona might be more unethical than we thought, if characters truly have a life of their own."

"That might only apply to e-books. Wouldn't altering a paperback only regulate that specific book?" Tanya asked.

"Send him into a children's book. Maybe something like *Green Eggs and Ham*," Jaiden joked.

"That's brilliant!" Imara stood again and started pacing the room.

"I was joking."

"No, no, that could work. We need to obtain a copy of the book. Then we'll need to add an extra suppression chant. No offense, Elle, but what happened to Gordon wasn't exactly a secret. What you did, Tanya, was the stuff of legend. I heard all about it, and I suspect Vlad did as well."

Jaiden glanced at Dani, who had a pained expression on her face. Jaiden didn't know what caused the grimace, but she didn't like seeing her discomfort.

Dani shifted in her seat. "How much time do we have before we can put this plan into action?"

"Why?" Char asked. "You got a hot date or something?"

"Can I have a little time with Jai before she goes back to…?"

Dani was special, and Jaiden felt an immediate sense of loss. A big part of her wanted Dani in her life, but that was selfish. Her feelings were convoluted and difficult to sort. Maybe Dani coming to life had taught her a lesson. Although she didn't think the lesson was the one originally intended for her.

Imara's brows knitted together, but she didn't say anything.

Char made soft eye contact with her sister. Jaiden could sense the compassionate connection between the two, which made her feel all the more bereft. "We need to find this children's book. We have a little time. Why don't you show Jai around? It isn't like we get the chance to play host to anyone, especially those from another dimension." Char chuckled. "God, even saying those words sounds incredibly nuts to me."

"Not to me." Toni stood and laid a hand on Char's shoulder. "Why don't Elle and Imara come with me to the lab? Val can take Tanya back to the infirmary while we work on this. I don't mean to be rude, but you're looking a little pale, Tanya." Toni grinned. "Cindy is the biggest badass of all of us. We're all afraid of her wrath."

Val and Sophie nodded their agreement.

"Dani, you can take Jai around the complex," Toni added.

"That's a great idea. Sophie, can you please find a copy of *Green Eggs and Ham*? Val, you be on alert for anyone acting strange or someone who doesn't belong here. I'm a bit uneasy about this Vlad character. Check out the perimeter of the property after you take Tanya back to the infirmary. I'll stay and join them in the lab. In this instance, shoot first. If your gut tells you something is wrong, go for it. The only other male hanging out in the complex is Antonio. Use that piece of information to your advantage. If you see a man, shoot him," Char said.

"It will be my pleasure." Val's eyes flickered with excitement.

"Why can't I stay behind and shoot the bad guy?" Sophie asked.

"Because Val won't hesitate to shoot and you might. You still have a tiny bit of integrity left," Char answered.

"Fine. I'm going," Sophie grumbled.

†

Dani hobbled slowly down the corridor in obvious pain, but staunchly refusing any assistance from Jaiden. Although Jaiden was impressed with Dani's fortitude, it was hard to see her struggle.

"I have an older set of crutches that I'll use until I can replace my sleek racing set," Dani said after her refusal to accept Jaiden's arm. "I'll take you on a full tour, but maybe we can drop by my room first and get those ancient sticks."

Jaiden simply acknowledged Dani's suggestion with a smile. When they reached Dani's pod, Jaiden was more impressed than when she'd read the descriptors of each person's compact domicile. The space was small but very cozy.

"This is nice."

"Yeah, home sweet home. I've tried to make these underground hovels more comfortable. In my spare time, I tweak the holographs to create a more realistic experience." Dani made her way to the couch and sat. She rubbed the back of her neck and looked at her lap before returning her eyes to Jaiden. "Realistic. Wow, now there's a loaded word."

Jaiden reached out to brush away the single eyelash on her cheek. She knew it was an intimate gesture, but somehow she wanted that touch to reassure Dani she was real.

"You have an eyelash." Jaiden took Dani's hand and gingerly laid the eyelash on top. "Okay, now you have to close your eyes, blow gently, and make a wish."

Dani looked as though a fond memory passed through her mind. "Char taught me that when we were kids. I always wished we'd find our way out of the trashy trailer park we lived in. We did. Thanks to Maggie."

Jaiden scrutinized Dani for a second, until an observation bubbled to the surface. "That was never in either book. You're adding to the story by your presence in our world. Or maybe you were always more real than we realized. The song that keeps running through my mind right about now is Natasha Bedingfield's, *Unwritten*. Your book is yet unwritten. Now close your eyes and blow before the eyelash develops a mind of its own and floats away without your wish."

"I wish you could stay." Dani looked earnestly at Jaiden. "You already know where we live, and Maggie wouldn't be able to forbid me from welcoming you to the family. My prospects for love are...limited. If I fall for someone who can't contribute to The Organization, the relationship is doomed from the start. Oh hell, what am I saying? I don't exist outside the pages of a book. I don't understand. How is it I feel real emotions, if I don't exist? Can you please explain that to me?"

"I can't other than to say you are real. Real enough that I find myself responding to you, but things are confusing for me right now. I can't lie about that."

"You're drawn to Imara, aren't you? I see the way you look at her. I guess that makes sense. Who wouldn't be? She has a powerful presence about her. Kinda like my sister. Women gallop to that. I'm just a crippled geek. Candy loved me for who I am, and I couldn't keep her from slipping through my grasp. Oh shit, that kinda sounded like I was holding her hostage or something."

Jaiden grabbed Dani's hands. "I can't stay, Dani. Even if I weren't drawn to Imara, as you so aptly noticed. I don't belong in your world any more than you belong in mine. Temporary visits are really all either one of us could hope for, without creating a whole shitload of complications. I will make a promise to you, though."

"You'll visit again?" Dani asked. The hope was evident in her voice.

"I don't know, maybe. Once I get back home, I'm going to work on finding a way for you and Candy to be together. I don't think that ship has sailed at all. Candy is the one you're meant to be with. I have an advantage. I've read the books, and I believe the author has that same vision. Maybe she is adamant about not wanting to write another story, but people change their minds all the time. How about if we make a deal? You continue to think positive thoughts and wish for Candy instead of me. I'll see what I can do to engineer a different kind of magic in my world."

"It's the age difference, right?" A smile tugged at Dani's lips and Jaiden was glad for the joke.

"Are you calling me old?" Jaiden teased back.

"Imara is a very lucky woman. I hope she appreciates you. For the record, I could have seen myself falling in love with you."

"Ditto, but I believe the universe has a different plan for both of us. Besides, I have a terrible track record. You're much better off without jumping into a relationship with me, regardless of which realm we're in. Promise me you won't write Candy off just yet."

"I promise."

†

Imara didn't want to think about what Dani and Jai were doing. She had a task to do, but her concentration was unraveling. What if Dani convinced Jai to stay in her world?

Or Dani decided she liked being in what Imara considered the true realm of existence? She'd come a long way, but Imara couldn't bring herself to believe the worlds authors created were anything beyond fantasy, despite some evidence to the contrary.

"Shit, I need Dani." Toni began chewing on the end of a pen. Toni's outburst pulled Imara from her obsessive thoughts.

Yes, let's bring Dani and Jai back. Imara thought less time for the two of them to spend alone together was a perfect idea. *I'm a selfish bitch. I don't deserve Jai.*

Char gently pulled the pen from her mouth. "Hon, you don't need Dani. You can do this."

"She sees code that I miss." A line etched Toni's forehead, as she began tapping on the computer keys. "Okay, maybe this will work. I've never put a message directly into someone's brain before. Audio in someone's ear is child's play, but this…this…is really complicated." Toni was mumbling to herself as she continued to type.

Imara began pacing the floor. Every minute that passed put everyone at risk. She wasn't sure what Vlad was waiting for. She was on edge anticipating his next move. Getting a jump on his plans was imperative if they were going to succeed. "Any chance you can hurry with this prototype? I'm not sure how much time we have before Vlad decides to act. Right now, he's toying with us. The sick bastard thinks he's showing us who has the power."

"I don't know how to test this out. Normally, I'd use myself, but I won't know if it truly works, because I'll already know the message I'm trying to send." Toni picked up the pen again and began to chew, as perspiration erupted on her brow.

"I don't think you should use yourself or anyone else from this realm. Use me. As a book magician, I'm the closest match to Gordon. Let Imara give you an uncomplicated chant to put in my head, and we'll see how it works." Elle bored her eyes into Imara. "Something basic, Imara. I'll get you back if you play a prank at my expense."

Imara touched her chest and widened her eyes. "Who me?" She cackled. "I've got the perfect chant to try out." Imara gestured to the corner of the lab. "Let me whisper it to you, then you can do your programming magic."

Toni and Imara made their way to the corner of the room. After Imara gave Toni the words, Toni burst out laughing. "Are you sure you don't want to stay here with us? You could add some fun."

After Toni added a few lines to the code, she stood and stretched. "Okay, now I need to transfer this to a nanobot and find a quick way into your body."

"You mean like me touching one of your special business cards or something?" Elle asked.

"Well sure, if you want to wait twenty-four hours for it to set. An injection is faster. The bot will quickly travel where it needs to, then attach itself to a neuron sending the correct electrical current to the brain. It works a bit like a neuroprosthetic device, only 1000 times more enhanced than current science allows. At least current science regulated by the National Institute of Health. They have a lot of pesky rules around the use of human subjects. Sometimes the side effects are a bitch. A little itching here and there, but it goes away after a while."

Elle blanched.

"Don't be a wuss, Elle. This is for the greater good." This was getting better and better for Imara. A mild diversion to take away her concerns over Dani and Jai's continued absence was just what the doctor ordered.

"Fine, but how are we going to get this into Gordon after you test it on me? It's not like he's going to let you inject a foreign substance into his body." Elle began scratching her arms.

Imara pushed Elle's hands away from her body. "Stop scratching. She hasn't injected the nanobot yet. You can't already feel itchy."

Toni laughed, as she walked to another part of the lab. Wires and vials of liquid hung together, looking like something in Dr. Frankenstein's lab. Imara wondered if some of Toni's ideas were born from that old classic. After drawing from one of the vials, Toni held up the needle and wagged it in Elle's direction.

Elle dragged her feet over to Toni and the long needle. Toni didn't give her time to reconsider, as she drove the needle into Elle's arm without warning.

"Ouch! You could have been a tad gentler with that thing."

"Okay, Elle, show us what you got." Toni smirked and glanced at Imara mimicking a long-distance fist bump.

The minute Toni said Elle's name, Elle gyrated her hips and thrust them forward, punctuating her gesture with an "Oorah!"

Imara burst out laughing. "Good one, Elle. You really got the moves, girl." On command, Elle repeated the move and yelled, "Oorah" a second time.

"I do believe our test is successful." Toni hurried back to her computer. "Okay let's program in the chant for Gordon."

"If any of you say my name over the next"—Elle turned to Toni. "How long before this nanobot juggles lose and I shit it out?"

Toni shrugged. "Two weeks maybe. Give or take a day."

"Two weeks!"

"Eye on the ball ladies. We need Cindy to surprise Gordon and inject him, or we'll have bigger problems than Elle's gyrating hips," Toni said.

On cue, Elle's body moved against her will and another oorah burst from her lips.

"Sorry." Toni held her hand over her mouth to keep from laughing. "I might have embellished a little. You should be free of the suggestion within 24 hours, give or take a few minutes."

Elle leaned over Toni and recited the simple chant Gordon had used to deflect her chant when she'd tried to send Tanya back from their first book adventure. She turned the words around to make Gordon's own thoughts work against him. "Stop my chant; it has no power. Instead, replace it with a cower." Imara added another verse to ensure the chant would remain in effect until Sophie returned with the book.

"Keep my will from coming back, I'm useless in Vlad's next attack." She tapped Toni's shoulder. "Don't ask me why, but book magicians have to say their chants three times for them to work. So can you program that in thrice?"

Toni rolled her eyes upward and tilted her head. "Sure, whatever. And I thought I was the freakazoid. You two make me look normal."

After Toni typed in the new message, she once again drew the pale-yellow liquid into a syringe. She handed it to Char. "Here, you'd better be the one to get Cindy to deliver the nanobot to the impostor. She'll do it for you."

"Don't worry, I'll make sure the fucker gets what's coming to him. He put my sister in danger. If it were up to me, I'd send him into that famous screaming-man painting. I don't see why that's not possible. If you people can send folks into books, why can't someone be permanently transported into a painting?"

Imara was impressed at Char's ability to do a 180 and accept the seemingly impossible nature of what they could do. The brick wall might have helped.

"You mean Edvard Munch's, *The Scream*?" Toni asked.

"Yeah, that's the one," Char answered.

Elle lifted her shoulders. "Maybe we can. Never heard of it before, but that doesn't mean it isn't possible. My Aunt Clara hinted she might know something about other mediums."

"Focus, people. We are running out of precious time." Imara felt a wave of darkness cross her path and sensed Vlad was near. His location was shifting; that was something she was sure of. "Vlad's on the move. We don't have much time. I hope Val shoots him, but honestly he's too clever to allow himself to get caught in her cross hairs."

"Don't be too sure of that. Val is very skilled at taking out the trash," Char answered.

†

It was time for Vlad to transport himself. Rattling the nerves of his conquests would provide an additional surge of energy. He relished seeing their surprised faces. A healer was the perfect ironic twist. He laughed loudly at the stupefied look on the explosive expert's face when she realized her beloved medicine woman was no longer present. His dark eyes peered from the borrowed body.

Vlad fully expected the group to send Gordon packing, which would convince the women they had the upper hand. Patience was usually a virtue reserved for the do-gooders, but Vlad possessed a fair amount of that skill himself. His ability to lie in wait and delay action until the perfect moment was a talent honed over many years. His powers grew exponentially with each new acquisition. That is how Vlad looked upon his followers, merely acquisitions in the game of power. Pawns really. Nothing more.

CHAPTER ELEVEN

After her talk with Dani, Jaiden was delighted with her short tour of the facility. They ended up in the lab, just as the group was making their move to the infirmary. Imara quickly informed Jaiden of their plan, but her usual bravado was missing. Jaiden suspected that beneath that cocky exterior was a genuinely good person.

More than a little jumpy, Jaiden wrapped her fingers around her crystal necklace and felt the familiar warmth. Since Franklin had broken the chain, she couldn't wear the protective stone around her neck where it belonged. The next best thing was to hold her talisman in her hand. Jaiden saw a whole new side to Imara, who chewed the edge of her cuticle, seemingly oblivious to what she was doing. The nervous tell seemed so...well...normal. Not something a powerful book witch would do. Ironically, this tiny gesture was endearing versus irritating. Jaiden reached up to move

Imara's hand from her mouth and clasp it with her own free hand.

As soon as the infirmary door was open, Jaiden knew something was seriously wrong. A tsunami of negative energy washed over her. When she stepped inside and closer to the group standing near Tanya, the energy appeared to flicker, as if its strength was waning a small amount. She quickly pressed the crystal in her palm and pulled Imara's hand on top, holding the powerful talisman in place.

The nurse practitioner, Cindy, whom she had briefly met when they brought Tanya to her, seemed peculiar. In an instant, Jaiden recognized those dark eyes. Ronda looked on helplessly, apparently rendered inactive by her warring emotions. Jaiden sensed Ronda knew the woman standing beside her was not her beloved but couldn't bring herself to harm the impostor.

Jaiden boldly took a step closer, and the impostor hissed. "Welcome to the party, ladies. I'll need you to set your necklace outside of the infirmary, Jaiden, or Tanya's health might take an unfortunate turn for the worse."

Tanya signaled to Jaiden she should do no such thing, then turned her gaze. Imara seemed to understand the private message. With a slight nod, she squeezed Jaiden's hand.

Complete pandemonium ensued, and Imara chanted.

Stop his progress with a wall;
on his ass he will fall.

Char charged the Antonio impostor and viciously jabbed the needle in his arm. Tanya scrambled off her bed to clasp Elle's hand. Imara was still holding Jaiden's, as she reached for Elle. Tanya stretched to reach Dani, who held her hand out and allowed herself to become part of the chain. Jaiden instinctively knew to take a step closer to the impostor and felt the rush of energy to her hand travel along each of their bodies in an unbroken chain of five.

Sophie charged into the lab and tossed the small hardback to Elle, who broke the chain only long enough to open the book to a page before reconnecting to Imara. With their hands barely touching along the spine, Elle began her chant at the same time Tanya recited her own.

The time has come to send us back,
Before the warlock's next attack.
Send us safely with my magic,
Lest we face something tragic.

Elle continued in sets of three, while Tanya spoke her own magic.

Bind the perpetrator to the book,
a fitting end to the crook.
No one else will know his fate,
No release to spew his hate.

Jaiden heard the Antonio impostor scream. "I will hunt you down from hell," before she landed on the floor of The Enchanted Page II.

Jaiden couldn't stop the volcanic bile. She did not ever want to travel in this manner again. "Ugh. I am so sorry."

"No, I'm the one who's sorry. I forgot to add the anti-nausea line." Elle pushed her fingers through her hair. "Crap! That was a close one. I like the shortened version, Tanya. Nice job!"

"Thanks, I knew we didn't have a lot of time to spare. If there is nothing else I've learned, I appreciate less is more."

Jaiden realized Dani was sitting next to Tanya, looking very green around the gills. She had barely managed to hold back her own vomit.

"I prefer the way Imara brings me to your world," Dani said.

"I'll get something to clean up the floor," Tanya caught Jaiden's eye, then looked sheepishly to the ground before going into the small bathroom attached to the store.

"I'm sorry. Am I missing something here? I'm not trying to be mean, but why did you bring Dani back? I thought you knew it wasn't her wish." Jaiden shifted her body and began to rise.

"It's okay. I knew you needed me. Five. You needed the power of five. A pentagon. There was only four of you. When Tanya reached out to me, I knew what I was agreeing to."

"You can send her back. Can't you?" Jaiden asked.

Imara looked away.

"Jesus Christ. You people stay away from me. You think you're God or something, playing with people's lives as if they're pawns in your own private chess game. I'm done. Dani, you're more than welcome to stay with me until we figure something out. This time, I prefer to do my own research into the occult. I'm not without resources. We'll find a way to get you where you belong." Jaiden grabbed Dani's hand and stalked out the door.

†

Tanya winced and tugged at her earlobe. Imara was too shell-shocked to say anything, as she watched Jai and Dani stomp out. Correction. Jai stomped. Dani sort of limped out the door.

"Well, that went okay." Elle's tone left no room for interpretation. Sarcasm at its finest.

"Shut it, Elle." Imara was not in the mood for Elle's quip.

On cue, Elle's hips gyrated and she called out the famous marine battle cry.

"Stop saying my name."

"Then stop being a bitch."

Tanya calmly cleaned up the vomit. "You didn't tell her that once she's back in her own book, she can't go back if you pull her into our world a second time."

"When was I going to do that? When she was having her special time with Jai?" Imara didn't mean to sound petty and jealous but suspected that was exactly how her retort came across. "Besides, you were the one who extended your hand."

"I thought she knew the consequences of her choice, and frankly, I didn't think we had another option."

"I don't think we did, but I suppose there was always a slight possibility we could have made do with four." Imara seriously doubted her own words. Even though the situation was less than optimal, she would have made the same decision.

"No sense crying over spilled milk. What are we going to do about our current dilemma? Isn't there some way we can return Dani to where she belongs?" Tanya asked.

"Any chance you know the author?" Imara countered.

"No, but I hear she's nice," Elle answered.

"Um, not to be another naysayer here, but don't we have another small problem with Vlad? Please tell me he won't remain in their world, occupying Cindy's body. I'd hate for Val to shoot her." Tanya looked calmly from Imara to Elle.

"Shit, I hadn't considered that. Let me think, please. There are too many wrinkles to consider all at once." Imara began nibbling the corner of her thumbnail.

"We need reinforcements. I suggest calling on Fay and Aunt Clara." Elle pushed herself off the ground and extended a hand to Imara. "Come on, get off your ass, and do some groveling. You need to mend the fence. If Jai didn't have feelings for you, she wouldn't have reacted with such fervor. For some people, intense reactions sometimes get mixed up. Hate and love are the two most powerful emotions. I don't think Jai knows what to do with how she's feeling."

"You really think so?" Imara felt a small amount of hope, as she stood and brushed her hands against her shorts.

"I do." Elle offered an encouraging smile. "Wow, I never thought I would see the great Imara fall in love."

Imara pondered Elle's offhand comment. *Am I in love?* She could admit to being interested, but love was a whole new cauldron of potions. "I do care about her."

"Go. Mend. We can all come together again and explore approaching the author if that is what will repair this situation. But first we'll need to figure out how to eject Vlad from Cindy's body without causing her harm." Elle gave a dismissive wave.

†

"That arrogant, cocky, self-centered, witch. How could she be so irresponsible?" Jaiden knew she was ranting, but her anger took control of her emotions. Even the crystal in her shorts pocket could not calm her negative sentiments.

"You love her."

"What? That's the most preposterous thing…" Jaiden slumped onto the stool in her store.

"It's okay. I've been thinking about what you said earlier. You were right. I do love Candy, and it's about time I got off my lazy ass to fight for her. Maggie's rules be damned. I should have come clean long ago. Perhaps it would have been easier to ask forgiveness than permission. You should learn from my mistakes. Don't let a few roadblocks get in the way of your happiness. Besides, we need those three to get me back where I belong. I get the sense they'll work hard to find the answer." Dani patted Jaiden's shoulder. "At least I'll be able to retrieve my souped-up crutches now."

"Oh shit, I'm a terrible host. Let me find you a comfortable chair." Jaiden quickly brought a rolling office chair from behind the register.

"It's okay. I'm fine, but I do appreciate the offer. Thank you."

The tinkle of the bell on the door caused Jaiden to turn her head. Imara entered, chewing on the edge of her thumbnail and looking everywhere but directly into Jaiden's eyes. "Um...can I...ah hell. I don't know what to say, but we'll find a solution. I promise. We aren't going to stop looking until we do. You have my word. I can't tell you how sorry I am. I never intended for anyone to be hurt. I only wanted..."

"What, what did you want, Imara?"

"I wanted you to let love inside." Imara kept chewing on her nail.

"I don't believe you or anyone else is responsible for where love finds a warm and cozy place to land, regardless of your overinflated egos that tell you otherwise. Love happens organically, when it's good and damn ready." Jaiden hadn't meant to be so pointed with her response and felt immediate regret when she saw Imara blanch at the comment.

"Touché. I guess I'll leave you two to..."

"Get your ass in here and tell us what you and your pals have rumbling around in your demented little heads." Jaiden let her lips turn up to take the sting out of her words.

"Um…we might have another problem. Elle went to bring back reinforcements." Imara shuffled her feet and began gnawing more voraciously on her nail.

"You need to stop biting your nails before you don't have anything left. Some women actually enjoy a little passionate scratching on the backside. Although I suspect that whatever happened to your back in the blast means no clawing on your backside for a while." Jaiden couldn't believe she'd blurted out that borderline flirty comment.

Imara opened her mouth to speak, then promptly closed it.

Dani chuckled. "Uh huh, they do indeed."

"Okay, spit it out. What's the other problem that has your knickers in a knot?" Jaiden leaned against the counter.

"Well…it seems that we may have left Vlad without a way back to this realm. He's still occupying Cindy's body, and that isn't good for her at all. Cindy is most at risk, but I don't think the other agents in The Organization are without some jeopardy."

Dani perked up and sat taller in her chair. "Well get him the fuck outta there."

"We don't quite know how, yet. I have some thoughts, but I'm not a book magician. This is their area of expertise. Mine is bringing characters to life. I may have the answer to Dani's dilemma. It requires some fast talking with the author. If she can pen a new story with you as the lead, I'm confident that will send you back."

"Books take months to write. That's your answer?" Jaiden's voice rose, and she reached into her pocket to stroke the crystal.

"You two seem particularly cozy. I thought you might enjoy the extra time." Imara's jaw clenched when the words burst out of her mouth.

Jaiden was ready to go all WWW smack down on Imara for that last remark, when the sound of the bell broke the tension. Tanya's eyes landed on Imara, then Jaiden, and she shook her head. "You were supposed to be making nice and groveling. What the heck is going on?"

"Jai is not very happy with my proposed solution to the first problem. And, I don't think Dani is relishing the fact that we left Vlad behind in Cindy's body."

"Oh. Well, that's what I was about to tell you. Fay and Aunt Clara are here." She explained to Dani and Jaiden, "Elle and I trust both of them with our lives and we wanted them fully briefed on the situation. They might have a solution. It's not without some risk but definitely worth trying. I can't say I like their suggestion, but Elle is willing. Elle wasn't the one who put him there and she has no special connection to Vlad, but that isn't the main problem." Tanya took a step inside of the store.

"You're babbling. What's everyone worried about?" Imara asked.

"Apparently, there's a good deal of risk when a book magician tries to remove someone from an adventure against their will. We're banking on Vlad not wanting to remain in the book or in Cindy's body. He could very well choose to bring Cindy with him. It's a different way to bring a character to life. Fay and Aunt Clara aren't exactly the experts on that part of the predicament. That's why we need you to weigh in. Then there's the little problem of dealing with him once Elle brings him back. Oh, and can you please not say Elle's name for the next twenty-four hours? She's a little sensitive to Toni's experiment right now."

Imara held her hand over her mouth and chuckled. Jaiden understood the inappropriate action was simply stress relief. She made a shooing gesture. "What are you waiting for? Take care of the more pressing issue with Vlad, then we'll talk."

"I really am very sorry. I'd do almost anything to make it up to you, but you probably want this whole issue resolved. Then I'm sure you'll never want to see my face, ever again. I get it."

"Wait." Jaiden jumped up and selected a beautiful amethyst crystal. She approached Imara and opened her hand, setting the gem in her palm. "Take this. It'll protect you. Seeing as how you don't seem to have the smoky quartz I gave you before."

"Um, I had to—"

"I might be a little pissed at you right now, but I don't want anything bad to happen to you. I know you're going to offer to go with Elle...and...well..." Jaiden pulled Imara into a gentle hug, careful to avoid what she suspected was a very large bruise on her back. "Good luck. My mother used to preach at me to never allow someone to leave without bringing closure to a disagreement. A swath of negative energy follows and that can have unfortunate consequences. I haven't always done such a grand job of letting go of irritation in the past."

Jaiden was shocked when Imara engulfed her in another embrace and crushed their lips together. Imara offered a quick, "Thank you," and left before Jaiden could react.

†

Imara figured she was already on Jai's shit list. Besides, if she was going to jump into a scalding cauldron of messiness, she deserved a final wish. Okay, maybe it wasn't

182

exactly a wish, more like acting on an impulse she'd had since her eyes first landed on the beautiful Jai. Vlad was extremely unpredictable, and Imara did not want him to take his frustrations out on the unsuspecting book magicians. Unfortunately, they were the only ones who could bring him back after sending Gordon into the children's book. Imara chuckled, as she thought about the pompous ass who would now spend eternity in a children's book with weird, little characters. That had to chafe his ass. He would be perfect as the grumpy old man named Sam, forever insisting he didn't like green eggs and ham, then changing his mind.

"Nice move, by the way. Kissing and running isn't normally what I'd recommend if you want to get the girl." Tanya pulled open the door to The Enchanted Page II. "By the look on her face, she liked it."

"Really?"

"Uh huh."

"Oh, and whatever injury you sustained in the big explosion is evident with Jai. It isn't anything serious, is it?" Tanya asked.

"Nah. A small bruise."

"What are you two jabbering about? You'd think neither of you has a care in the world. Bad warlock on the loose. Remember?" Elle shook her head.

"Whatever the solution, I'm not letting you go back into the book alone. I don't trust Vlad. He might have found a way to hold you hostage. Hey Fay, Clara. I'm happy you were both so willing to drop what you were doing to help us out." Imara crossed the room and briefly hugged both women.

"Vlad has been a major pain in my arse for years. He thinks he can simply pull that donkeyhole, Gordon, from banishment without any pushback from the Magicians' Council. Well, he's got another think coming. I also heard about the wall ears. I am not at all pleased by that. There may be another wizard helping besides Gordon. I'm going to get to the bottom of that. I've no doubt he's the one who got them all worked up to begin with, convincing the wizards we were inferior and only good enough to support and serve them." Fay absently pushed back her hair as she spoke.

"Yeah, that sounds about right. So what's the plan?" Imara asked.

"Well, you know how book magicians depend on the power of three. Three of you must remove Vlad from the book with a chant you say together. I will go with you. Elle and I will both touch Vlad, forming a point. Imara, you must connect to both Elle and myself to complete the triangle of power. Did you get a crystal from Jai?"

Elle's hips thrust forward. "Oorah." She groaned. "Please, don't say my name."

"Oh, right, I heard about that. The crystal?" Fay asked again.

Imara's brow furrowed. "Yeah. How did you know?"

"Jai is more than meets the eye. Her crystals hold a lot of power. That will help to truss him up while we bring him back. The chant Clara and I learned in South America has a great deal of power. I feel relatively confident it will work. The risky part is adding an occlusion chant to the end. It won't hold him for long but should give us a little breathing room to put in place a more permanent solution to our shared problem. His influence is gaining, and that does not please me. I suppose I knew this day would come, and I must fulfill a promise to a friend." Fay began to look around the store. "Do you have paper? The chant is very precise and must be said in unison with a strong voice."

Tanya rooted around the store until she found a pen and paper. She handed both to Fay. "Here. Please make sure you bring my girlfriend back in one piece."

Fay printed the words they would need to say the minute the three arrived inside the book.

The warlock has no choice;
return him without a voice.
Let him stew without his power,
until the nightly witching hour.

Imara leaned over Fay and read the chant. "So we basically have until tonight to figure out how to neutralize Vlad once and for all."

"Precisely." Fay gave the group a curt nod. "Let me know when you have memorized the chant. The fortunate thing about the three of us saying the chant together is that we don't have to repeat it two more times."

"Oh, that is a nice benefit," Elle said. "I'll drive, Fay. I know the location in the book we'll likely find Vlad. I hope he hasn't had enough time to wreak havoc on those poor women."

"That's why we need to hurry," Fay answered. "Have you both memorized the words?"

Elle and Imara nodded, and the three clasped their hands together.

"Hey, do I need to say my chant three times to get us there or will once work since we're connected?" Elle asked.

"Once will do." Fay smiled.

"Wish I'd known that before. Okay, ready?"

Before Imara had time to prepare for the journey, Elle began,

Take us to the sick bay,
time for us to save the day.

CHAPTER TWELVE

Imara couldn't decide if it was better to prepare herself for the journey or to abruptly transport into the book. Either way the scene before her was unsettling enough to stir the bile again. She fingered the amethyst in her pocket that Jai had given her. The small rock sent a jolt of assurance throughout her body. Elle and Fay had materialized behind Cindy. Val stood in front of Cindy with a gun to her head, while Ronda pleaded for Val not to shoot. Ronda's eyes were overflowing with tears, and Imara thought it was the most heartbreaking thing she'd ever seen.

"Ah, you've returned to view your handy work. I must admit, I was close to taking action. This one's sniveling is getting on my nerves." Cindy, or rather Vlad, pointed to Ronda. "Although, I confess to a certain fascination with Val. I have half a mind to bring her to life. Someone like her would come in handy. Don't you agree, Imara?"

"Bout fucking time you returned. I wasn't sure I would be able to stop my twitching finger from shooting this piece of shit. I figured you could fix things after the fact with some of your magic, and we could get Cindy's body back from this parasite."

Gone was the efficient nurse practitioner, as Vlad's cold, appraising eyes peered from Cindy's face.

"What do you want, Vlad? Why are you toying with these characters? Surely you have another way out?" Imara was tired of the cat and mouse game he was playing. She had a niggling feeling he could have left the book at any time, but since she wasn't positive she'd called on the assistance of the book magicians. The warmth spreading through her body from the powerful amethyst she curled her fingers around gave her the confidence she needed to confront the arrogant asswipe.

"Why you, my dear. I want you, and of course, Jaiden. I want you both groveling at my feet and serving me in every way you can possibly imagine. Jaiden is simply the bonus round, but she is not to be forgotten in this. I have an old score to settle. Ah but you, my dear, are the main attraction." He narrowed his eyes. "I don't think you really want to test me, do you? I did make a small miscalculation. I should have jumped into Val's character. I do believe that would have been a better fit."

Val grabbed his throat. "Shut the fuck up, because my notable hair trigger temper causes me to act rashly." She turned her glare toward Imara. "You'd better do whatever it is you were planning and bring Dani back unharmed, or I swear I'll learn everything there is to know about magic and chase all of you to the bowels of hades."

With one last squeeze on the amethyst, Imara removed her hand from her pocket and moved into the power position. "Now!"

The three women stepped close and clasped their hands together, as they surrounded Vlad and recited the chant. Vlad's eyes went wide, and Imara knew he hadn't expected both the power and protection of her crystal, as the final, binding line of the chant rendered him without power. She couldn't help the self-satisfied smile, as she looked him squarely in the eye. Perhaps this chant wouldn't keep him out of their hair for long, but hopefully it would be enough time to find a more permanent solution.

†

Jaiden paced back and forth, watching out her store window. Dani was her responsibility until they found a way to send her back. She felt protective of Dani. Imara had pushed her into this insanity and placed her squarely in Vlad's line of sight, all to teach Jaiden a life lesson.

"Why don't you go next door and get an update? You know you want to," Dani said.

"Do you think that might jar their concentration or something? Maybe they need a quiet space to deal with everything."

Dani chuckled. "I doubt it. The past several hours have been anything but quiet, and they seem to have overcome all distractions. Bombs, sniping women, jealousy, skeptics. I'd say it's been downright chaotic. Go on, I'm not too proud to admit that my legs need a tiny rest. I've been pushing it lately without my forearm crutches, and my legs are sort of revolting on me. I'll be anxious to get my good set back."

"Oh, shit. I should run home and get those for you. Maybe that will take my mind off the impending apocalypse."

"No really, go next door and check on their progress. It can't have taken too long to rip Vlad out of my world. I'm not looking forward to making his acquaintance. I sure hope they found a way to neutralize him."

"I'll just pop in for a minute and get an update."

"What'll I do if a customer comes round?"

"Sell them everything you can at full price. It won't even be a lie for you to inform them there's a nasty warlock hanging around and creating a massive amount of negative energy. My crystals will come in handy as a sturdy layer of protection. You're probably used to good food and drink. I'll need the money to keep you in the lifestyle you're accustomed to while you hang with us crazies." Jaiden grinned.

Dani saluted her. "Will do."

Jaiden was a little sad that eventually Dani would return to her own world and secretly happy she was stuck in Coupeville for a while. The jumble of feelings easily surpassed a set of Christmas lights haphazardly thrown into a box. She always imagined them eagerly waiting for the unsuspecting person to attempt unraveling them when it was time to put them up again. If inanimate objects had an evil streak, she was sure Christmas lights were at the top of the heap.

Who will unravel my emotions and make sense of this situation so I can shine my light?

†

When Imara saw Jai standing next to Tanya, she felt a rush of exuberance. Jai's presence at The Enchanted Page II could mean only one thing. She cared.

Vlad's mouth continued to open and close without a single sound pushing through, despite his many efforts. Imara had to tamp down her urge to gloat. She knew they only had until midnight, then all bets were off. His face had turned a bright shade of red.

"Stop trying to speak, Vlad. You look like a fish. Your ability to toss nasty spells our way is finito. I do love Italian. Such a beautiful language, don't you agree? Oh right, cat's got your tongue right now." Fay laughed.

Imara wasn't sure Fay should be prodding the bear like that, especially since they hadn't talked about a permanent solution yet. Maybe Fay knew something Imara wasn't privy to. Apparently neither were the others, judging by the wide-eyed blinking contest.

"Now what?" Tanya asked.

"We'll get to that." Fay turned her attention to Jai. "You must be Jai. I am Fay, Grand Magician and leader of the book magicians. I know your mother, Zelda."

Jai quirked her eyebrow. "You do?"

"Yes, lovely woman. Clara, do you mind warlock sitting while we move this party next door? I, for one, will appreciate recharging amidst the abundant positive energy in Jai's shop. You..." Fay pointed to Elle. "Tanya, Imara come along. We've work to do. Clara, feel free to use that nifty incontinence spell we learned in South America if you feel at all uncomfortable. If he moves a millimeter, he'll be pissing and shitting all over himself." Fay grabbed Jai's arm and escorted her out of the bookshop.

Clara was laughing loudly as they exited.

This is all getting more interesting by the minute. Maybe I was simply the bait and the real fish is Jai. Imara vowed to protect Jai with her last breath. Vlad was not going to sink his black claws into her.

Jai kept looking back at Imara as if to say, *will someone please tell me what the hell is going on?*

Outside and out of Vlad's earshot, Fay continued prattling on about Jai's mother. "Everyone was trying to recruit your mother. She decided against joining the book witches. We weren't a good fit for her either. Apparently, she felt a different calling. I can't say I blame her. Too much politics between book witches and book magicians. We used to play very nicely in the cauldron. I blame the rift on the wizards and warlocks. Your mother is the sole reason Vlad hasn't won his little war yet."

"I seriously doubt that. My mother is a pacifist and the gentlest, most loving soul on this planet. She would never involve herself in whatever power struggles are occurring."

"Oh, I agree that Zelda is a gentle soul. I learned a great deal from her. Alas, our styles inevitably took us on different routes, as she knew they would. Yet, we did not possess competing goals. During my banishment, it was a privilege to be in her presence. She offered a very special gift to me at a pivotal moment in my life. She knew there would come a time when I could repay her kindness, and here I am."

Imara was riveted to the conversation. Although she was anxious about Vlad, something about Fay's command of the situation put her at ease. The universe had a plan. Of that she was sure.

†

Jaiden had a lot of unanswered questions. At the top of that list was why her mother had never told her about book magicians and book witches. Jaiden had a hard time synthesizing her view of her mother with the woman Fay was describing, not to mention imagining the two of them as great friends. Fay had such an air of royalty and confidence about her. Jaiden's mother always reminded her of a butterfly, beautiful but extremely fragile, with a presence that was fleeting. At least her existence in Jaiden's life had always been temporary. Jaiden treasured the moments her

191

mother spent with her, but her gentle soul did not remain in one location for long. Jaiden didn't exactly consider her flighty, more like transient.

"We need to transport everyone to Jai's home. That will be a more comfortable location to have this conversation. Besides, Dani looks distressed. I presume you are Dani. I am Fay, Grand Magician. It is a pleasure to meet you."

"Um, yeah, nice to meet you too, but I'm fi—"

"Nonsense. There aren't enough chairs, and I'll be damned if I'll plop my old, out of shape ass on the floor and sit crossed-legged like the young people. The dark one will be fine with Clara. She's got mad skills. Isn't that how you young people say it?"

"Um, I hope you aren't lumping me into that young un' category. I doubt very much that you are a great deal older than me," Jaiden said.

"Oh I know, but I still have a few years on you. Besides, you're like your mother. You hold your age well, along with your health and flexibility. I look younger than I feel. My bones did not get the same memo as my face. They protest every single time I try to keep up with those healthier than myself. Good thing Oren loves me the way I am. Come, let us join hands. Shall I do the honors?"

"Can we add the line I used before, make the flight a peaceful trip, even at a hasty clip? I'd prefer to avoid the normal motion sickness," Imara said. Jaiden and Dani added their agreement.

"Oh that would be lovely. I must admit I don't enjoy the journey as much as I used to. Another result of getting older." Fay took Jaiden's hand and reached for Dani with her other hand.

"Well, I guess visiting the world's largest roller coaster for vacation is out for all you wusses." Elle joined hands with Tanya.

Imara maneuvered herself to Jaiden's side and clasped her free hand, while accepting a connection on her other side with Elle. This left Tanya to close the loop by accepting Dani's outstretched hand.

Jaiden felt the familiar tug, and soon the entire group landed in the middle of her living room. Dissipating from one space and appearing somewhere else blocks or miles away, not to mention into another realm, was something to freak out the calmest person. Yet, Jaiden surmised these outlandish experiences would stop feeling foreign if done often enough. Would this be old hat if she continued to socialize with these women and they thought nothing of bringing her along for the ride?

The group was rather large for her relatively small space, and Jaiden chose to sit on the edge of the couch near Imara. The European recliner was the closest thing to a throne for the Grand Magician. Clearly Fay would direct the group, unless Imara began to vie for the spotlight. Jaiden could see them jockeying for that position, but since Fay seemed to possess information that was clearly a surprise to Imara, the confident book witch had yielded to her lead.

Jaiden's head whipped around. Amidst Fay's prattling, she'd said something about Jaiden's father. Jaiden had been distracted watching Imara and needed to pay closer attention to what Fay was saying.

"Your father was a big asshat when he met your mother, but she wove her magic, and honestly, he was probably one of her greatest successes."

"My father?" Jaiden had wondered about him. Her mother hadn't spent much time talking about any of her ex-lovers. Jaiden saw them come and go and wondered why her mother always seemed to attract the biggest losers. Just as they started to grow on Jaiden and become decent human beings around her gracious and loving mother, they would leave. Jaiden had asked about her father, but her mother never wanted to talk about him.

"Yes, letting him go was the biggest sacrifice your mother ever made. He was the only one to worm his way into your mother's heart. She'd done such a grand job with him and ended up falling in love, but the greater good won out in the end."

"What are you talking about?" Jaiden shifted on the edge of the sofa.

"Your mother is the most skilled of the Sanguine, a very rare and hidden group, who work mostly in the background. Imara, you are not Vlad's true target. You are merely a means to an end. He was hoping to fold Jai into one of his covens. You were purely the cherry on top. I'm sure he told you quite the opposite, but Vlad has a very personal score to settle with your mother, Jai." Fay paused, allowing Jaiden time to let the first part of her story settle.

"I don't understand."

"Vlad's older brother, Aaron, is your father. Your mother influenced Aaron's original path. Vlad was winning the conflict and collecting more to his vast network until recently. I've got my theory on what's happening, but I've no hard evidence. I would have sought out your mother to ask, but Imara requested my help before I had the chance to explore my hypothesis. More people are starting to align with Aaron, and Vlad is not at all happy about that. This is the real reason Vlad is here causing havoc and toying with both of you. He wishes to tip the balance of power in his favor."

Dani started laughing. "Shit, this is better than a soap opera. Are you sure this isn't some outrageous fiction? Maybe I'm having a really crazy dream. Perhaps all of you are the true book characters."

Fay pursed her lips. "This is no laughing matter, young lady. Everyone's future is at stake."

"Okay, back the info train up a bit and fill in some gaps you've left," Jaiden said.

"Imara knows there's been a conflict going for centuries between those who choose to rule by hate, revenge, and unchecked power, and those who prefer love, compassion, and forgiveness. History shows how the balance often changes, shifting slightly in one direction or another. The Sanguine are a small but mighty group who have helped to tip the scales in the direction of love and light. The old cliché of good versus evil certainly applies here."

"How exactly does my mother influence this conflict, and why was I never told about this?"

"Your mother never wanted you to be part of the whole messy situation, especially after she learned about Aaron's younger brother Vlad and his growing influence. Besides, your talent is not sanguine. She believed your unique gifts would be ample protection against the dark magic. She didn't foresee Vlad tapping into the skills of the book wizards. We've mainly stayed out of witch business until now. We had our own struggles with the power-hungry book wizards led by that buffoon, Gordon. Nice work on that, by the way. *Green Eggs and Ham*. Brilliant. Positively brilliant. I couldn't have thought up a more fitting punishment." Fay started laughing.

"You still haven't explained how the Sanguine work." Jaiden stood and began pacing her wood floor.

"I don't exactly know how it works, but I'll give you the condensed version as I understand it. Mean, awful people who would normally gravitate to warlocks like Vlad, are sucked into the positive energy and light your mother exudes, without any effort at all. Jai dear, while you pace, do you think you can wrestle up some libations for us? I do enjoy a good glass of wine, now and again."

"Um, sure." Jaiden stopped her nervous feet and looked at the rest of the group. "Anyone else?"

"Sure, I never turn down wine." Imara's bravado appeared to return as she leaned back on the couch and finally seemed to relax.

"Do you think it's a good idea to drink wine while we still have the little matter of neutralizing Vlad beyond this temporary reprieve?" Elle asked.

"Most definitely," Imara responded. "Wine helps lubricate my brain. I do my best work under the influence." She waggled her eyebrows at Jaiden.

"Or loosens inhibitions and lubricates other parts of your body," Elle muttered.

"Please continue, while I get the wine and help to lubricate Imara." Jaiden couldn't help herself.

"Right, let me continue. Your mother takes them under her wing, so to speak. I suppose that is an appropriate analogy, because those in the Sanguine are truly angels on earth. Over time, those dregs of society become productive, loving, compassionate people. Human, witch, or warlock, they're transformed after they've spent time with Zelda. The amount of time it takes, varies, but once they make their way to your mother's gravitational pull, the change is inevitable. Some like your father, have a tremendous impact on the world."

Jaiden set the bottle of wine down on the counter. "Why do they all leave if she is such a positive influence? I would like to have known my father or at least had another parent to lean on growing up. I would finally get to like her latest fling, then they were gone."

"I suppose it is a bit like roasting a turkey. The indicator pops up and they're done. They've evolved to the best person

196

they can be. Moving on is the only right thing to do so that others may bask in Zelda's light."

Jaiden picked up the corkscrew and jabbed the sharp end into the top. "Well I wish her positive light would have made me a better person. I probably fit more nicely into Vlad's evil network. It's no wonder he's attracted to my essence."

Imara ran to Jaiden's side. "Don't say that. You are perfect just the way you are. Nothing wrong with being a bit discriminatory in your selection of partners."

"Right, I thought that was the whole reason you brought Dani to life. I needed to be taught a lesson in love and acceptance, because clearly I didn't get that memo from Mom."

"Zelda has faith in you and believes the right one will come along."

"Why should I find someone when my mother doesn't get to keep any of her lovers?" Jaiden pulled out the cork and brushed a tear away. "I've been so hard on Mom. Not that I've ever said anything to her, but I've certainly judged her without words."

Imara wrapped her arms around Jaiden and murmured, "That is a sad tale. I wish I could do something to change your mother's life. Love potions are definitely not my forte, or I might have used one on you." Imara separated from Jaiden, and her lips turned up in a mischievous smile.

"Don't worry about your mother. Zelda is retiring. Rumor on the vine is she's been seen in the company of a certain dashing, older man. Apparently, they positively glow together."

Jaiden's head popped up. "What? Who?"

"Why your father, of course. Neither ever got over the other, even though they were predestined to travel different paths for the greater good. I believe Vlad caught wind of the rumor and is using the news to settle an old score. His power is growing, and the last piece in the puzzle is you, dear. Imara and Jai would lock in his leverage in the struggle. We cannot let that happen. The world of book witches isn't the only concern. I am sure you can see the impact of his influence, with what is happening with the US presidency and around the world."

"Not that this history lesson is unimportant, but can we focus on what needs to happen now?" Dani asked.

"Lovely. I am so glad you brought Dani to life. She is a clever addition to this hodgepodge team. Many people are depending on us," Fay answered.

"Um, thanks. I think." Dani squirmed in her chair.

Fay clapped her hands together. "Brainstorming session. We have until midnight to engineer a permanent answer. Jai, the wine is not going to pour itself unless Imara issues a pouring spell."

Jaiden grabbed several glasses from the cabinet to her left and began filling the glasses. "No magic. I've had enough in the last twenty-four hours."

CHAPTER THIRTEEN

"Can we use Tanya's suggestion of jumping from e-book to e-book to buy us more time?" Elle asked.

Imara caught herself before she began to bite her nail. *Goddess, is this hormones or what? I'm getting whiplash.* One minute she was nervous, the next she was confident and playful. She wondered how Jai perceived her constant shifts. She was sure Jai was more attracted to the confident, borderline arrogant Imara.

"I'd rather deal with this once and for all and not simply stall for more time. Besides, I have this feeling that Vlad is still influencing our emotions. I seem to be all over the place, and earlier we were all behaving uncharacteristically. Even Dani's behavior was impacted." Imara dove her hand into the pocket of her shorts to keep from nibbling on her cuticle.

"Send him into the same children's book. He could become the weird little character with the red hat. They deserve to spend eternity with each other," Jai quipped.

Imara could tell Jai wasn't serious but still thought the idea was brilliant. "Why didn't any of us think of that?"

"Because it won't work on him. He's already thrown up a protection spell after seeing you do that to Gordon. I get the impression he wanted you to dispose of Gordon for him. He's playing a dangerous game of chess with us." Fay paused as she took a large swallow of her wine.

"What about the character chant that Aunt Clara told you about?" Tanya asked. "You could turn him into a new character and put him into a brand new story that is truly horrific."

"We only have until tonight. I doubt an author could write a new story that quickly," Elle answered.

"What about what Char suggested? Can't you find a witch or magician to send him into Edvard Munch's painting?" Dani asked. "He won't be expecting that."

"Now that is truly inspired. Clara and I heard rumors about that. I think it can be done." Fay clapped her hands. "For added insurance, do you think you can produce another mind control spell and place it directly into his brain? Before this one wears off?"

Dani looked down. "Oh, I don't know. I'm not even in the same universe as Toni's brilliance with nanobots."

"Should we bring her to life, then?" Imara asked.

"No!" The resounding response from her friends startled Imara.

"Okay, bringing Toni to life is out," Fay said. "Tanya or Elle, can we find that author? She needs to write a scene where Toni teaches Dani her nanobot technology."

"Oorah!" Elle grimaced, when once again, her hips thrust out. "My name, remember. Can you please refer to me as something else for the next twenty-four hours?"

Imara smirked. "How about BM, short for book magician?"

"Do not even think to name me a gross bodily function."

"How about BBM, beautiful book magician," Tanya innocently suggested.

"I guess that'll work for now," Elle agreed.

"Can we please stop with the name debate? BBM and Tanya, go get that author and bring her here. I don't generally advocate for scaring the crap out of a nonmag without warning, but we're desperate and don't have much time."

"Um…am I missing something here? I thought we didn't have time for that," Tanya said.

"It's not a complete story, so it shouldn't take her as much time. She can write that scene and transfer it to paper or a computer in a manner of hours, not days or weeks. We'll have to hope that it works without publishing a new book or short."

"Tanya, you keep up with her on social media. Where is she living now?" Elle asked.

"Some tiny town in this state. Forks, I think. Or at least she was planning to move there." Tanya picked up the glass of wine in front of her.

"Oh yeah, I forgot, you already said that didn't you, Imara. The rainy, vampire town, right?" Elle asked.

Fay ignored the vampire comment. "Well if the town is that small, it can't be hard to track her down." Fay waved her hand in a dismissive manner. "Go."

Imara decided to take a chance and ask to spend a few moments alone with Jai, while Tanya and Elle went on their mission. She wanted to make sure Jai was okay with all the revelations about her mother and father. She also wanted to make sure Jai didn't hold a grudge for bringing Dani to life.

Knowing she hadn't been the one to deliver all the danger that had come crashing down on Jai wasn't a huge consolation to Imara. She still wanted to protect her.

"Jai, can we go onto your deck and talk please?"

"Sure, but I'm opening more wine."

"Perfect."

†

Gone were any reminders of Imara's magic; only familiar furniture remained. Jaiden set the full bottle of wine on the small table between the two chairs. "I'm sorry for laying all the blame on you earlier. I guess I'm the one who brought his evil to the island, not you."

"Oh, I share some of the responsibility for this whole mess. I didn't need to involve Dani or the rest of the gang from those books. That's squarely on my head. I had the best of intentions, but you know the old saying."

Jaiden filled the empty glasses with wine and held her glass in her hand, swirling the liquid. "I can't believe it. All these years… I've thought of my mother as a lovable person but a major doormat. I never knew, and she never corrected my perception."

Imara turned to face Jaiden. "Fay kept alluding to how special you are. I've felt that all along, since the very first moment I laid eyes on you. It's why you became my chosen one."

"I don't feel special. I'm just a lowly teacher who runs a crystal shop in the summer."

"I don't think so."

Jaiden sipped her wine. "Do you suppose Fay is right and there is someone out there for me? Someone I won't nitpick to death."

Imara smiled. "I certainly hope so, or I wouldn't have kissed you."

"Why did you kiss me?"

"Why does anyone kiss another person? Because they are wildly attracted to them and can't make it through another second without feeling the other person's satiny lips. Yours were like cotton candy, sugary tasting, and soft, like puffs of a cloud."

"That is a sickeningly sweet statement to make. Worse than a terrible romance novel could ever put in black and white."

"Okay, try this. If I could send Dani back and have her never grace your presence again, I would. Major miscalculation on my part."

"That sounds a bit like jealousy to me."

"Oh, make no mistake. That is exactly what it is, and I won't apologize for that. Don't care if it's an unattractive trait." Imara shrugged.

"I do like your confidence. Borderline arrogance, if I'm completely honest."

"Yeah, I know. Another unattractive trait I won't apologize for."

"Don't. I find it…refreshing."

"Refreshing, I'll take it. Just don't ever fake an orgasm with me. That would not be refreshing to me."

Jaiden spurted wine from her mouth. "What? Do you spy on your chosen ones?"

"I wouldn't exactly call it spying. More like research."

"I was starting to warm to you. Now I'm irritated all over again. How could you eavesdrop on such a private moment? And what makes you think we'll ever move to the intimacy stage for me to even try faking orgasm?"

"Whoops. Another small miscalculation. I'd hoped that was where we were heading once all this craziness is past. I'm not going to lie to you. I think I'm the one your mother was hoping for. I feel it deep in my bones. Come on. You have to feel it too."

"Argh. Sometimes I really hate your arrogance."

Imara stood. She pulled Jaiden to a standing position and kissed her with such passion that Jaiden knew she'd never felt before. The tingling was certainly new, but so was the absolute belief that she fit perfectly in Imara's arms. Her mouth opened to let Imara inside, and Imara took her time exploring every inch. Imara brought her hand down over Jaiden's clavicle and stopped short of the curve of her breasts. "No, you don't."

Jaiden could not stop her body from reacting or wanting more. The teasing touch was almost her undoing, as she moaned and protested without real force in her voice. "Yes I do."

"I'd like nothing better than to prove you wrong with a night of unbridled passion, but unfortunately we have to resolve our troubles first. I want us both to get what we deserve, a happy, healthy relationship. I won't stop trying, despite your feeble attempts to push me away."

"Oh." Jaiden didn't have anything else to say, because the tingling in her body was still front and center.

"See, I've won you over already. We have a future date in the bedroom. Soon. Very soon."

"You're awfully sure of yourself. We'd better head back inside before they wonder if we're gossiping about them."

"I am sure of myself, and don't worry, Elle knows I wouldn't waste this precious time on such meaningless drivel. You and I are all that's important to me at this particular moment. Just so we're clear." Imara stroked Jaiden's face. "So are we good? You've forgiven me? I believe you're enamored with me, but I must know I've been forgiven."

Jaiden grabbed Imara's arm. "Come on, before your inflated head won't make it through the doorway."

†

"What the hell just happened to me? Who are you people?" Dressed in a tailored suit, the dark-haired woman blinked rapidly.

She didn't look like she was about to upchuck all over Jai's living room. Imara smiled. "You added the anti-nausea line, didn't you?"

"Maybe," Elle answered.

"She did," Tanya confirmed.

"Thanks for writing me into your books," Dani said. "I know now is not the right time, but I was hoping to ask another favor after we're done here."

"And you are?" the author asked.

"Dani, Char's sister."

"I'm having a nightmare. A nightmare. I've finally lost my shit, and my characters are talking to me as if it's the most normal thing in the world. I know I joke about that happening, but not like this…"

Fay motioned for the author to take a seat. "Let me get right to the point. We need you to sit down and write a scene. I'll help lay it out, but you see we don't have much time. A very bad man is planning on making our lives a living hell, unless you help us out."

"Okay, I'll bite. As long as I'm having a vivid dream, I should pay close attention. Maybe I'll get a best seller out of this. Since I'm dreaming, I might as well wish for that."

"We need you to write about Toni teaching Dani nanobot code and how to inject a nanobot that will deliver an instant message to the brain. Specifically, a chant we wish to implant into this asshat's head." Fay waived her hand. "Well go ahead, start writing."

"Um, and if it's not too much trouble, can you also think of a way to put Dani back into the story?" Imara asked. "Maybe you can work on that after you write the first scene."

"Um, can I please have a computer? One with Scrivener on it. I've lost pages with Word when my computer crashed."

"I have a laptop, but I don't have this Scrivener program." Jai ran into her bedroom and brought out a laptop that she quickly booted up.

"Screw the program, just write the damn thing in Word. We'll take our chances that you won't lose your work," Imara said.

"Do I have to pay attention to errors as I write?"

"God, no. The thing doesn't need to be perfect, just legible, and plausible," Fay answered.

"Well, some readers don't exactly think my books are plausible. The suspension of disbelief thing doesn't quite work for them."

"Fucktwads. Less talk, more writing," Imara ordered.

The author nodded and began typing.

"Do you think we will irreparably affect her sanity?" Tanya whispered to Elle.

"I don't think so. Isn't she a bit odd anyway?" Elle lowered her voice to respond.

"Aren't all writers?" Fay asked.

"I can hear you talking about me. Normally, I don't get distracted by others, but you aren't making it easy."

"Everyone on Jai's deck now. Come get us when you're done. You too, Dani. Someone find her crutches," Fay ordered.

"They're right here." Tanya lifted them from the corner and handed over the forearm crutches to Dani.

"Make sure you write in your scene that all the materials needed are found in the Coupeville High School science lab.

Now that will be a huge suspension of disbelief, but Imara here is a powerful witch. Just have her offer up a spell. Her specialty is bringing characters to life, but you can stretch those boundaries, can't you?" Fay asked.

"A book witch who brings characters to life. Hmm, I like it." The author nodded and continued typing.

"Concentrate on the scene we need. Later you can write a book about her. She'll love being the main character in a book. Feeds that huge ego of hers," Fay said.

"Hey now." Imara felt the need to clarify even though she thought Fay's grin meant she was joking. "I don't possess the skills for that."

"Shhh. She doesn't know that and I'm not kidding," Fay answered under her breath before pushing open the door.

The group of women marched dutifully outside. Imara directed Fay and Dani to the empty chairs, while the others milled about.

†

Dani stretched her legs out in front of her and turned her head to catch a peek at the author typing away in Jai's living room. "Do any of you know much about her?"

"Tanya follows her," Elle said.

"Facebook is sort of a false place. I don't know how much following her reveals. People who have met her say she's nice, down to earth and genuine. Cares about people and social issues," Tanya said.

"You think she would consider writing one more book, so I can have my happily ever after?" Dani asked.

Jai crouched in front of Dani and took her hands. "I promise, we won't stop haranguing her until she does. Screw that I'm-not-a-sequel-writer rule. If you love Candy and she loves you, it will happen."

"She's big on writing stories based on her dreams. If she really believes this is a dream, we have a lot of power to influence her next project." Tanya touched Dani's arm. "I know I wouldn't mind reading another in the series, especially if you're the main character. Now that I've met you, I can't imagine not hearing about how you make out." Tanya blushed. "Not make out like high school fumbling in the back seat of a car...oh...you know what I mean."

Dani chuckled. "I do, but I wouldn't mind a bit of heavy petting in the story." Dani's face flushed. "Candy and I haven't...um...been intimate yet."

"Wow, really? There isn't a whole lot about your relationship, other than you grumbling about not being honest and having to break dates with her all the time. You did manage to bring her to a Thanksgiving get-together. Things seemed to go well there."

Dani looked at the ground. "Yeah, that was before the whole Leonid mess. Life got crazy, and I had to focus on our prototypes. Val was in danger. That was top priority. Candy kept reaching out, trying to make it work. I...well, I couldn't be honest with her. She thought I was seeing someone else. I let her believe that so she would move on."

"Want me to bring Candy to life?" Imara asked.

"No!" everyone shouted at once.

"It was just a thought," Imara answered.

"Candy was the first person who didn't see the crutches first. She had a shit for an ex and yet didn't have trust issues at all with me. Who knows now? Emotional abuse is as bad as physical abuse, and I let her believe I was cheating on her. I didn't tell Char because she would have chewed on my ass for that. She has a soft spot for Candy."

"Isn't Char sliding into the top spot in The Organization? Surely she would let you fill Candy in on what you really do," Tanya said.

"See, there you go, a major plot point already solved," Jai said.

"My sister does love me and wants me to be happy. Toni's my best friend, and she revels in breaking the rules. Val is ready to go toe-to-toe with Maggie over the plans she and Gina have for their life with a new bundle of joy on the way." Dani began to feel optimistic about her love life, as she thought of what the changing variables could mean for her. "Things could really work, couldn't they?"

"Absolutely!" Jai kissed Dani's forehead.

Imara narrowed her eyes, and Dani worried what a book witch might do in a fit of jealousy. She'd be lucky if she returned without a terrible case of crabs.

Jai stood and brought her hand seductively down Imara's arm, then briefly caressed her behind. "Stop thinking evil thoughts, you have nothing to worry about. Don't even think of showing that unattractive green hue of jealousy."

The women continued to talk as if they were all good friends at a lesbian pot luck. One hour stretched into two, then three. Their final conversation about the ethics of what they did was cut short as a dark head poked out the door. "Okay, it might not be the best writing I've ever done, but this is a dream. It'll do in a pinch. I didn't know how to print out a copy. Is your laptop connected to a wireless printer?" She held it out for Jai.

"It is. Here let me take that from you, and I'll print out a copy for all of us." Jai balanced the laptop in her hand and pressed a few keys, as she began walking back inside.

"After I perform that little miracle and engineer the nanobot, do y'all think you can hold off on sending her back? While you do your thing with Vlad, I'd like to talk to her about writing another story in the series," Dani said.

"Sure, Dani. We can do that," Tanya answered for the group, as Elle nodded her agreement.

Imara smacked her hands together. "Wonderful, as soon as Jai has the printed copies, let's all head to the high school." She touched her watch. "Time is running out. We only have another hour and a half to make this happen. I don't like cutting this so close."

Jai returned to the porch and began handing out the printed scene. She scanned the paper and began nodding. "Oh, this is good."

"As long as I'm having such a vivid dream here, do you think I could come along, even though the longer this lasts, the harder it will be to record the dream for later use? Wow, a self-aware dream, I've never had one of those before."

"Sure, why not," Fay answered.

"Let's walk there, okay? It's not far." Jai looked up from her paper.

"Sorry, dear, not with Dani's, uh…" Fay glanced at Dani who opened her mouth to argue, then quickly closed it. "Besides, we don't have any time to spare."

"Oh right. I guess we have to do the handholding thing again. Please retain the line that keeps the motion sickness at bay." Jai held her hand out to Imara and smiled.

CHAPTER FOURTEEN

Coupeville High School was just down the road from where Clara was watching Vlad in the bookstore. The red building with the decorative brick base wasn't much to look at, but the small structure wasn't horrible either. No peeling paint or ancient appearance. The school looked like it was built in this century. That was a plus.

Jai was able to let the group into the school, even though everything had closed for the summer. Imara was moderately impressed with the lab. She knew a high school wouldn't have the kind of equipment needed for nanobots. She would have to refer to the story and hope Fay knew what she was doing. Imara had her doubts.

"I know this room isn't as impressive as the lab at your complex, Dani, but we're very proud of the school's achievements in the sciences. The school is well known for their Science Olympiad team that does quite well in competitions," Jai said.

"Hmm, really. That's impressive." Imara was studying the scene that described what she needed to do to create the right kind of equipment for Dani. The author had written several scenes to accomplish their ultimate task.

The author was nodding her head. "So vivid. I am loving this dream."

When Imara got to the part where she recited the spell, she was equally impressed with the author's grasp of how things might work. *No time like the present.* "Okay here goes nothing."

Make this very basic lab
far, far away from anything drab.
State of the art is what we need,
enable the nanobot to plant the seed.

"I really could not have come up with a better chant. Nicely done," Elle said.

"Thank you." Imara breathed a sigh of relief. A large computer appeared, along with vials and wires that looked suspiciously similar to the high-tech lab at The Organization's base. So far, so good.

Dani was reading from her draft. The story did not exactly explain how to perform the miracle, but something must have come over her like a wave. She hobbled over to the computer and began typing in code. "I need the chant to program in," she called over her shoulder.

"Isn't it in the story?" Tanya was flipping through the pages.

"No, I figured you didn't need me to write that."

"She's right, we don't. Crap sandwich. We forgot to obtain a print of the painting, and no stores are open now. I don't suppose your bookstore has a copy?" Imara asked.

"Um, nope. We're a bookstore. We wouldn't have had a copy of *Green Eggs and Ham* to offer up either. We have a limited selection of children's books. I don't suppose, *Heather Has Two Mommies* will work?" Elle sucked in her lip.

"I'd really rather send him to that awful painting," Fay said.

Imara rolled her eyes. "Okay, where in the world can we get this print? Please don't suggest a country like China or Japan. I can't read those symbols. Somewhere that English is the first language."

"Australia? New Zealand? Let me check my phone. I know there's a world clock app." Tanya began scrolling on her phone that she had dug from her pocket.

"Just go, go, while Dani finishes everything else for the syringe. Try Australia first. That would be the right time frame, if memory serves me well." Fay made a shooing gesture at Elle.

"Okay, I'm on it." Elle disappeared in a fog.

"Wow, I am loving this dream!" the author exclaimed.

†

Jaiden noticed Imara biting the edge of her cuticle again and wondered what had sparked a new round of agitation. She pulled Imara's hand from her mouth and intertwined their fingers. "Tell me what's causing your jitters. Except for not having the print, everything seems like it's going well."

"I don't like how close we are cutting this. Time is sometimes a little mushy when we create our spells. The witching hour could be midnight or before. There's always a bit of imprecision. A half an hour here or there makes quite a bit of difference when we cut this so close."

"Oh, that's not good. Do the book magicians know that?" Jaiden asked.

"No and we're not going to tell them either. That will only serve to ratchet up the negative energy, and none of us need that."

"No, we don't."

Fay raised her eyebrow. "What are you two whispering about over there in the corner?"

"Apparently, the witching hour might come a half hour early, and they don't want us fretting over that little fact," Tanya answered.

"Shit, I forgot about your supersensitive hearing," Jaiden said.

"Do not ever withhold critical information. Elle thinks she has more time than she does and that is not good. No, not good at all," Fay muttered.

"I know, I know. I thought I was keeping everyone from climbing the walls or pressuring her to write faster." Imara pointed at the author.

"Ooh, a cliffhanger. I like it. I can't wait to wake up and write this all down."

Elle reappeared, scroll in hand, and saved the group from Fay's tongue-lashing. "I got it in Western Australia at this novelty shop. It was not easy to find, I'll tell you that."

"Do we have the syringe ready?" Fay asked.

"Yeah, right here." Dani held up the needle with the pale-yellow liquid inside. "God, I hope this works. It was like I was on autopilot and knew exactly what to do. Weird? I guess the power of the printed word is truly amazing. Not only does it have influence on social mores, but look what it helped me accomplish. Knowledge I didn't possess a few hours ago, and I might not even be real!"

"Let's do this." Imara's confidence had apparently returned.

214

†

The first clue that an important miscalculation had occurred was Vlad's self-satisfied smile. As soon as Imara stepped into the store, the very air she needed to breathe became elusive. She wasn't sure if her face was turning blue yet, but it wouldn't take long.

The next words she heard, sent a chill up her spine.

"She will be dead in less than a minute. I can spare her, but only if you agree to join my coven, Jaiden. I don't much care one way or another if Imara dies, but I wouldn't mind her attaching to your coattails when you join me against my spineless brother."

Jai spit on Vlad and yelled, "Never." She wrapped her arms around Imara, providing an instant wave of warmth through her body.

Imara gasped for air, which now began to flow through her bronchi with life-saving speed. The heat started with the amethyst still in her pocket and seemed to travel up her spine and move outward. She felt the healing power extend to her injured backside and knew that whatever bruise had marred her body earlier was gone.

Imara jumped into action on autopilot, as she joined the pentagon surrounding Vlad and plunged the needle into his shoulder. Of one mind and voice, they chanted the message now traveling to Vlad's brain.

For those who dare to seek harm,
these words will act to disarm.
Their evil motive will turn within,
counteract malicious sin.
Tie the perpetrator to The Scream.
Heed the power of our team.

After all is said and done,
the print will know the evil one,
then it will demand a cost,
and for evermore Vlad is lost.

No one else will know his fate;
No release to spew his hate.

They repeated the chant two more times, watching Vlad's face contort before he disappeared. Imara was sure the expression on his face was as close to the one in the print as could feasibly occur. This was indeed a fitting end to Vlad.

They jumped up and down like girls in a schoolyard, swinging their still-joined hands. "We did it!"

Fay stepped back, leaving the couples still holding hands with one another.

"Why do you suppose, we all began to chant together what Dani had programmed into the nanobot? That wasn't part of either scene," Tanya said.

Jai smiled at Imara. "Not everything is predestined. It's like I told Dani, our lives are a blank page. They're unwritten. Authors are not the only ones who get to write down what happens and change the course of events. Everyone can write their own script in the play of their life. Intuition is a powerful thing. I believe we intuitively knew that extra push was needed."

"I sure am glad you have refined intuition. I don't know how you literally breathed life back into me, but I'm very grateful," Imara said.

"That is your power, Jai. You are a protector. When you wrap your arms around someone you love, you can bat away any pain or harm that may come to the person like an annoying mosquito. Vlad wanted your strength to keep him from harm, but you would never have loved him. Not even as your uncle. Although, I am not sure he knew that fact."

"Why didn't anyone tell him and save us all from this bucket of shit we found ourselves in?" Jai asked.

"He would not have believed any of us, and he would have made you and everyone you love pay for your assumed disobedience," Fay explained.

"Quite right. I am sorry I was not able to keep Vlad from performing that evil spell, but it looks like all's well that ends well. Jai you certainly showed us what you are made of." Clara grinned. "Well done, well done. Now, if you all don't mind, I have a mai tai waiting for me on the beach, and a certain stud who enjoys a bit of afternoon delight."

Tanya groaned. "Ugh, I will never remove that picture from my head. My father, the stud?"

†

Dani didn't quite know how to start the conversation with the author. She was worried about Jai and the rest of the group, even Imara, but she desperately wanted her happily ever after. "Can I ask you something?"

"Sure. Why not?"

"Not to sound ungrateful or anything, because you did create me, but Char has Toni, Ronda has Cindy, Sophie has Kim, and Maggie has Antonio. Even surly Val now has Gina. Why did you leave things hanging with me? Am I such an unlovable character that I don't deserve my happily ever after?"

"Oh God, no. In fact, you are a fan favorite. I don't really know the answer to that question. I was going to write a whole book with you front and center, then it occurred to me that Val was a more appropriate choice for another action adventure. I couldn't quite work out in my head how I would weave your story into something that was a page turner. Readers would rake me over the coals if I produced a romance with serious, social commentary instead of romantic intrigue."

"Okay, I guess I get that. Perhaps a short or novella? Something along the lines of that Thanksgiving story. Valentine's Day maybe? That's a particularly good holiday for romance."

"Fair enough. You absolutely deserve your happily ever after. If I can remember this wacky dream, I promise I'll jot down some notes to help my muse get started."

"Thank you."

The door to the science lab opened, and Dani was happy to see the relaxed and smiling faces of the women as they surrounded her and the author.

"I take it everything went well?" Dani asked.

"A tiny glitch that Jai rapidly resolved," Imara answered.

"That's great. So Vlad is in the print now?" Dani asked.

"Yup and his face looked unbelievably similar to the one in *The Scream*. Hopefully he is screaming for all eternity," Elle said.

"Good. I'm ready to go back now."

Jai walked over and hugged her. "I'm not sure I'm ready for you to leave just yet." She stepped back and brushed away a tear. "Damn, I'm going to miss you. Don't forget what I said. Blank page for you to write on. If she doesn't write your story the way you like, figure out a way to write your own. I believe in you. Go get Candy. Make her understand the real score."

"She's going to write the story. I do hope there's a steamy sex scene. I'd like that. I'm going to miss you too. Imara is a very lucky woman. Don't nitpick, okay?"

"Okay." Jai kissed Dani's cheek, then immediately went to Imara's side and looped their arms together. Imara's scowl turned into a smile.

"Are you ready, Dani?" Imara asked.

"I am. Be good to her, and don't let your arrogant side overshadow everything and screw it up."

Imara laughed and hugged Dani. "I am going to miss you. We needed you for completely different reasons than I originally anticipated. Thanks."

"You're welcome."

"I really like the final scene, absolutely brilliant. I think I'll add one more line to the spell. I'm so glad I'm the one who gets to say the chant after being the one who fucked this up in the first place. So, I'll take care of Dani if BBM"—Imara smirked—"takes care of our illustrious author. Do you need me to remove her clothes?"

"What the hell?" Jai asked.

Imara held out her palms. "Only to make it appear as though she's been asleep. I doubt very much that she wears work clothes to bed."

"Oh."

"Nah, we'll take care of it. I'll tell her to get ready for bed like she normally does, and it will all seem like part of her vivid dream," Elle answered.

"This is all positively delightful. I can't believe a full-blown story is playing out in my dreams. I wonder what I ate last night to cause this, because I'm buying out the store next time."

Imara turned to Dani. "Get ready."

Return this woman to home base,
secure and settled in her space.
Make the journey quick and fluid,

then send to her a savvy cupid.

Imara finished her spell with a wink.

CHAPTER FIFTEEN

Tanya and Fay had mumbled about needing to attend to something and made a quick exit, leaving Imara alone with Jai. They started the short walk back to Jai's home.

"Nice last line in the spell, by the way. You old softy. You want Dani to get her happily ever after as much as me, don't you?"

"Of course I do. Everyone deserves that. No one is more worthy than Dani. The universe has given her a shit playing hand for quite some time. First in the book, and now here in our world. I played a part in that, so it's only fair I nudged her future in the right direction. Combine whatever the author writes, your pep talk, and my spell...I figure we have that triple covered. Book magicians swear by threes. So..."

"Yeah, so...here we are. Alone at last." Jai took Imara's hand.

"About blinking time. I mean, I love Elle and Tanya. I also respect Fay, more than I ever thought possible, but while

221

five might be the perfect number to cement certain spells, it is most definitely a crowd. I don't want a mob for what I have planned."

"You're not exhausted? I am positively drained."

"Oh, I thought we could get to know each other a little better." Imara waggled her eyebrows.

"Is that code for make love?"

"Well yeah. Don't you think that's better than saying fuck like bunnies all night long?"

Jai smacked Imara's chest. "You are not exactly making your case right about now."

"Well, poopbiscuits." Imara tilted her head and captured Jai's eyes. "You do look a little ragged. I suppose a good night's sleep would improve the bags under your eyes. I'll find my way back to the inn."

"Oh no you don't. You're joining me in that big bed of mine. We're going to start out sleeping together, not 'sleeping together.' We're going to wake up with morning breath and our hair all kittywampus. If, and only if, neither of us go screaming in the other direction, then we'll fuck like bunnies all night long. I'm not starting anything with you based solely on lust."

They reached Jai's front door, and Jai turned the knob to lead them inside.

"It's cattywampus, and I'll have you know my hair is damn near perfect when I awaken each day."

"Whatever. Maybe you should be the one to teach my English classes then. Kitty sounds so much nicer than catty. Catty has very negative connotations, and I'm not into all that negative energy." Jai laughed. "Come on, I'll get you a toothbrush so you can start off the night with minty fresh breath. You're probably one of those who insists on brushing before a morning kiss."

"But of course. It is the only civil thing to do. Were you brought up in a barn or something?"

"You are seriously mixing your figures of speech. We'll work on that."

Imara raised an eyebrow, as Jai tugged at her hand and led her into the master bath. "Says the woman who changes words she doesn't like. Does kittywampus ring a bell? Never mind. So, morning delight then. I can adjust. Morning, afternoon, evening. Makes no difference to me. I will rock your world regardless of the time of day. Oh, and I sleep in the nude. I sure hope that doesn't tempt you too much."

"You are a cocky little shit. I think I can handle it. Can you? I don't wear clothes to bed either."

"This should be fun to see who breaks first." Imara nearly skipped into the bedroom following Jai. She wasn't the least bit tired. A second wind activated her imagination, as she envisioned multiple ways to ravish Jai's body.

Imara started her seduction when she grazed past Jai to take her place at the second sink. She caressed a very fine ass and earned a cautionary finger wagging. It was all fun and games until Imara caught Jai's weary face reflected in the mirror. Jai hadn't exaggerated. Her sleep deprived eyes were clearly fighting to remain open. At that moment, all Imara wanted to do was wrap her arms around Jai and snuggle until her own energy waned and allowed sleep to come.

Jai wasn't joking. Without showing a bit of modesty, she stripped and pulled back the covers of the bed. Her dirty clothes found their way into the hamper, and she indicated with her hand that Imara should toss hers on top. "Don't think I didn't notice how you borrowed shorts and a t-shirt from my drawers. Did you also steal a thong from me?"

Imara was trying not to ogle Jai too much and not exactly succeeding. *Cuddle only. I can do this.*

"Nope, went commando. I sensed when you and Dani were in danger, and I ended up pounding on Tanya and Elle's door wearing not a stitch of clothing. That's why I wasn't carrying the smoky quartz. They lent me a robe, but I didn't think traipsing through a potentially dangerous situation in just a robe was appropriate." Imara stripped off her borrowed clothes and followed Jai to the bed.

Imara took her time to get under the covers and didn't miss Jai's fleeting look of appreciation. She wanted Jai to get a good, long look at her unclothed body.

"Okay, I'll admit the mind is willing and wound up, but my old, weary body won't follow. I'm afraid I'd fall asleep on you, and we can't have that. I don't want to start this whole rocking-my-world thing in any one-sided fashion."

Imara pulled Jai into her arms and began rubbing her back and massaging her head. Not even one minute had passed, and she knew Jai was fast asleep. Imara sighed and decided to enjoy the moment. Passion and mind-blowing sex were important, but this comfortable feeling of holding the person you loved all night long was what she sought. Tiny snoring sounds from Jai made their slice of time perfect. Yeah, she'd fallen in love with Jai and only hoped Jai wouldn't uncover all her imperfections and toss her aside.

†

Jaiden thought she heard the low murmur of a voice beside her. She smiled as she remembered Imara holding her all night. She could definitely get used to head rubs and gentle caresses to her back. She knew she'd fallen asleep quickly and hoped that hadn't turned Imara off. *She's still here beside me, so something must have kept her interested.* As her waking state grew, she caught the tail end of a spell. *What the hell?*

And make it so my hair is tame.

"You cheater." Jaiden poked the naked form next to her. She brought her nose to Imara's mouth and sniffed. "Aha, I caught you. No fair murmuring a grooming spell so you can greet me with perfect hair and minty fresh breath. Rewind, this instant. I insist on dragon breath and hair that sticks up everywhere."

Imara hmphed. "Even without the spell, I can assure you that long hair never sticks up everywhere. Sometimes it isn't quite as fluffy and luxurious, but *I* am never spiky."

"I am dead serious. If you do not neutralize the spell, I'm not kissing you this morning."

Imara grinned. "That's okay, there are a whole lot more choices—"

"And none of those either."

"You can't be serious. How about if I include you in my morning-after spell?"

Jaiden tossed the covers aside and stalked into the bathroom, where she began brushing her teeth. After running her fingers through her hair, she called out, "Coffee? I need coffee. I'll make us some."

"Wait, wait, wait. I'll do a reverse spell right now."

"Too late. I've already brushed my teeth." Jaiden pulled open a drawer in her dresser and retrieved her bra, a t-shirt, and shorts. She grabbed a second set and tossed them to Imara. She wondered how Imara had managed to fit into her clothes. Imara was considerably larger than Jaiden, and the temptation to bring her mouth to Imara's ample breasts was starting to wear her resolve down. Jaiden needed Imara in clothing before she brought her back to bed and gave in to temptation.

Expand these clothes a little bit,
to help achieve a perfect fit.

"So that's how you made my clothes work. Do you have a spell for everything? Never mind. Don't forget to return them to their original size, please. Well, stop looking at me like I'm an alien and get dressed."

"Son of a bitch. I am going to have my hands full with you, aren't I?" Imara grumbled. "Okay, if I don't get nookie this morning, can we have a proper date tonight? I'll pull out all the stops to make it as romantic as you like."

"You don't get it, do you?"

Imara crinkled her nose. "No, I guess not."

"I want complete imperfection. See, I think we fit. Better than those clothes you altered." Jaiden smirked then turned serious. "I've never thought that before about anyone, and now I want to prove my theory by tossing every conceivable imperfection into the mix. I want to see how I handle it. No spells. I want the raw, unvarnished you. I accept the date. It's a beautiful day. Let's not waste it, okay? I've decided not to open my shop today. I'm going to play hooky with you." Jaiden left the bedroom, heading for the kitchen.

"Oooh. I'll bet Tanya would agree to watch your store, if you want. She's a total sweetheart." Imara appeared in the great room fully clothed.

"We can walk to Main Street and see how they're doing, maybe grab some breakfast at Knead & Feed. I could cook a breakfast for you, but why mess with perfection? Their baked goods are to die for. I don't mind closing my store for one day. The island is fickle that way. None of us are beholden to tourists."

"Conjuring up a boat to explore the sound might be a bit out of my range." Imara pursed her lips.

"Don't want or need a boat. Walking along the rocky beach or on the pier and simply enjoying the day is fine with me. Maybe we can grab two books from your store and sit comfortably in the sun. That is usually what I do with my time off. I wonder if that's too tame for you."

"Are you trying to find ways to push me away? For the record, I enjoy a good book as much as a day filled with excitement. Toss another challenge my way. I can tell I've already wormed my way into your heart, so you might as well give up now."

Jaiden chuckled. "I do find your overconfidence charming. Go figure. You know, I went to a conference once, where this speaker said something I will never forget."

"What was that?"

"There is absolutely no correlation between confidence and performance." Jaiden began laughing.

"Fine, go ahead and yuk it up. Wait 'til I prove that yahoo wrong. There will absolutely be a connection. You'll see."

"Oh, I look forward to that research."

Imara grabbed Jaiden's hand, twirled her around, and dipped her with a brief kiss. When she stood Jaiden upright, she brought their lips together in a kiss that left Jaiden panting for more. She abruptly broke the kiss. "Come on, I'm starved. We can get coffee at the restaurant."

†

Sunrise came early during island summers, a definite benefit to living so far north. The sun had already warmed the outside air, as Jai and Imara walked along Main Street. Imara had a hard time remembering how scary yesterday had started and continued to enjoy the morning with the birds singing their songs and the light breeze coming off the water. The conditions were idyllic for a stroll along the bay.

The island was definitely growing on her, especially with Jai walking alongside her. Imara needed to ask her two friends about their plans for the bookstore. She wasn't a book magician, but maybe she could convert and learn that trade. After her experience bringing Dani to life, she wasn't sure if her heart was in it anymore. If characters were something more, then essentially playing God didn't seem right to her. She took away their free will. Perhaps, as Tanya suggested, book witches and book magicians could combine their skills. They could jump into the books to ask those characters for their permission. But what if they truly fell in love? Was that cruel to send them back? Everything was all so topsy turvy now. She'd never had to consider the ethics of what she did for a living. Imara began to chew on her nail, as she considered her future.

"What's stressing you now? I don't see any bad guy lurking behind the bushes. I haven't even seen that sniveling douchebag, Franklin, lately. Speaking of which, he needs one of us to teach him a lesson. I don't care if he was under Vlad's spell. He broke my necklace, the little worm."

"I was thinking about my future. How would you feel if I looked for a more permanent residence here on the island? I like it here. I'm not sure what Tanya or Elle are planning, but maybe they'll let me run the bookstore. Or maybe they'll decide to settle permanently on the island. Regardless, I can't stay at Captain Whidbey Inn forever. I know Tanya misses her cat, Tolstoy. Although, I bet he'll miss his feral, little girlfriend. I should make friends with her and bring her here."

"Wow. That was a lot of random thoughts all linked together in a surprisingly logical fashion. How come you don't already have a cat of your own? Aren't witches supposed to have familiars hanging about?" Jai deftly avoided the original question.

"My special little girl recently passed away. I haven't felt a connection to any other yet. I mean, no connection to another cat," Imara amended.

"Mmhmm, finding the right familiar is important."

"Speaking of witches and their familiars. Where's your familiar? You do recognize that you're one of us. Not a book witch, but from what I experienced, you're a very powerful protection witch. I suppose I could do worse than falling for someone in that particular sect." Imara tried to bring Jai back on track about a possible relationship.

"Falling for?" Jai seemed to choke on the question.

"What else do you think we've been doing? I would have bedded you and moved on by now if I hadn't fallen. And you would have started to find fault with me already. I've certainly given you enough ammunition."

"Not quite. We haven't had a proper morning after. I did have a cat, and she was a perfect companion. I was ready to go to the shelter to pick out another when all this excitement occurred. I still would like to do that."

"Let me tame Tolstoy's girlfriend. She's a beautiful little tabby, unless you want to find the stereotypical black cat. Unfortunately, black cats aren't adopted enough, because they get a bad rap. I am bound and determined to find a way to cement our future. Nothing says commitment like adopting a cat together. Don't think I haven't noticed how you keep dodging the topic."

"I haven't been avoiding the subject," Jai sputtered.

Imara stopped walking and turned Jai to face her. "Let me be clear. I'm confident I've fallen in love with you, and it's only a matter of time before you admit you're equally enamored with me."

"I'll agree we do seem to fit, but I'm not declaring anything until you prove you can really rock my world. I want a taste of that milk before I buy the cow. I'll also admit the idea of you finding a more permanent place to stay is certainly not unappealing to me."

Imara quickly kissed Jai and lingered for a while, as she nibbled and sucked on her lower lip. "Not exactly a rousing endorsement of my thoughts on future living arrangements, but at least I've moved the needle."

"Oh you have, you definitely have." Jai tugged on her hand and they descended the stairs leading to Knead & Feed.

†

Jaiden didn't know why she'd held off on making love with Imara that morning. She was well rested after waking. Her libido certainly had not taken a vacation either. She wasn't sure if Imara's teasing touches and kissing throughout the day was intentional or not. She wondered if she was whipping Imara into a frenzy to match her own. She could barely hold herself back from slamming her book shut and taking her right there on the incredibly uncomfortable rocky beach. They hadn't gone back to her house to shower. Instead, they chose to grab a couple of books from The Enchanted Page II.

Imara stretched her long legs and leaned back. The simple movement was the sexiest thing Jaiden had ever seen. Imara turned her head, and the satisfied look on her face revealed that she'd known exactly what effect her movements had.

"Okay, you win. Time to head back to my place."

Imara grinned. "About damn time. However, there is one thing I am going to insist on. Either I get to perform a small grooming spell or we shower together."

"Normally, that would have been a mood killer for me, but I'm oddly aroused by the notion of a grooming spell. I kinda want to know what that feels like, but don't get any ideas about that being the norm."

"I can accept those conditions." Imara jumped up and took Jaiden's hand, then pulled her up too. "Come on, I'll race you back to the house."

Jaiden pushed her back onto the beach and began running, laughing as the breeze pushed her hair back. Imara's long legs gave her a distinct advantage, and she was leaning against Jaiden's door with that satisfied smirk on her face.

Jaiden didn't want to waste another minute. She opened the door and nearly dragged Imara inside. She was pulling off her clothes while tugging on the bottom of Imara's t-shirt.

Imara grabbed her wrist and stopped their forward motion. "Wait. Just give me thirty seconds, please.

Bless these two with a magical shower,
soft and sensual petals of a flower,
a tingle here across our skin,
preparation for our afternoon sin.
The scent is sure to tempt the nose,
more sweet than the fragrance of a rose.

Jaiden's body felt like a thousand tiny feathers were caressing her skin. She couldn't believe how much her arousal soared with the sensation caused by Imara's spell.

"I hope you meant sinfully good," Jaiden said.

"But of course. How'd you like my magical shower?" Imara asked.

"That was...um...really nice. Can I amend my earlier declaration? I may never want a normal shower again." Jaiden continued her forward motion until they stood at the foot of her bed. She quickly pulled her shirt over her head and tossed it on the floor.

"Really?" Imara moved her hands up Jaiden's side and slid the tops of her fingers under Jaiden's sports bra, carefully nudging the tight-fitting garment.

"No, I'm joking. Please don't use any sexual sorcery today while we make love." Jaiden was impatient to let her breasts free and yanked her bra up and over her head. "What are you waiting for? Get naked already."

Imara laughed. "I wouldn't dream of using…what did you call it? Sexual sorcery. I'll have to remember that." She removed her own t-shirt and bra. "I must say, I like wearing your clothes, but honestly, I'd rather not have to continue performing alteration spells."

"Less talk, more undressing please."

"Why aren't we doing the provocative strip tease bit or how about removing each other's clothes? Doesn't that add to the burgeoning excitement?" Imara tossed her shorts onto the same pile of clothes littering on the floor.

"Only in the movies and cheesy romance novels. I'm too mature for that kind of foreplay. Besides, I don't think I could be wound any tighter than I already am. If your hands and tongue do not find their way onto my body in less than fifteen seconds, I'm pulling out my handy vibrator and releasing the coil."

Imara pushed Jaiden onto the bed and grinned. Jaiden scooted her body back until she was almost to the headboard and quickly pushed down the covers.

Imara looked like a sleek cat, as she crawled on top and began kissing and nibbling on Jaiden's earlobe and her very sensitive neck. Jaiden wondered how Imara knew this was one of her favorite erogenous zones. She could damn near have an orgasm with the right amount of attention there and a few quick strokes somewhere else. Jaiden wondered why getting her off was such a problem for her ex-lovers. If she was properly teased, all they would have had to do was blow on her and she'd explode.

"Mmm," Jaiden said. This was the only feedback she was providing to Imara.

Imara didn't appear to be in any great hurry to move to any other area of her body. "I'm going to take my time. By the end of my worship, you'll be screaming my name at the top of your lungs."

Jaiden was already squirming under Imara, trying to make another connection by grinding into her. Imara stilled those movements with a gentle hand. Jaiden tried to maneuver her hand, repositioning their bodies and reaching around to Imara's backside. She managed a few strokes upward where she knew she'd reached Imara's clit. Her fingers slid easily along the folds, and she knew Imara was just as excited as she was. "So wet for me."

"You don't really want me to recite a binding spell do you? Of course, I could always deploy the old-fashioned cuffs and ties."

Jaiden grunted her frustration but decided to let go and give in to the wonderful sensations traveling up and down her body. Eventually, Imara began to move downward. She gathered Jaiden's nipple in her mouth, sucking gently. Jaiden didn't enjoy hard breast play. What Imara was doing was pleasurable instead of slightly uncomfortable. Jaiden felt an overwhelming need for something, anything, to touch her clit, and she wanted Imara's fingers inside at the same time. "Please, Imara."

"Please what?"

"I need your touch."

"I am touching you."

"You know what I mean."

Imara moved further down Jaiden's body and spread Jaiden's legs. The tips of her fingers brushed the inside of Jaiden's thighs and toyed with the hair covering her mound. Jaiden neither shaved her pussy nor had close-cropped pubic hair. She'd always thought it felt like stubble, and that was too much like kissing a man.

"Mmm, your hair is so soft. Don't ever shave. I hate that. If I wanted to feel stubble, I'd date men."

"I know, right?" Jaiden had barely said those words when she felt Imara's tongue in just the right spot. Jaiden knew she wouldn't last long. She felt the most glorious sensation. Imara must have curled her tongue, which she was slowly pushing in and out of Jaiden's vagina. Something was also hitting her most sensitive spot, and Jaiden kept lifting her hips to enhance the sensation.

"Mmmmmm." A low rumble from Imara that sounded almost like a moan created barely enough vibration to bring Jaiden over the top, and a wave of release erupted from her tightly wound body.

"Oh God, that is so damn good, Imara," Jaiden said. She let her body relax and return to a relatively normal state, as her heart rate continued to race. "Just give me a few moments. I'm dying to get my hands on your body. I am so turned on by your red hair and am most definitely impressed by the fact that you are a natural redhead."

Imara crawled up Jaiden's body and captured her lips. Jaiden's scent was all over Imara, and for once she wasn't turned off by that. Oddly, this caused another wave of arousal and she couldn't wait to touch and taste Imara.

"I would have liked a bit more vocal acknowledgment of my talents. Well? Did I pass your first critical test?" Imara sounded disappointed.

I suppose I'm not as demonstrative as her previous lovers. Jaiden wasn't sure what she needed to do to assure

Imara. *If she only knew the truth.* Very few had ever taken Jaiden this far before. Imara had sparked not only a physical reaction, but an emotional one as well.

"I'm not a screamer, but I'd give you an A plus. I don't think physical intimacy will be an issue for us."

"I should hope not." Imara rolled to the side and propped her head in her hand, as she continued to stroke Jaiden's body lightly.

"Hey, what did you do with your tongue? My God, that was incredible." Jaiden turned to face Imara.

"A little rolling of the tongue can go a long way." Imara winked.

"I can't roll my tongue, damn genetics."

"That's a myth."

"It is not."

"Oh, yes it is. If it was all genetics, then identical twins would share that same trait and they don't in every case."

"Hmm, you'll have to teach me that trick then. I guess I'd better figure out a way to develop those rolling muscles." Jaiden tried rolling her tongue.

Imara chuckled. "Sorry, it looks like you're sticking your tongue out at me. But when you do learn how to roll your tongue, I'll be a very lucky woman. You seem to have an exceptionally long tongue."

"Really?"

"Oh yeah, you'd give Steven Tyler a run for his money."

Jaiden pushed Imara on her back. "Well, I think I'll put that very long tongue of mine to work now."

"Oh yes, please do. Can I say your playful side makes up for your lack of screaming, even though it was a slight blow to my ego?"

Jaiden saw the small smile and began her playful assault on Imara's lips and what she hoped were Imara's optimal pleasure spots. By the sounds coming out of her new lover, she thought she might be hitting everyone.

CHAPTER SIXTEEN

Elle glanced out the front window of The Enchanted Page II and saw Franklin hovering on the other side of the street. Imara and Jai had stopped by earlier, on their way to Knead & Feed, and they looked like they were in love. Elle was happy for her old friend, but she didn't particularly like her separation from Tanya. Tanya had offered to keep Jai's store open while Imara and Jai spent the day together. Tanya had whispered in Elle's ear that she thought they deserved this time together and needed to cement their developing relationship.

Seeing Vlad's puppet slithering around on Main Street unsettled Elle. She wanted to give him a little leeway. Vlad had unduly influenced him, but he was a creepy man who wouldn't accept Jai's constant rebuffing of his overtures. When Jai had told them it was Franklin who'd broken her necklace, Elle could sense the irritation and desire to send him packing once and for all.

Elle marched outside and confronted Franklin. "Why don't you take your creepy, stalking self far away from Jai, before I decide to send your smarmy ass somewhere you definitely don't want to be."

"It's a free country. I'm not afraid of you. Gordon told me—"

Elle laughed. "Gordon isn't going to help you and I'm feeling rather—"

"Elle?" Tanya crossed the street and joined Elle, who was glaring at Franklin. "What's going on?"

"Oh, Franklin here thinks he's grown some balls. He doesn't know that neither Gordon nor Vlad is going to come to his rescue or fulfill whatever promises they made to him." When her hips hadn't moved of their own volition, she sighed in relief. The experiment must have finally worn off.

"This is none of your business. If you and that redheaded whore hadn't come to town, Jaiden might have agreed to start dating me. We have a lot more in common than what's her name."

"Imara. And don't be too sure about that. You still call her Jaiden. Ever wonder why she lets all of us shorten her name, but not you? Oh, and I wouldn't want to be you if Imara or Jai catches you hanging around after what you did to Jai. Imara has a very bad temper. You know what they say about redheads. Here's my advice to you; find another teaching job and leave the island before Imara decides to act on her emotions. Or maybe I'll—"

"Elle." Tanya touched Elle's arm. "Not in anger, never in anger. We don't send people into books unless it's a last resort. Franklin is not a real threat. You know that. Let Jai deal with him."

"Fine, but I don't think I can control Imara. She's always been a little impetuous. Potential consequences don't impact her rash actions." Elle spun around. "You're lucky Tanya is so kindhearted. I don't believe Jai will help to save your ass and might choose her own brand of justice. Good luck, Franklin. You're going to need it."

Franklin's evil grin was his only response. It seemed like there was something he knew that neither Tanya nor Elle were privy to.

As they began to walk away, Elle asked, "Do you think we should warn Jai and Imara that Franklin is still hanging around? His negative energy is nearly palpable."

"Maybe. Let's close up the stores and head to Jai's house. I do get an uncomfortable sensation. I like her shop. The crystals give me this warm feeling, like a protective blanket or something, but the minute I stepped outside." Tanya shivered.

"I know. It's like evil is hanging on for dear life. Almost like there's residual material dripping off of Franklin." Elle grabbed Tanya's hand and squeezed.

"I miss your Elvis-as-a-Marine routine. Too bad the spell dissipated so soon. It might have come in handy when screaming your name in ecstasy. You know, a little extra thrust at just the right moment."

"You are bad. I think a little bit of evil infiltrated your body." Elle laughed. "I kinda like this side of you, but no, I don't want Elvis to return."

†

Imara was making lazy circles on Jai's stomach, when she heard the loud knock on Jai's front door. She sighed. "I don't suppose we can ignore that and hope whoever it is will go away."

"Oh suppose away, because that is exactly what I intend to do."

Bang, bang, bang.

"Come on, open up. I know you're in there, and this is important. So get dressed and answer the door," Elle yelled from outside.

Imara put her finger to Jai's lips. "Don't say a thing. She's just assuming. Besides, I think she's trying to get back at me for when I banged on the wall when she was having her own moment with Tanya."

Jai giggled.

Bang, bang, bang.

"Seriously, Imara, you'd better open up, or you'll force us to interrupt whatever you're doing."

"She wouldn't," Jai whispered.

"Nah, she's all bluster. I'm sure she's bluffing." Imara continued walking her fingers up and down Jai's body in a playful manner.

Jai grabbed the sheets and pulled them up over her naked body and gasped. Tanya and Elle had appeared in the bedroom. "Sorry, Jai, but I warned you both. And no, this is not about payback, Imara."

"So what the hell is so important you had to come barging in someone's bedroom? That's especially rude, Elle." Imara pushed the sheets aside and emerged from the bed, as she crossed her arms over her chest.

"There's a bit of unfinished business. Franklin was slithering across from the shops just now. Something is definitely off about him," Elle answered.

Imara frowned. "I forgot about the little weasel. I need to teach him a lesson."

"I have a better idea. Remember what Fay told us about your mother and the Sanguine? Jai, I think it's time for you to get in touch with your mother. Honestly, I believe Franklin is salvageable," Tanya said.

"I'd rather bring back Val to dispose of the cretin," Imara said.

240

"A little over the top, don't you think?" Jai asked. "He's irritating, not life threatening. He needs a lesson, not an execution."

"He put his hands on you without your permission, I call that a bit more than irritating." Imara began putting on clothes. "I know a few handy spells to make him think twice about doing that again."

"Your jealous side is mildly arousing." Jai laughed. "On anyone else, I would start thinking that was a perfectly logical reason to dump your ass, but I find your faults appealing in an odd sort of way."

"Really? Well I can ratchet that jealously up a few notches—"

"Do not encourage her bad behavior and stop talking about how her idiosyncrasies are arousing to you. That's just...ew," Elle said.

"I think it's sweet. It shows how love is conquering all." Tanya impulsively kissed Elle's cheek, and she reacted with a goofy grin.

Love. Yes that was definitely what Imara felt for Jai. Did Jai really love her back? Maybe, just maybe, everything would work out as it should. But this latest piece of information concerned her. What Elle was not saying had her worried. "You think Franklin is more of a danger than we've been led to believe, don't you?" Imara asked.

"Not exactly, but he was far too confident for my liking, even after learning Vlad and Gordon would not be coming to his rescue. That does concern me," Elle answered.

"Tanya's idea is a good one. I've wanted to connect with my mom anyway. Can you two please wait outside while I get dressed? I'm a bit more modest than Imara."

Tanya looked embarrassed as she mumbled, "Sure." She tugged on Elle, and they left the bedroom.

Imara grinned. "Oh, goody. We're at the meeting-the-parents stage. I'd say our relationship is progressing nicely."

Jai laughed. "You'll love Mom, and you know she loves everyone. She sees whatever good might be lurking within."

"Hey, didn't I recently prove how much good is hiding inside of me? Wasn't I spectacular a short time ago?"

Jai grabbed her clothes from the floor. "When do I get to meet your parents?"

"There's only Mother, and never. She's far too self-involved. Bea is like the mother I should have had, and you've already met her. Can we leave it at that?" Imara hadn't wanted to reveal her sensitivity on this topic, but her feelings slipped out.

Jai pulled Imara into her arms and gently kissed her lips. That kiss was like a salve, and Imara felt the strength of Jai's protection. At that moment, Imara knew Jai would not only safeguard her physical self, but that armor would extend to Imara's emotional fragility as well.

†

Jaiden was nervous as she made the call to her mother. She knew she'd avoided contact because she'd judged her harshly. She'd vowed to never end up like her mom. She'd erroneously viewed her mother as a kind of doormat. Those unkind thoughts reverberated, as she heard her mother say hello.

"Um, Mom, I met your friend, Fay."

"Oh," Zelda answered.

"I've been so wrong about you. Can you ever forgive me?"

"Oh, honey, there was never anything to forgive."

"I've met someone, Mom. I want you to meet her, but we also need help from you or someone in the Sanguine." Jaiden shuddered. "I really don't want to see you get together with Franklin, even if it is for the greater good."

"That's good, honey, because I've decided to retire. I…uh…well… Would you like to meet your father? We've sort of reconnected. I do have an apprentice that could take on a new project."

Jaiden stumbled backward into Imara's loving arms. Imara adopted a quizzical expression, as she turned Jaiden around to look in her eyes.

"I don't know," Jaiden answered honestly.

"He's kept everything a secret, because I asked him to. I didn't want to add more confusion from the choices I made. He's always been there in the background, watching over you. He's the one who sent Imara to you, and I might have helped by calling on my old friend, Fay."

The pieces finally fell into place for Jaiden and she blurted out, "Aaron Busam is my father. Isn't he? The superintendent of our school district! He simply rearranged his last name. Right? Instead of Ambus, he changed it to Busam," Jaiden exclaimed.

"Aaron Busam is your father?" Imara sounded more than a little surprised.

"Just a minute, Mom." Jaiden moved her cell phone from her ear. "You know Aaron?"

Imara nodded. "Sorry, I didn't know. I swear."

Jaiden put the phone back to her ear. "We need a pow wow. Right now. Mom, do you think you can drive down?"

"I'm here at Aaron's and so is Hallie, my apprentice. She, uh, just moved to Coupeville."

Jaiden groaned. "Okay, I'm going to take a wild guess here. Hallie is the science teacher we recently hired. Isn't she?"

"Yes, she is. Don't be angry, honey. Everything that happens in this world is meant to be. It's all been foretold, and we are simply pawns in the big plan. There are only rare moments in history when the balance of good and evil teeters on the edge, and it can go either way. I had to make sure the seesaw did not tip in favor of evil. I do hope you understand that. Your father did."

Jaiden sat on the stool in her kitchen. "I do, Mother. I do. Just come over and we'll talk about it, okay?"

"We'll be there in about fifteen minutes. I love you, Jaiden, and so does your father. We never, ever wanted you to judge love so harshly because of the choices we made."

"I know you didn't, Mom. It's okay. Everything seems to be righting itself." Jaiden smiled as she looked at Imara. "See you soon."

"I can explain—"

Jaiden placed her finger on Imara's lips. "Wait for Mom and Aaron. I guess I should call him Father now."

"Aaron is a good guy," Imara said.

"I know," Jaiden answered.

"Wow, a real-life soap opera unfolding in front of us. Where's the popcorn when you need it?" Elle quipped.

"Shut it, Elle," Imara snipped.

Jaiden loved her for turning the tables and playing protector.

"Sorry," Elle mumbled. "I'm just trying to lighten the mood."

†

Imara should have seen it earlier. Aaron Busam had been so kind to her growing up and had remained a friend and supporter. The man who'd been like a father to her walked into Jai's house and offered a sad smile. He had Jai's eyes.

"Hello. Imara, Jaiden, I'm glad everything is almost completely out in the open. I know I should have told you more, but I made a promise," Aaron said.

Jai gestured to the couch, where Tanya and Elle were sitting and taking in the scene. "Come on in. Mom, Hallie, and uh, Aaron, these are our good friends, Tanya and Elle. Hallie, it's nice to see you again. They're book magicians. Can I get anyone a drink? Wine, water…"

The group nodded to each other and stood awkwardly in the living room.

"Relax, honey." Zelda pulled Jai into a hug and stroked her back. Imara was glad when Jai appeared to settle into her mother's embrace. Zelda's whole being exuded positive energy.

Aaron wisely held back, and Imara missed his usual greeting. She understood this might be awkward for him. Jai might feel slighted if he hugged Imara yet held back from embracing his own daughter.

Zelda turned to Imara. "You must be Imara. I've heard so much about you, and I am delighted you are in my daughter's life now." She swiveled to Jai. "This is the woman you were speaking about, right? I do hope you're a hugger." Zelda took Imara's hands in her own and pulled her tightly for a hug. Imara liked the woman immediately.

"Yes, Mom. Imara is the woman I wanted you to meet. I also wanted you to meet Tanya and Elle, but they're a couple. Oh…" Jai blushed. "You know what I mean."

After Zelda released Imara, she lovingly stroked Aaron's arm. "Aaron, darling, go hug your daughter. I know how special Imara is to you, so you must greet her properly as well. She'll think you don't care about her anymore, and I know that is the furthest thing from the truth."

Aaron took Zelda's hand, then let go. The look in his eyes was pure love, as he let his eyes fall briefly on Zelda, then turned his attention to Jai. Imara had certainly never seen him look at Serafina with that same adoration. She'd always known her mother wouldn't keep Aaron in her life for long, especially after he started taking an interest in her daughter.

Serafina always had to be the center of attention. Imara had often joked with Elle that some crazy book witch had brought to life the queen from *Snow White*, and Imara was the unlucky recipient. Aaron was one of the few suitors who took the time to get to know Imara and form a lasting friendship with her. Nothing was untoward about how he treated her; her mother's jealousy wasn't logical or appropriate. The nail in the coffin was when she'd accused him of wanting to screw her own daughter. He'd kept in touch with Imara, despite her mother's foul accusations.

When Jai looked at her with concern after her awkward embrace with her father, Imara knew she must have telegraphed her uncomfortable trip back in time. Aaron shifted his attention and opened his arms. Imara let him wrap her in a hug. "Did you put a spell on me so I would pick Jai as my chosen one?"

Aaron smiled.

"How devious of you. I have a whole new appreciation for your talents. I guess you sensed she'd be the one." Imara patted him on the arm.

Aaron's deep, baritone laugh punctuated the silence. "Well, someone had to tame you. When I would tell Zelda about you, she thought you'd be the perfect match for our daughter. She was right."

"You two have been playing matchmaker?" Jai's voice held a tinge of irritation. "Go on, sit down. I'm getting some wine. I believe I either need it or deserve it."

Hallie made a beeline for Tanya, and Elle narrowed her eyes at the new woman. "I am so happy I have a chance to talk with you, Tanya. We've heard all about the nonmag Director of E-books. I love to read. Even though I've chosen the Sanguine, I'm fascinated by book magicians, especially how you all have managed to get with the times and send nonmags into e-books."

"She doesn't like when you call her a nonmag," Elle tersely added.

"I am so sorry. I'm supposed to add positive energy. I have so much to learn. I do hope I will be able to help Franklin. I see that tiny amount of good and wish to bring that forward." Hallie folded her hands in her lap. "But…uh…I don't think I can…uh …get intimate with him."

"There are times when intimacy is necessary for the transformation. In this case, Hallie, the opposite is true. Franklin needs to learn he can be friends with a woman and treat her respectfully, without the relationship turning romantic. He also needs to learn acceptance for those who are on the opposite end of the sexuality spectrum. I've always felt comfortable swinging either way, but you, my dear, do not need to change who you are to be effective with heterosexual men." Zelda smiled at Hallie.

Aaron and Zelda settled on the love seat and held hands, as if the connection was the most important thing to them at that moment.

Imara pushed aside the ottoman in front of the European recliner and sat on the floor, leaning against the empty chair. She thought they made a handsome couple. "Aaron, why did you start seeing my mother when you are so clearly in love with Zelda? Weren't you jealous of her other lovers? Zelda, weren't you unhappy to learn he'd moved on?"

Jai grabbed the open bottle of wine, filled her glass, and took both bottle and glass with her to the living room. "That's an excellent question." She set the wine on the coffee table and settled into the chair Imara was leaning against.

247

"Jealousy is a useless emotion and so negative," Zelda answered. "I knew that eventually Aaron and I would make our way back to each other after the important work was done."

"Besides, we kind of broke the rules over the years and never quite stopped seeing one another." Aaron had a mischievous look in his eyes. "No one knew of course. That would have been dangerous to Jai, until she came into her own power and met the person intended to complete her. I should have known when I first met you, Imara, but it took the growing danger with my brother to force my hand and take the chance. We did play matchmaker, but seeing you two together has confirmed this was the right move to finally right the imbalance of power."

"Came into my own power? I know that Fay said I'm some kind of protector. Surely you aren't suggesting I join a stupid sect or coven?" Jai asked.

"Oh no, dear. You aren't expected to join our sect or a coven. Protectors have but one job. To protect the ones they love. Imara is very important to keeping the balance. The characters she must bring to life in the future will not be for the sake of a chosen one, but rather for the fight against evil. You must protect her with your very life. In fact, you are the only one who can truly protect her. To a lesser degree, you must also protect Tanya and Elle, who will play a role in this battle as well."

Elle's and Tanya's heads spun in Zelda's direction and in unison they asked, "What?"

"Books are very valuable tools in our arsenal. We intend to make the most of this resource. The Sanguine has been losing ground for years now. It is only since the book witches and book magicians have come together that we see hope for the future. You four are at the forefront." Aaron looked each member of the team in the eye.

"Holy crap," Tanya exclaimed.

"I'm definitely in. Ooh this is going to be so exciting. We'll be like epic, crime-fighting superheroines." Imara pumped her fist in the air.

"Oh yeah. I like it. Besides, book witches and witches in general throw excellent solstice parties. The Paganicon was really something," Elle added.

"You two would, being the adrenaline junkies you are." Jai took a large gulp of her wine.

For the next two hours, Aaron and Zelda filled the group in on everything they'd discussed during a gathering of witches, warlocks, magicians, and wizards, who were fighting for a positive future filled with love, compassion, and kindness.

†

Jaiden and Imara lay in bed together, talking about what they'd learned. They were only slightly worried about Hallie's ability to turn Franklin away from the dark influences. She was so green and seemingly naive, but desperately wanted to prove herself.

Jaiden was becoming more comfortable with the notion that, whether she liked it or not, she was responsible for protecting Imara. She'd found "the one" for her, complete with imperfections. Imara's brashness and tendency toward impulsive acts were bound to cause a massive headache for Jaiden. But she was duty bound to protect the one she loved. *I do love Imara.*

"Move in with me," Jaiden blurted out.

"What?"

"Do you love me?" Jaiden asked.

Imara turned, and Jaiden saw the same love in Imara's eyes that she'd seen when Aaron looked at her mother. "I do, more than I thought I was ever capable of. I am trying to wrap my head around being the one who needs protection, rather than me being the protector."

"We'll probably end up protecting one another, although I do kinda love knowing I'm the badass in our love equation." Jaiden chuckled. "I love you, Imara. Warts and all. I want us to live together and do that lesbian thing."

"I do not have warts." Imara hmphed.

"It's an expression. Well?"

Imara grinned. "I was hoping for an invitation. I'd love to settle here, or rather make this our base of operations. All we need to do is convince Tanya and Elle that moving here permanently makes perfect sense. They can ask Bea to run their bookstore in Moses Lake. I know her and Scott, Elle's dad, would love to take over. They are basking in their own reunion of sorts, and Scott loves books. Besides the notion of living in sin might be our only walk on the dark side, since we're now fighting for all that positive light shit."

"It's only living in sin if we do a lot of what we have been doing in the last twenty-four hours. Speaking of which…a certain part of my body is ready again."

"Insatiable, that's what you are. I love it, my big, badass, protector. How about if I do that rolling tongue thing again?"

"Oh yes, do that again, my gorgeous, sinfully good, book witch."

ABOUT THE AUTHOR

ANNETTE MORI

Annette is an award-winning author, published by Affinity Rainbow Publications, who lives in the beautiful Pacific Northwest with her wife and their five furry kids. With fourteen published novels and one Goldie Award for her fourth novel, Locked Inside, she finally feels like a real author. Annette is as much a reader as a writer and is always looking for the next lesfic novel to queue up. She came up with the One Fan at a Time tagline, because it rolled off the tongue much better than One Reader at a Time. After pondering who she was at her core, it was all about connecting to each reader on a personal level. Annette would be the first to admit she doesn't do well with the masses. If someone picks up her book and it touches them, she believes she has achieved what she wants with her writing by reaching each reader. It is who she is at her core. Drop her a line, she loves to hear from readers:

annettemori0859@gmail.com

Sign up for her mailing list
Check out her blog: Everyday Occurrences
Visit the Affinity Rainbow Publications website for her books
and many other outstanding authors:
https://www.affinityebooks.com

251

OTHER AFFINITY BOOKS

<u>Calling Home</u> by Jen Silver

Sarah Frost enjoys her dream job as director of the Frost Foundation making her home at one of their writers' retreats, The Lodge on the Lake. Galen Thomas, taking an extended break from her vet's practice arrives at the island to fill the post of handy person. The island idyll is soon undermined by the revelation of events from forty years earlier, threatening the lives and loves of Sarah, Berry, and Galen. Calling home and what they now call home—all are affected by the disturbing legacy from the past.

<u>Reach of the Heron</u> by Angela Koenig

After an automobile accident takes the lives of her parents and nearly her own, Arkadia O'Malley faces a painful recovery. As she seeks custody of her younger sister, Rini, she must also contend with the obstruction of Irish law. When Rini is moved from a harsh orphanage to one of the notoriously cruel Magdalene homes, Arkadia's efforts to reunite with her sister are aided by powerful women from this reality as well as from Elsewhere.

From Wind and Water by Laura Kovack
The Seventh Kingdom is surrounded by the Lands of Earth, Fire, Water and Wind. All but Earth have rulers. When a new enemy threatens all of the Lands, it is imperative to find the last ruler of Earth. Morgayne, ruler in Land of Water and Ventus, ruler of Land of Wind, form a tentative yet skeptical relationship—everything depends on them. Will that tie survive the battles ahead? Will they allow or deny their feelings in this fantasy adventure that will have you urging them on to victory on all fronts.

The Book Addict by Annette Mori
From award-winning author Annette Mori comes the captivating story of Tanya, a young woman whose life is unremarkable without any friends or lovers. Then she meets Elle, the alluring owner of the new bookstore, The Enchanted Page. Elle looks like she stepped out of a Nordic adventure and Tanya is immediately infatuated with the mysterious woman. Join the colorful characters as they try to right the wrongs created by Elle's fiercest foe. And just maybe, the books won't be the only thing enchanted if Elle allows the magic of love to enter her heart.

Colors of Rage by Nanisi Barrett D'Arnuk
Dr. Kailyn DeKendran, head of the Acoustic Research Department, and her sister Jayanta, are drawn into the fray of unrest during the election season when the participants can't remember why they are rioting. When Kailyn disappears, family and friends band together to find her. Time is running out, and the riots are getting more violent. Will they find

Kailyn before it is too late to put an end to the madness that has overtaken them?

<u>Naomi's Soul</u> by Renee MacKenzie
This second book in the Karst Series picks up the Peace Movement where Kai's Heart left off. Everyone is still struggling to find the balance between reconciliation and guarding. Control must remain in the hands of those working diligently for peace in the war and disease ravaged New America. Warrior Naomi Adams is on a routine mission for the Peace Movement when tragedy strikes her contingent. She will need to dig deep to find the strength to move past the devastating earthquake that has split up her party.

<u>My Starlight</u> by Loryn Stone
If only we could have met sooner…
Orly Kochav likes nerdy things. A huge fan of Japanese animation, cosplay, and playing the bass, she's convinced she can use her natural charisma and swagger to get anything she wants. Including beautiful girls. When her judgmental mother catches her kissing a girl and asks her a hideous question, Orly goes into a state of emotional hiding. Now sixteen, Orly is itching to reclaim her prior life and when a new friend informs her that a secret club dedicated to their favorite Japanese Anime, Lovely Starlight Fighter, is at their high school, Orly thinks she'll be able to slip back into the world of fandom without issue. Until she meets the club's vice president, Danielle Cohen and the rising attraction to her threatens to make Orly question every choice she's about to make.

<u>True North</u> by Ali Spooner
Cam's story continues as the Gator Girlz business continues to thrive under her leadership, but will self-doubt jeopardize

her relationship when Bugsy reveals the family moonshine business to an unsuspecting Luce? Will a devastating injury to Sandy end her career as a gator hunter or will it open a door to love? Join the St. Angelo family for a third adventure to find out more about life, loving, and family in Bayou Country.

The Dream Catcher by Annette Mori
What if all your dreams—the good ones and the nightmares—came to life in the real world?
Heaven is a Dream Weaver, and that is her reality. When she wakes up, she never knows what will greet her or her best friend and roommate, Syl. It could be a sexy stripper or a monster from another dimension. When Syl suggests a Dream Catcher to help her control the dreams, Heaven is wary until she meets the alluring Maya. Between the government and the powerful Dream Catching sisters, time is running out for Heaven. She wonders who she can trust. Can this lovely Dream Catcher protect her or is Heaven truly on her own?

Gator Girlz by Ali Spooner
In the sequel to Diamond Dreams, Cam St. Angelo finished her freshman year on a high. Her softball career is on path. Everything seems to fall in place for Cam and Tab as the new school year and softball season take off. All too soon, unfortunate events at the home front force Cam to leave college and her softball dreams behind. As always, it's family first.

The Tempest by JM Dragon
Doctor Alana Cameron has dedicated her life to working on the family legacy, a transportation device which will change the world for everyone, called Tempest. Tragedy has dogged

the project over the years, causing military intervention. Super soldier Major Denise Tranter, who loyally defends Earth in any way possible, finds herself drawn into the Tempest program. Emotional bonding is not in her remit, although she finds herself inexplicably drawn to Alana.

Trusting Hearts by Samantha Hicks
When successful advertising executive Carrie-Ann Stedman is tasked to train a new hire, she is reluctant. She has never forgiven Holly Fletcher, the newbie, for stealing an important client away from her. Holly doesn't know what Carrie's problem with her is. When the two are thrown together, can they build a working relationship without business getting in the way of the growing attraction between them?

Free to Love by Ali Spooner and Annette Mori
Captain Hillary Blythe loves sailing the ocean. Her journeys along the Atlantic Coast and Caribbean to deliver goods contain many adventures. When she brings a small group of rescued Africans to the Methodist mission on Antigua, challenges to deeply ingrained beliefs arise when devoted Christian, Elizabeth Allen, is drawn to one of the women, Kia. Will Kia and Elizabeth be free to love among the harsh laws of the land and Elizabeth's struggles with her faith?

Kai's Heart by Renee MacKenzie
The time has come for the Resistance to take back control of New America from the Anointed tyrants. Growing up as the daughter of a Resistance Army General, Kai Brodie's focus is keenly on the upcoming Revolution. So how is it then that she can't take her eyes off the beautiful Anointed guard? Can Kai break free from tradition and find love in the arms of

someone her upbringing tells her she should hate? Can she protect her love from those who hunt them? Will Kai and Rachel survive the battle over the fate of their beloved New America?

Diamond Dreams by Ali Spooner
Cameron St. Angelo dreams of playing softball in the College World Series. Earning a scholarship to play ball for her beloved LSU brings Cam one step closer to achieving this dream. When Cam arrives on campus, she joins a family of women who share her love of the sport, and she realizes there is room in her life for another love.

Unconventional Lovers by Annette Mori
Bri and Siera are young women with huge hearts and strong wills; they want nothing more than to find a peaceful and secure space to be themselves. But the world is a harsh place for anyone who is different. Bri's Aunt Olivia is a vet who channels her emotions into her work and her love of Bri. Siera has her Aunt Deb who adores her. Despite their individual battles against hurt, prejudice, and rejection, can these four women find love against the odds?

Affinity
Rainbow Publications

ebooks, Print, Free eBooks

Visit our website for more publications available online.

www.affinityrainbowpublications.com

Published by Affinity Rainbow Publications
A Division of Affinity eBook Press NZ LTD
Canterbury, New Zealand

Registered Company 2517228

www.ingramcontent.com/pod-product-compliance
Lightning Source LLC
Chambersburg PA
CBHW052024020726
47501CB00004B/1240